KINGDOM OF FLAMES & FLOWERS

RAVEN STORM

RAVEN STORM

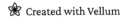

ALSO BY RAVEN STORM

The Lost Siren

The Lost Alliance

The Lost Kingdom

The Lost Nation

The Lost Princess

The Lost Child

The Lost King **Coming Fall 2023**

Rise of the Alpha Series

Chained: Rise of the Alpha Book 1

Claimed: Rise of the Alpha Book 2

Changed: Rise of the Alpha Book 3

Box Set with Bonus Scenes

Aggie's Boys

The 40-Year-Old Virgin Witch

The Witch Who Couldn't Give Amuck

Hex Appeal

The Demon Chronicles (YA)

Descent

Feud

Royal Hunt

Kingdom of Flames & Flowers

TRIGGER WARNING

This book contains a scene of sexual assault on female victims in the form of an involuntary medical examination. This scene takes place halfway through chapter six. There will be another warning in the chapter just before the scene begins, and another break when the scene ends.

CHAPTER

ONE

The first time I saw the fireguards, I was only a year old.

According to my mother, I had been a squalling infant with a bald head and crying constantly. The guard had frowned at me as we stood in line with my older brother and everyone on my street, his red and gold armor flashing like liquid fire in the sunlight. He had made a tick on his scroll to mark my existence, and another guard had stepped forward to put the brand on my shoulder—MM3—and went on his way.

Mother said I screamed for days afterwards as it healed.

The second time I saw the fireguards, I'd been six. I'd started asking questions by then and had heard stories and rumors. Not from my mother, of course, but from the other girls who ran the dirty streets with me. All my mother would say was that the fireguards were doing their duty; every five years they must take a census of all the children in the kingdom. It was for our safety and the overall wellness of our people to know which women were the most beautiful, the most fit, the most likely to bear many children ... and which ones weren't. In addition, they were looking for which boys would make suitable pupils for the Seat, and which ones would be condemned to stay forever in the mud quarter. The girls deemed not good enough had to stay here for the rest of their lives, prey to the fireguards that roamed the alleys and the men who hadn't been deemed good enough either. Those men were angry and mean, and they liked to grab girls and haul them away to their huts. You had to be quick if you wanted to stay safe from them. The boys weren't much better: the teenagers who roamed the streets and took in the younger boys who'd also been kicked out of the Seat for a deficiency of some kind. Together, they formed awful gangs that bullied their way into taking what they could from others.

As we raced between the alleys and nooks of the twelve dirty streets that made up the mud quarter, the girls whispered to me about the ones lucky enough to make it out.

The girls were wives of nobles who wore jewels and ate so much that they grew fat and lazy.

The girls served the king himself, and went to sleep each night on a real bed with a warm blanket.

The girls were companions of the queen and got to travel beyond the wall.

Beyond the wall.

I lifted my eyes to the gargantuan stone and mortar barrier to my left. The wall went one hundred feet up, and was wide enough at the top to allow the fireguards to patrol at all hours. There was only a small gap above their heads before the great dome started—our enormous shield made of iron, steel, and a newer metal called dragonsbane. It was necessary to keep us safe from the dragon, of course.

"Quick, to the market. It's almost time for rations." Shava pointed ahead, easily outstripping the rest of us as the oldest girl with the longest legs. Shava was tough and kept our little gang of girls safe. I'd seen her beat boys and even a grown man bloody once for cornering another girl and trying to touch her.

Most days Shava felt like my real mother. Mothers fought for and protected their kids. They didn't hide away in a mud hut, huddled into corners. And yet, I couldn't hate my mother. I knew she was just sad. Like everyone else.

We raced under the large, faded canopies thrown up between each cramped, squashed, little hut. Rain never reached us because of the dome, but water always rose from the ground, occasionally turning the alleys into dangerous cesspits of mud and muck. It covered everyone who lived here in the dirt and grime. Clean water was only accessible from the large communal well, guarded constantly by a fireguard.

"Wait for me!" I cried out, one of the youngest out of our prowling group. If I didn't get there in time, there wouldn't be any food. Mother didn't care to get any for herself or me, so if I wanted something, I had to take it.

Mother had been sad ever since they'd taken my brother. It was up to me to care for her.

Luckily, I made it with time to spare. I was small, but I was fast.

"And what would the little flower want today?"

My favorite fireguard stood in front of the crates from the Seat, in charge of distribution for today. He was older, but he was always kind to me and called me 'flower.' It made me feel special. And he always snuck me an extra bit for my mother.

I gazed up at him hopefully, my eyes darting between the bread and fruit. Mud girls weren't allowed to talk to the fireguards. I'd seen a girl whipped for doing so before.

A gray eyebrow rose. "No meat today?" he asked quietly so that no one around us heard.

I shrugged. If I asked for meat, I wouldn't be able to get as much of the other foods. Bread filled you up the best, after all.

"One chicken, a loaf of bread, a wedge of cheese, and two pieces of fruit," he proclaimed loudly, and a younger fireguard handed them down to me, wrapped in a cloth.

I didn't wait to see the reaction of the other girls. If I didn't get going quickly I'd get mugged in the streets. This was enough to last for almost a week if my mom and I were careful! I took off running down the streets, my prizes in hand. I wished I was a boy. They were at least allowed to travel between quarters for trade and messages, or they were allowed to until they surrendered to the Seat.

That happened when they turned five. At the Seat they began their education and training, and found their purpose in service of the king and queen. Well, unless they were found unworthy. Then they were stuck in the mud quarter with no other choices than joining a gang. My mother had broken the day they'd forced my brother from her. At least, that's what the other girls had told me, and that was what their mothers had told them. I had only been two, so I had no real memory of him or that day. All I knew was that my mother was sad and nothing helped.

My brother never came back so that meant he'd been found worthy.

Whatever worthy means.

Men in the mud quarter were divided into two groups; the fireguards who fed us and protected us, and the rejected men who tried to hurt us and steal from us.

Luckily, today the bad men were far away since there were so many fireguards, and my run home was safe. I had a feast of food in my arms, but Mother didn't react when I brought it home. She never did. I tried not to let it bother me.

A week later, when the fireguards came for the census, I was angry and not speaking to Shava, who'd said the fireguards called every girl 'flower,' and that I was just another dirty mud rat like her. She said I wasn't special. When I started crying, she relented and gave me a few nuts from her store. That's how I knew she wasn't trying to be mean; she was just miserable like the rest of us.

I was angry because deep down, I knew she was right. 'Flower' was a stupid name, anyway. Why couldn't I be called a 'flame' like the boys were?

Flowers were weak and died easily. You couldn't eat them without gagging. Shava claimed the royal family had an entire garden of them up at the castle, just for *looking at and smelling*. It was wasteful; that was space we could use to grow crops.

And now the fireguards were back, but not to give out food. I stood before them for the reaping.

They paused as they went down the line, full of children and young women alike from my street.

"Marigold Mudthrice."

I stomped my foot and scowled. In that moment, my rage was so great I forgot the rule about not talking to the fireguards. "That's not my name! My name is MARI!"

The unfamiliar fireguard bent down to get a better look at me. My mother wasn't fast enough to pin my arms back to my side, and I punched him as hard as I could in the face with my six year-old muscles.

He flinched and wheeled back, surprised. Then he laughed and laughed, the other fireguards joining him.

Then he turned and hit me so hard I saw stars.

Pain was the only thing I knew, along with my mother's gasps and sobs as she hovered over me. They pulled her away, and the fireguard added a few kicks for good measure.

"You're lucky I don't have her whipped. Insolent brat."

He spit on me for good measure.

My mother bowed her head in apology as the second fireguard made a mark on his paper, his hand shaking, and face pale. The guards who came for the reaping weren't kind like the everyday fireguards were. It was a hard lesson to learn. My mother's grip on my wrist was like iron as she hauled me to my feet. I twisted away at the strength of her grip, but she held me firm.

Above the dome, the dragon roared in fury. The dragonsbane metal that protected us all hummed as the beast landed heavily on top of it, the metal glowing as it rained down fire and brimstone to no effect on the people below.

The fireguards moved on.

Mother sent me to bed without supper for my actions that day. Not like I missed much since it was only dirt cakes for dinner. I hated dirt cakes. They were bits of flour mixed with dirt and whatever herbs could be traded and spared between the women. My head hurt horribly, and it was a week before I could run the streets again.

When I was eleven, the fireguard had to hunt me down for the reaping. I'd hidden in the old tunnels that used to be mineshafts before they had built the wall and everyone had to stay inside of it.

I wasn't the only one who knew of the tunnels. Shava was the one who'd first introduced me to them, saying they were a great place to hide if any of the men bothered or chased you. I knew my absence would cause trouble, but I wasn't going without a fight. It'd taken four fireguards to haul me out of my hole, covered in mud and dirt. The one who'd beat me five years ago was gone, but the others were the same, including my favorite, older fireguard. He'd laughed at me like the other fireguard had, but his laugh was different. Bits of gray hair peeked out from below his helmet. I saw the look of pride in his eyes. He *liked* how I fought.

Another damn tick went next to my name.

When I was sixteen, I was deathly ill with the flux. It was

a stomach sickness that was common in my quarter. The fire-guards hadn't even bothered to stick their heads in the door to confirm I was ill—except for the older fireguard. He'd frowned when he saw me lying in a dirty corner of our hut, covered in sweat and clutching tightly to our only matted fur blanket.

I recovered, but many didn't. They dragged the dead in front of each hut door and fireguards collected them on a cart. Rumors flew, saying they fed the bodies to the dragon. We didn't hear any roaring from the dragon for an entire year, so perhaps that was true.

I hoped not.

I'd gotten lucky that day. That's because that year the fire-guards took all the older girls to make up for the dead ones, and in one fell swoop, all my friends were gone.

Including Shava.

I never really cried, but that day, I did. I'd lost my only protector and the closest thing I'd had to a friend all at once.

Only the ugly and sick remained, along with the mothers and their children. And the old crones. And the boys and men no one wanted. No one had any use for any of them.

Today I was a woman of one and twenty.

I wasn't a child any longer. I wouldn't run and hide or try to fight a fruitless battle. I wasn't sick either, though I'd tried. My mother had caught me adding the pergainsa berries to my water, which would have made me violently ill. She'd cracked me across the face and pointed to the door in a silent order to go stand in line with the others. It was the most alive I'd seen her in months.

It was slim pickings this year. Most of the women my age were gone, taken five years ago, or had died from stomach illness. My friends had been gone for ages. There was a fresh slew of babies held by women with sad eyes and faraway looks. There were no men standing next to them, meaning they were just victims like my mother had been.

It infuriated me.

I hadn't bothered trying to tidy myself for the fireguards. My black hair hung down my shoulders, snarled and tangled. The skirt of my dress was indecently short, but it wasn't my fault that the edges kept fraying and had to be cut off. I think the dress itself had been red at one point, but it was brown now, caked with mud and dirt like every other piece of clothing here. It made little sense to keep anything clean.

As one of the oldest girls left, I stood head and shoulders above everyone else, sticking out as a woman in the prime of her life amongst the children, mothers, and crones who made up the rest of my line.

The fireguards came as they always did, trudging through our quarter with armor and shields gleaming. Three of them had mostly gray and black hair sticking out from their helmets, but the other three were young, their movements crisp and efficient. Two had brown hair, one was blond.

I tried to breathe. Maybe the stories of old were right, and a wonderful life awaited me in the Seat. The other girls had to have gone *somewhere,* after all.

The same kind guard paused before me. At least it was him, and not the one who'd hit me all those years ago. "Ah yes. Marigold Mudthrice. Mud for the quarter, thrice for the third street down the line. We missed you five years ago."

I said nothing. These men now held my fate in their hands. I wouldn't antagonize them. Not today.

"Nothing to say today? No punches to throw? No grand chases through derelict mines and muddy alleys?"

I remained silent. He pushed my dress roughly down my shoulder, reading my brand and confirming I was who he thought.

"How dull," he remarked, eyeing the rest of the line. All were mothers, old women, or girls too young to be taken. "Just the one?" he asked incredulously, one eyebrow raised at us.

"The rest you took last time. Those that didn't have the flux," my mother offered in a soft voice. The fireguard's eyes lingered on her for a long, long moment before he looked away. My gaze sharpened. I'd only fight back if he hurt my mother.

He didn't.

Instead, he gave her a lingering looking, and glanced away. I frowned. No one had ever looked at my mother like that.

"Very well. Let's go."

I felt the eyes of the others on me. I wouldn't go fighting and screaming. I was too old for that. Or at least that's what I wanted them to think. What I really wanted was to see the top of the wall, and way beyond it. I'd never seen the world outside of these high stone walls. I wanted to see it all.

Next to me a young girl started crying. She couldn't have been more than two. Her mother was young; only a few years older than me at most. She'd likely been caught in an alley by a fireguard like my mother had been all those years ago.

My hands bunched into fists.

The fireguard checked his list and must have seen something that confirmed what my mother said. He sighed and waved me forward.

I turned to my mother and hugged her. I knew this day was coming, so I'd been making a cache of food for months. I wasn't sure how long it would last, but I had hopes that the kind fireguard would see to her. He seemed to like her, just as he liked me.

"Take care of yourself," I muttered into her ear, knowing it was likely a lost cause. I had to give her a bit of hope, didn't I? "If I marry well, I'll bring you to the Seat with me. I can't do that if you starve yourself."

I felt my mother nod against me, our tears making tracts down our faces as they took a bit of mud and dust with them.

"That's enough. Time to go," the fireguard bit out, but with no venom or malice. We separated, but my feet felt glued to the hard, dried dirt beneath me. I couldn't leave her here. Not when I had no real assurances she would be looked after, or look after herself.

The fireguard's hand came down heavily on my shoulder. "I will see to it that she eats," he muttered into my ear so no one else heard, and the vice grip around my heart eased, allowing me to take a few steps forward to join the fireguards.

I gave my mother one last glance over my shoulder, then faced forward. They marched me past my mother and out of the mud quarter. With no words of goodbye, we headed off.

I wouldn't look back. I couldn't look back. Fireguards flanked either side of me, and I wouldn't put it past any of them to beat me if I stopped moving or turned around.

My mother would be fine. The fireguard had promised; and he was kind. He'd always been kind.

I told myself that because I couldn't think of her giving up on life now that her last remaining child had been taken from her. So I marched forward.

The bread quarter was next to ours. You'd think we'd eat well being next door to them, but few of us could afford their prices with no way to earn income. Instead, we had to rely on the fireguard's handouts. Usually it comprised the palace's leftovers and any food deemed unsellable from the bread quarter bakers.

Still, it captivated me how different it was just a few streets over. The most immediate difference was the houses. Unlike our mud huts, they made these with stone and mortar, mixed with sand and stone borrowed from the stone quarter to stand the test of time. They had given thought and care to placing each house, leading to neat, orderly streets. Up high, plants and greenery sprang from each roof, serving as a personal garden for each family. I'd give anything to have my own source of fresh fruits and vegetables. My mother would have probably loved to have her own garden, though it was hard imagining her doing anything other than sitting in the corner of our hut, staring at the wall.

The people who glanced up at the fireguards as we marched by were plump, not one had a bone or rib showing. Men and women walked side by side as equals instead of one running in fear from the other. I burned with envy.

The fireguards called a halt, and we stopped right in the middle of the street. The cobblestones under my feet were smooth from the wear and tear of actual shoes and boots. It felt much better on my feet than the rough, cracked surfaces in the mud quarter.

We waited for five minutes, then ten. I counted the number of people around me out of sheer boredom. I wondered if the other girls had brands on their shoulders like I did.

Finally, a small company of four fireguards appeared with five girls in tow. Most had brown hair, but two were blonde. One was perhaps eighteen, with bright blonde hair that made her stand out among the brown hair of everyone else, and the other blonde looked extremely young Thirteen? Twelve? The rest of the girls were around sixteen or seventeen. All younger than me, of course. They stared at me in my filthy clothes and bare feet, but no one dared to say anything.

We crossed into the stone quarter, and I couldn't help but gawk.

The stone quarter people were great miners, bringing in a wealth of resources for the kingdom. Shava had said the mud people use to mine too, but it was hard to believe. It had been lucky for the stone quarter when a miner had dug down into his own home and found a wealth of jewels. The king gave permission for each family to have a small mine under their houses, as long as they gave a good portion to the crown.

As a result, the houses were large and spacious, and the children here looked happy and well-fed. They ran around with leather sandals and colorful tunics, grasping actual toys in their hands. There were just as many fathers as mothers strewn about. I wondered how different my life would have been if I'd had a father. Maybe mother wouldn't be so sad all the time if she had someone to share her life with, and help look after her. *My* life would have been much different.

From this quarter they took seven girls, all ranging from ages thirteen to seventeen. *Children,* I thought with disdain though I knew this would be the likely outcome. Very few girls made it to my age before being taken.

Their hair was all brown except for one who looked older and could be around my age. She sneered at everyone and kept her nose in the air, as if all of this was beneath her. Her hair was white. I gawked a bit, having never seen such a color before. Everyone in the mud quarter had black hair.

Maybe we could be friends if she quit glaring at me.

A few of the younger girls openly sobbed, but most let silent tears fall down their cheeks. All looked hale and healthy.

Did everyone get to eat except the mud quarter?

We walked for a long while until we hit the rock wall of the Seat at the very center of the kingdom. The castle loomed before us, high upon a giant cliff that rose straight up. It hurt my neck to try and look at it.

"Come."

The fireguards escorted us through an iron gate and into a large shaft that went straight up into the belly of the rock. A giant cage made of iron greeted us with a chain that ran all the way to the top of the stone mountain. Once up top, I knew there were walkways and battlements that reached over the quarters and ran all the way to the wall. It was how the fireguards patrolled and kept us safe.

The only thing left between us and the Seat were the great iron cages.

There were ten spread about at the bottom of the massive shaft. It was the only way to reach the Seat itself. The entire noble quarter lived on top, as well as the castle and the king and queen's court.

To my despair, the fireguards herded us all into one cage like cats and abandoned us. There were nine more! Couldn't they space us out?

"There will be more guards at the top," the familiar guard told us, though his eyes lingered on me. Then, as one unit, the six of them turned and headed back toward the city to patrol.

The older girl with white hair shoved me toward the back and I elbowed her in the face, which was conveniently at eye level, though it was difficult with all of us shoved so closely together. So much for that burgeoning friendship. She quit pushing after that, merely scowling at everyone around her to back off, but there was no room. There were thirteen of us: me from the mud quarter, five from the bread quarter, and seven from the stone quarter. I wondered if they took any girls from the remaining quarters.

We barely fit as it was into the cage, crowded uncomfortably up against iron bars. We all flinched and a few even screamed as the cage made a horrible lurching sound, then began its ascent up the shaft, straight up into the air.

TWO

It was the most terrifying yet exhilarating thing I'd ever done in my life.

As we came out from the shaft and rose over the kingdom, I set eyes on the remaining two quarters I'd never seen before: the artist's quarter, which was wedged between the stone and bread quarters, and the noble's quarter which awaited us high on the Seat. The art quarter was beautiful, a shimmering jewel compared to the dark streets of the mud quarter and the simplicity of the stone and bread. The artist quarter was all the way to the east, the gilded tops of their buildings shining in the sun. I bet they lined their streets with gold too, and beautiful mosaics of every color. Maybe they even shit gold.

I vowed to hate anyone I met from there.

With a loud grinding sound, the cage came to a halt at the top of the cliff, swaying ominously in the mild breeze. Girls screamed all around me and clutched the iron bars as if they would somehow save us should we fall. A fireguard at the top unlatched the cage and held it steady. A second one held out a hand to assist us out onto solid rock. There was a gap between the cage and the ground of about three lengths of my foot.

"Grab my hand and I'll haul you over."

This fireguard was younger than the ones who patrolled my quarter, possibly even my age. His black hair marked him as someone who had mud descent like me. Nobles usually guarded desirable characteristics for their bloodlines, like blonde hair—that's likely why the blonde girl was here despite being so young.

He seemed handsome from what I saw under his helmet, but I didn't think I had good judgment on that, having only ever seen a handful of men in my life and usually running from any I encountered. He surveyed all of us with silver eyes tinged with green, his face showing interest in us instead of the usual disdain the other fireguards had. All fireguards wore their helmets at all times, so unless their hair was longer, it was hard to make out much more of them.

"Let's begin. Remain calm."

Unfortunately, the younger girls took this as their cue to rush the entrance of the cage, each wanting to be the first to take this handsome fireguard's hand, or just afraid to be swinging in the cage for any longer.

I stumbled and tripped as the cage tilted dangerously, wrapping my hand around an iron bar to keep from tumbling into the pile of girls near the door. Two other fireguards yanked the first man back, but he kept his grip on the lucky girl who'd snagged his hand first. He pulled her with him as he fell, and she landed safely on top of him. The two girls after her weren't as lucky, slipping into the gap and reaching back to grab the cage too late. If they had committed to going forward and leaped, perhaps they would have made it. As it was, they fell screaming to their deaths far below us.

One fireguard cursed and ripped a horn from his waist, giving two short blasts.

They had a special call for every time someone fell, I realized.

Screaming was all around me as girls clawed and fought each other, desperately trying to find something to cling to. All the while, the cage swung back and forth wildly in the wind. Death had reared its ugly head, and I froze as the others panicked. I couldn't even remember what quarter the dead girls had come from, and now they were gone.

I refused to be next.

"Stop it!" I screamed. "Let the cage settle!"

The girls went still, freezing under my authoritative growl as they hung on tight to anything, including each other. I don't know if it was because I was older, my rough appearance, or because I simply scared them, but they quit fighting. As we held our breaths, the cage slowed until finally a new fireguard could grab hold of it again.

"One at a time," I barked at them from the back of the cage. "If you rush it again, I'll chuck you off the rock myself!"

The girls bowed their heads and listened, still shaking and crying as they waited to be carried one by one over the open air and onto solid rock. Mr. Handsome stayed in the back, eyes stormy. The girl my age pushed in front of me rudely, and I let her. I would not fall to my doom because of her.

Finally, it was my turn.

I kept my eyes on my feet, not trusting myself to not turn an ankle in the empty slats. I got to the edge of the cage and glanced up, startled to see Mr. Handsome reaching out for me.

I'd throw myself into the void before I let another fireguard touch me.

I narrowed my eyes, judged the distance, and jumped. The stones on the other side were sharp, and I hadn't taken that into consideration. My foot landed, slicing open on my heel. I staggered and fell backwards toward the gap.

The girls gasped as I teetered, wobbling dangerously. The only thought in my mind was how I'd finally gotten free of the mud quarter only to trip and fall to my death like a simpleton.

A hand grabbed my wrist and held on, strong and solid as a rock, pulling me forward.

The guard.

The moment he touched me, revulsion and nausea reared their head, threatening to overwhelm me. *He will not hurt you. He's trying to save you.*

The other fireguards rushed to drag him back, tugging us both to safety over the other edge. Embarrassed, I popped up quickly, ignoring the pain in my heel and desperately trying to control my rapid breathing. The fireguard in charge looked pissed as hell, but only glared at the young guard who'd risked himself to save me. When none of them spared a glance my way, I relaxed. Slightly.

"See? Nothing to panic over," I chastised the girls, trying to put on a brave face. I crossed my arms over my chest, waiting for further instructions. My wrist tingled where the guard had grasped me tightly.

I tried to ignore how the other girls shot glances over the side of the cliff. I refused to look.

"What an interesting group this year," the captain noted dryly. "Let's get them to the bathhouses."

The fireguards formed ranks around us, including Mr. Handsome, who went toward the back. Without another word for the dead girls we were leaving below, they led us up a winding path up with thousands of spiraling stone steps. It was high. It was steep. But the final quarter of our city lay at the top, as well as the castle and a new life. I wanted to see the noble's quarter for myself. I wanted to eat the food and sleep in a real bed.

"Walk. Those who cannot make the journey stay behind."

I didn't want to be left behind because of an injury, so I hurried along with the rest, ignoring the bloody footprints that trailed behind me. My feet were tough, and I was strong. I couldn't help but wonder what my mother would think about all this. Would she be terrified for me and want me back, or would she feel the risk was worth the reward in the end? She probably would have loved the chance to move up in life, but hadn't had the opportunity when she'd fallen pregnant with my brother. And then me.

I ended up toward the front of the group hiking, which soon became a nuisance.

The eighteen-year-old blonde was at the front, doing well and consistently putting one foot in front of the other. Like me, she was lean and mostly muscle. The more plump girls from the stone quarters behind her were soon huffing and puffing, clearly unused to so much activity. They slowed and slowed, and we came almost to a halt. Sweat stained their pretty silk dresses.

I wondered what they did all day in their stone houses.

"What is the holdup?" a girl asked from behind me. The girls from the bread quarter were all lined up at my back, wondering what the problem was. They were just as stout as the stone girls, but clearly more used to physical work. With determined faces, they had hiked up their dresses and faced the steps patiently, one at a time.

"Halt," came the command from the fireguard up front. He was nearly an entire staircase ahead of us, the older blonde girl nearly at his heels. She stood still while he descended back down to the rest of the line, beginning with the red-faced stone quarter girls.

"You must continue," the fireguard captain warned the stone girls.

Or else what? I wanted to ask.

"Move it, piggies!"

I knew without turning around that the insult came from the girl my age, who was toward the back. The rest of the girls were between her and me.

We all ignored her, even the fireguards, who were yelling at the stone quarter girls to pick up the pace. I rolled my eyes. If they could go any faster, they would. I certainly wouldn't complain at having to follow behind at a slower pace. Begrudgingly, they continued the climb.

We kept at it for a bit more, getting only a quarter of the way up the stone steps. The stone quarter girls in the front openly sobbed, begging to rest. I glanced at their feet and saw silk slippers stained with blood. My own feet were bare but callused from years of running through the streets. My injured heel hurt, but I'd deal with it. I'd dealt with worse before.

These girls clearly hadn't.

Mr. Handsome raced past me, taking the stairs two to three at a time. I gawked at his speed and fitness, and in no time he was at the front of the line, arguing with the fireguards. I couldn't hear what they were saying over the wind. He must be someone important, despite his youth, if he was able to argue with older fireguards like that.

He must not be winning the argument, though. He growled and suddenly swept one stone quarter girl's legs out from under her and climbed the steps with her in his arms.

The other guards grumbled, but each one up front took one of the stone girls, and in short order, we were moving again.

The girl my age toward the back with white hair had plenty to say about this. "We should leave them behind if they can't make it up; only the strong should succeed!"

I rolled my eyes and shoved my irritation down. The side of a cliff was no place for a fight. I'd wait until we were safely above, then demand to know what her problem was.

"Fat pigs have no place in the noble's quarters!"

Screw waiting. I whirled around. "But you do?" I shouted down to her, sick of her voice. "Shut up or I'll come back there and make you." I raised my fist for good measure.

Her mouth dropped open in stunned silence, then she closed it angrily and kept climbing. I knew I'd have to watch my back when we reached the top, but that was fine. At least she shut up, and for now, I was too far ahead of her for her to retaliate.

An hour or two later, the top of the hill crested, great white stone buildings bore down on us as we staggered to the very top. I immediately moved inward toward the fireguards, shooting the tall girl a wary look. The fireguards gingerly set down the stone girls. The girls whimpered and whispered words of thanks.

I rolled my eyes, then kept them pointing toward the heavens. Up this high, the giant dome that protected us from dragon fire was so *close*.

THUMP.

We all flinched and crouched down as the massive shadow of the dragon landed on the dome and started crawling over it. The dome itself was only three building's height from me.

"Come," said the fireguard captain, pulling our attention away from the roosting dragon.

We followed them as they led us to a white stone building shorter than the others, but much longer. I tried to keep up, but I couldn't stop staring at the gleaming city around us. It was so clean and tidy! And the people wore bright, white linen robes that weren't dirty and frayed! And I wasn't the only one gawking.

"It's made of gold. Look at that!" A bread girl pointed at a gleaming building with a giant dome, the top gilded so it flashed in the sunlight. Beyond it lay the white stone castle itself, sprawling and large over the Seat itself, like a regal guardian. I blinked in disbelief as the dome thinned over the castle, leaving holes and spots open to the bare sky. The edges of the palace were gold from the roof to the windowsills. It hurt to look at, but I squinted my eyes and fought away my tears, determined to stare at it, anyway. I had to memorize every detail because one day I'd get back to my mother and describe everything, down to the worn patches of metal on the doorways from generations of hands wearing down the threshold into a smooth groove.

"Don't be foolish. Gold melts. It only looks gold," sneered the older girl, but she too couldn't look away from this very intimate view of the dome.

Even the stone girls gawked. Precious gems were embedded in the road at my feet, making wondrous patterns and spirals that led away to various buildings. I noticed some of the patterns led to particular buildings. Was it a marking or a sign system?

"You're bleeding."

I jerked, not noticing the handsome fireguard sneaking up on me. I would have to be more alert. If a guard in loud armor could sneak up on me, the taller girl would have no problem strangling me or pushing me off the cliff when I wasn't paying attention.

The fireguard bent down toward me, but I stumbled back.

"If you pick me up, I'll scream and punch you," I promised, refusing to look weak in a new place surrounded by strangers. Weakness killed you in the mud quarter.

His eyes sparked with interest. "Is that so?" His voice was smooth like cool water on a hot day, washing away the dirt from your eyes and soothing everything that burned hot. I'd never seen eyes like his before, all that green bursting from a silver outline. Then again, it could be the most common eye color in the Seat and I wouldn't know.

I couldn't stop looking at them, though.

"The others are leaving. We're taking you to the bathhouses."

Before I could protest, he scooped me in his arms and strode forward. I considered following through on my promise to beat him, but it didn't seem fair, and my foot hurt. Wasn't there a saying about finding trouble where there was none?

Grumbling, my arms found themselves around his neck, hanging on for dear life. His hurried gait was anything but smooth, and his armor felt slightly warm against my skin. He smelled like leather and some spice I'd never smelled before, along with ashes and fire.

Quickly, we caught up to the others as they passed underneath a large stone overhang beneath eight large, shining pillars that swirled with green and black material mixed into the gleaming white.

"It's called marble. Like a jewel, it has the most marvelous shine when rubbed."

I glanced up at the fireguard. I wanted to ask him why he was talking to me, but that would require talking to him. Was he trying to bait me into chatting, and then he'd smack me?

I shivered as the memory of being smacked across the mouth surfaced again in my mind, sharp and clear as the day it had happened. It was being around all these fireguards. It was driving me mad.

The sound of running water happily distracted me. We walked through a ring of more fireguards into the great stone building, which was full of large tubs set into the ground.

Oh. A *bathhouse*. Like a house that had baths in it. It had never occurred to me that such a thing existed. Why would it? It was a tremendous waste of space and precious fresh water. In the mud quarter, we had to use rags and dirty basins to clean ourselves, not that there was much point. You'd only be dirty again five minutes later.

My face flushed as we were the last ones to file through, leaving the other girls to stare as I came in cradled in the fireguard's arms. There were a few other girls already here, including one with fiery red hair. We all glanced at each other, uncertain. We had started with thirteen, then two died from the cliff. Now there were four more girls, putting us at fifteen. No one else had black hair. No one else had come from the mud quarter.

From further back in the building, a line of older women came forth, immediately swarming us. Clothed head to toe in swirling robes somewhere between red and purple, they had large cowls covering their hair. The color was so vibrant it hurt my eyes, reminding me of wine. In the mud quarter, water was in short supply, but the fireguards would give you as much wine as you wanted.

I never took it. I saw what it did to my mother.

My fireguard set me down gently and backed away to resume his rank.

The women moved gracefully in jeweled slippers, offering each girl our own goblet of wine. A kindly older woman offered an emerald-encrusted cup to me, a knowing smile on her face. The moment the scent reached me, my stomach flipped, and I turned her away. I wanted no part of it.

Not to be dissuaded, she held the wine out in one hand and pushed me toward one tub with the others. All around me, the women were stripping the girls naked in full sight and plain view of everyone. Even the guards.

I made my muscles rigid and sat down on the cold floor. I

would be the only one with a brand on my shoulder since I didn't see any on anyone else's. The other girls all had smooth, unmarred skin on their shoulders. I pulled my limbs in and made a ball, refusing to move.

"They marked this one as troublesome," I heard the captain remark to one of the robed women. The one escorting me backed away as the fireguard descended upon me.

Three on one. I'd had worse odds, but the boys in the mud quarter I'd routinely fought for food didn't wear armor or carry swords.

"Come, child. Let's get you into the bath and scrape that mud away."

I tucked my body tighter, sneering.

"Girl, do as the prima commands. You would go before her highness covered in filth?" the captain exclaimed, a sneer twisting his face.

"Rather that then go before all of you naked," I grumbled back, glaring at the 'prima' and daring her to try. The older woman sighed, then shot a look at the captain. Before I could protest, he picked me up and threw me into the nearest pool.

The water was more than warm; it was scalding hot. I screamed, but no one heard it. Steaming water rushed in all around me and I flailed helplessly. It filled my eyes and ears, my nose and mouth. I choked, realizing I couldn't breathe. Never had I been fully submerged in water like this!

Don't panic. Stretch out and feel what's around you.

I resisted the urge to breathe in since water was running down my throat, and instead I stretched out my arms and legs as far as I could. My toes scraped the bottom, and on instinct I pushed against it as hard as I could.

My face broke the water, and I gasped, choking and coughing.

The ledge. Grab the ledge.

I wasn't sure how I managed it, but my hand grasped the stone edge and I pulled my body over to it. I held onto it like a lifeline, coughing and hacking, and trying desperately to regain my breath. Water dripped through my hair, plastering it flat against my face. With one hand, I brushed it away and looked around. I expected to see the other girls flailing in the water like I had. As far as I was aware, no one in the kingdom knew how to swim. Well, maybe those up here who used these bathhouses, but certainly no one from the districts below.

Cries rang out and then were quickly cut off as the fireguards bodily threw each girl into the water. As I hung onto the side of the pool like a half-drowned rat, I watched helplessly as other girls flailed and splashed in tandem. Not a single fireguard twitched from their perimeter, and the primas watched serenely with no panic or surprise in their eyes. Where was the kind fireguard now?

I thought of the two girls who had fallen to their deaths. I thought of how none of the stone girls would have made it up the steps without the young guard fighting to carry them. And now this.

My realization hit me all at once. This wasn't a selection process.

It was a carefully planned execution.

Screams and cries for help became muffled until the only sounds were frantic splashing, and then nothing. In the end, most of the girls flailed over to the edge or were tall enough to get their feet under them eventually.

But not everyone.

"There. She doesn't move."

The captain of the fireguards pointed toward a pool in the middle. One of the bread girls floated serenely in the middle, her face completely submerged in the water. She was still.

"And there."

The same in a far pool, but a stone girl. Shame, that was the young blonde, only thirteen or so by my estimate. Her blonde hair floated on top of the water, surrounding her body like a halo.

To my horror, there were more. Six girls in total. The fire-guards dragged the dead girls out of the water and carried them away, and the primas began washing the survivors. Bundled in the arms of fireguards, it looked as though they were only sleeping.

There were nine of us left.

I must have gawked for too long because the prima tending to me broke her silence. "You'll learn to obey or else."

My wet hair smacked my face again as I turned abruptly to face her. I clawed it out of my eyes just in time to see her kneel at the side of the tub, a small jar of oil in her hands.

"Or else what?" I demanded rudely.

"You aren't chosen," she shot back. Her voice was firm, but not angry. It didn't seem like a threat, but the way she said it had me wary.

"What happens if you aren't chosen?" I asked instead as the prima rubbed oil from the jar onto her hands, then into my scalp. Everyone knew the entire purpose of being taken from your homes was to be chosen as a wife up on the Seat. I'd given no thought to the possibility of a girl being taken and *not* being chosen for a wife. It didn't seem so bad. I could go back and take care of my mother, and protect her.

Then again, if they killed all of us before we made it ...

Survival was my number one goal. If not for myself, but for my mother. The prima didn't answer, instead putting the jar down and lifting a wiry brush. All of my questions fled as she attacked my skin, scraping off years of mud and muck and turning the clear water around me into a thick, clouded soup.

It hurt. It burned. I bared it all with grit teeth, remembering my ultimate goal to survive.

"Get up. To the next bath."

It was empty because they'd just hauled a dead girl out of it. She pointed to a small set of stairs at the edge of my pool. I pulled myself along on the edge of the water, my toes just touching the bottom. I climbed up the steps and tried to cover myself. The prima couldn't care less, shoving me forward. I shot a glance at the fireguards, but they were still standing still, rimming the outskirts of the bathing house and facing away.

The other girls stared as my prima shoved me into the next pool where a dead girl had been minutes ago. It was smaller, and easier for the prima to reach me once I was in. Luckily this one wasn't as deep, and I could stand.

"I guess it's true what they say about mud girls," laughed the older girl from across the room. The others tittered, the primas even giving them small little smiles. Heat flushed my face, but nothing clever came to my tongue. Why would it? She was right: I was filthy. The brand on my back burned from the heat of their stares.

I submitted to the prima meekly after that, even when the prima called over to the others in an annoyed tone, and it took two more to help finish scrubbing me off while a fourth woman worked on my hair. She eyed the choppily shorn edges with disdain, and I tried not to wince. In the mud quarter, we took a knife to our hair every so often. If it grew too long, it was simply in the way and would be used against you in a fight.

"We shall ... put it in a knot and braid it. I will inform the royal dresser you will need a personal visit."

Even with four primas on me, the other girls finished way ahead of me. They were all dressed in sheer robes and led away. The fireguards went with them, all except for my handsome friend. I snatched my robe from a waiting prima and clutched it to my chest, curling up in a ball and covering all the important bits.

"Are you following me?" I grit, wincing in pain as the prima attacked a stubborn knot in my hair.

She then pulled my hair on purpose, pulling my head back so I could see her wrinkled face. "Do not talk to the fireguards."

She let go, and my hands went to massage my scalp.

"I am assigned to see you safe with the others." His green and silver eyes flashed at me, but his helmet obscured any other feature. Thinner metal wrapped around the front, covering the cheeks. The thinnest strip came straight down from the forehead, covering his nose. The only bits I could see of my fireguard were his eyes and his smile. He backed away and took up his post, which was behind me.

"See me safely? Or off me where no one can see?" I shot back.

The prima whipped around and slapped me across my lip, splitting it open. So it wasn't just fireguards who liked to watch me bleed, was it? What was everyone's fascination with hitting me? Did I imagine it, or did the corner of his eyes wrinkle in sorrow at what I said?

"The deaths are regrettable. And you should speak more respectfully." He nodded toward the prima, who gave him a doting smile. He glared at her. None of it helped my throbbing lip.

Fully clean for the first time in years, I turned my back to him as the primas grabbed my robe from me and held it out to help me into it. Dainty leather sandals followed, and I frowned as I donned shoes for the first time in my memory. The prima twisted what hair I had into a bun and tucked the edges under, forgoing their idea of a braid. She secured everything with silver pins.

I felt the fireguard's eyes trace the muscles of my back and caress the curve of my ass underneath the sheer robe. For no reason at all, I blushed.

"All of you must speak respectfully, or you won't be chosen," my prima scolded.

I kept my mouth shut this time, turning back to face the fireguard. He made a gesture, and the primas walked further into the temple where the others had disappeared to. For one moment, the fireguard and I were alone.

"I like your filthy mouth," he muttered, his breath warm on my neck.

I nearly tripped, not realizing he'd been that close behind me.

The spell broke, and I swore at him, hurrying after the primas and the other girls like a chastened child. His laugh behind me was loud and boisterous, warming something deep inside my chest.

THREE

I rushed to catch up, but the inside of this temple was a maze of marble columns and stone floors. The fireguards disappeared, one by one, until I saw the older blonde girl trailing at the end of the line. I don't know if I'd ever get the image of the young blonde girl's dead face out of my mind.

I ran up to the older one as fast as I could with my wounded foot and tried to act like I'd been there the entire time. She turned her head and raised an eyebrow, but didn't otherwise say anything.

I was thankful.

In a line, they led us through the temple and back out onto the streets. A massive crowd greeted us as the fireguards lined either side of us, keeping us separate from everyone else. A few little girls threw petals between their legs, dusting our path with beautiful reds and purples. The guards blocked the view of most of the crowd; all of the men were taller than me. I could only see the blonde girl ahead of me. The sun was setting, further blinding everyone who faced the west.

"The flowers are here! They are going to the castle!"

The cheers grew louder and the crowd swelled. Everyone threw petals now, and I wondered how they could waste such a luxurious item on us. The delicate blossoms tossed haphazardly into the air were only going to be pressed into the dirt by our feet. I wondered if I could shove a few in my pocket and save them for my mother. But no, they would only wilt and die, leaving me with nothing but brown, dried out carcasses.

High above us, the dragon continued to lounge on the large dome, quiet and content for now. I stared as we passed directly underneath him.

"We're going to the castle!" The older (and now the only) blonde craned her head around to look at me, excitement building in her eyes. The castle itself rose in front of us, the obvious destination as we continued our winding, slow progress through town.

"Flowers! Flowers! Flowers!"

I couldn't help the smile that crept onto my face. Admiration wasn't something that came easy to me: I was just some dirty girl from the mud quarter like all the others. Someone like me had no business being in a castle. What if they expected me to act like I'd been born in the Seat? Worry and dread twisted my gut.

"Budge up, flower. Act like you've been here before. Otherwise they'll eat you alive."

I glanced to my left, my skin erupting in goosebumps as the handsome young guard marched right next to me. The guard on my right made a huffing sound as if he was chastising the other for daring to speak with me.

My fireguard gave a dark chuckle, so I risked one question. I was willing to bet they wouldn't dare hit me in front of a large crowd like this.

"What is your name?" I asked breathlessly, barely louder than a whisper.

The castle towered over us as a delegation of the most elaborately dressed people I'd even seen waited, standing high above us all at the top of the stone steps. Gems and gold glinted at us from their wrists, hands, neck, and the crowns on their heads.

The king and queen!

The fireguards halted at the bottom, keeping themselves between us and the royal family.

My fireguard's breath was hot on my neck, bared to him with my hair styled up. "Zariah," he whispered, and slipped away from my side.

I didn't get to see where he went. I had to pay attention to stay up with the other girls. We formed a straight line in front of the steps, all nine of us.

The king had black hair like mine, which immediately took me aback. Was he from the mud quarter? That was impossible though, wasn't it? The surrounding crowd was a sea of browns, blondes, and even a few reds, but he and I (and a few of the fireguards, I supposed) were the only ones with truly black hair. His face showed deep lines and wrinkles, but his smile was genuine as he looked down on all of us with twinkling blue eyes. He wore a simple tunic down to his knees, but with intricate designs in gold and silver on his chest. A crown of fire sat on his head, red and gold and bronze metals twining together to create the illusion of flames in his hair.

Next to him, the queen wore a similar crown, though it was smaller to accommodate her features. She looked down at us from on high, her white hair done in intricate braids and knots. I envied the length of it, which trailed down past her waist. No one had obviously ever tried to grab it to steal from *her*. The queen's dress was pure silver to match her eyes, which glared down at us with ill-concealed disdain. She was perfect, with no lines or creases marring her delicate face. How old was she?

Twenty? Fifty? I wouldn't be able to put a number on it if my life depended on it.

"So few," she said, raising her chin and tilting her head to the side. Perhaps it was a trick of the light, but was the corner of her mouth smirking?

The fireguard captain walked up three steps and bowed. "My queen, I brought all I could. Remember the flux that swept through the quarters five years ago?"

The queen's eyes narrowed, a corner of her mouth lifting. "Ah, yes. Now I remember. How sad. Perhaps we should have abandoned the usual trials."

That small gesture at the corner of her mouth said otherwise.

"How many were pruned?" she asked nonchalantly.

It took me a moment to understand what she meant. *Pruned.*

"Eight, my queen. It would have been more, but ..." he trailed away, giving the queen a significant look, and then glanced at the row of fireguards behind us.

Was he implying fewer girls died because of my fireguard's actions? Surely those stone girls would have perished on those steps, moaning and holding their delicate feet the entire time, had he not stepped in?

The queen huffed. "We are thankful good sense prevailed, then." her white hair glowed in the rapidly approaching twilight. Her nose lifted in the air, furthering the impression she was looking down on us.

"Get them to their rooms."

With a flourish of her hand, she dismissed us.

Including the captain, they left only four fireguards to escort us into the castle and through to our chambers. We couldn't help but gawk at the gilded portraits lining the halls, and the rich fabrics under our feet. They gilded the walls with gold and silver embellishments, and there was enough wealth on one square inch to feed my mother and me for months.

It was such a waste.

"Through these doors are your rooms. You may share them as you see fit. Do not leave for any reason. We will escort you anywhere you need to go." The captain glared at us as if to impress upon us his seriousness. Two of the other fireguards opened the heavy wooden doors, and we passed through them in two lines.

Once the last pair crossed the threshold, the doors slammed shut behind us with an unnerving finality.

"Wow," said one girl, summing up my thoughts nicely.

The room wasn't a single room, but a few rooms interconnected to each other. We stood in a large common area with pillows and couches arranged facing each other. Small tables were scattered here and there. A large balcony stood directly in front of us, long strips of gauzy fabric fluttering in the breeze on either side. Half of the girls ran to it immediately, making delighted sounds as they took in the view of the Seat below us, and beyond that, the entire kingdom. Or what they could see of it, anyway. Darkness was quickly slipping over us, making it hard to see the entirety of the view below.

Look at me now, I thought. *A flower among real flowers.*

I left most of them to the balcony and their gawking, and explored the other areas. Four bedrooms were off to the left with individual beds that were surrounded with the same gauzy fabric as the balcony. They looked soft and comfortable, covered in velvet and with so many pillows that I didn't know whether to laugh or cry at it all. I claimed the one furthest on the left, slipping off my silk slippers to feel the fur rug in between my bare toes. My heart hurt imagining my mother with just *one* of these items of luxury, let alone an entire room. Everything was so clean. I hesitated on touching the bed, then

I remembered I was clean as well. That would take a while to get used to.

Candles were lit everywhere, providing a warm, comforting glow. We didn't have candles in the mud quarter. When it got dark, it was dark.

"It's a lot, isn't it?" whispered a voice.

I glanced up to see the blonde flop on the bed next to me, grinning mischievously. I smiled back and touched my palm to my forehead in greeting.

"My name is Marigold Mudthrice, but please call me Mari."

She held out a hand toward me. "Leilani Breadtwice."

I stared at her hand suspiciously.

She laughed. "What, you don't do handshakes in the mud quarter?"

My brow furrowed. "It seems foolish to offer your hand like that. What if the person you are meeting grabs it and pulls you down, stealing your food?"

I crossed my arms over my chest. It was a stupid greeting that left you vulnerable.

Leilani withdrew her hand, instead using it to comb through her hair instead. "Oh. I suppose." She frowned. "Things are rough in the mud quarter, aren't they?"

I sighed, not really wanting to get into it. "We survive," was all I offered. "Did you see what's on the other side of the rooms?" I asked instead, desperate to change the subject.

Leilani waved a hand dismissively. "More beds. There are nine of us, after all."

A red-headed girl poked her head around the corner of our room and shyly made her way in. "Is it alright if I take this bed? All the others are taken."

I shrugged.

"Of course not. Make yourself at home," Leilani beamed as

if the red-head were some long-lost sister of hers. "I'm Leilani, and this is Mari." She pointed at me.

My esteem for Leilani rose slightly when she used the preferred version of my name. Almost no one did.

"Stone quarter, right?" I asked. Most of the girls were from there. I wondered if it was purposeful.

"I'm Azalea, actually from the art district," she said. "They grabbed me earliest and mixed me in with the others," she offered, neither offering a hand or touching her forehead, but giving us a deep bow of her head. It was a better greeting than the bread quarter's, but it still left you vulnerable when you took your eyes off the person in front of you. I reconsidered my vow to hate everyone from the art district. She seemed kind like the bread girl.

Was my quarter the only one with any common sense?

"Is that it? For your name?" I clarified. She hadn't specified a row she was born on. Surely she wasn't the only Azalea in her quarter. I had been one of seven other Marigolds my birth year, for crying out loud. That's why we had our second names; to tell us apart.

"As far as I'm aware." Azalea shrugged, looking mystified I'd even asked. She shook her head. "Freesia's called a meeting. She wants everyone to meet in the big room," Azalea muttered, running her hands over the velvet blanket on her bed.

"Who's Freesia?" I asked, wondering who that was, and why she thought she was in charge.

Leilani shot me a look. "The tall one you yelled at on the steps. White hair."

Ah, yes. Her. I shot a longing look toward the bed. Soon enough I'd lay in it.

"Let's go see what she wants, shall we?"

The other two girls followed me out to the open sitting area, where the other six had already assembled. I flopped down onto a bunch of pillows next to two similar-looking brown-haired girls from the stone district, who were holding tightly onto each other. They looked away when I turned to them. I ignored them to savor the feel of such soft fabrics against my skin. I could have easily fallen asleep against such luxury!

Freesia stood among the gaggle of girls, head high and her hands on her hips. Her white hair was identical to the queen's. "I just wanted to make it clear to everyone here that I plan to win. If you want to survive this and come out on the other end, stay out of my way."

She glared at each of us, but I didn't give her a chance to get to me. I stood, reluctantly leaving the soft fabrics. "You're not the queen. Though I think it's a good idea to meet and get to know each other. Maybe share what we know about what's going on."

Freesia laughed. "You're such a stupid little mud girl. You don't know what's going on?"

My face burned, and half the girls looked away. Leilani glanced at me, then raised her hand in the air. "Well, I'd like to know what's going on. All I know is that they choose a crop of girls every five years to marry off to the nobles in the Seat. This seems to have ... more to it." Girls around her nodded. That was a mild way to put odd death trials.

Freesia flipped her white hair over her shoulders. "And why should I share what I know with you? Isn't it obvious why we're here?"

I grinned inwardly. Freesia couldn't help herself; she was too smug in her own knowledge to hoard it. She'd dangle it before us to feign superiority while giving away prize pieces in the attempt.

"You don't know any more than us," I goaded, leaning back in my pillows once more.

Freesia whipped her head back around to me. The primas had braided her long white hair and then pulled at it, creating the illusion of large braids in a flower pattern.

Flowers. Always flowers.

"I certainly know more about it than any of you," she insisted. "My father is the head mason and in charge of overseeing all the family mines. I have royal blood in me, you know."

I tried not to barf as she outwardly preened, tilting her head here and there to ensure we saw her hair. If that were true, she'd be a noble living in the Seat and not another girl in the stone quarter.

Then her words played again in my head. She'd said her *father*. I wasn't sure if I was angry, jealous, or just mystified at knowing someone who'd actually had a father. I opened my mouth to ask, then shut it. I could discreetly ask Azalea and Leilani if they had fathers. I didn't need to embarrass myself in front of Freesia, who was still talking.

"He knows things the others don't," she continued. "The choosing is usually for brides of the nobles who live here in the Seat," she explained. "But this year is different. It's special." Her voice lowered to a whisper. "They're looking for a bride for the prince."

Excited muttering greeted this pronouncement.

I rolled my eyes. "Are you forgetting how they're actively trying to kill us off?" I pointed out. "Remember the cage? Remember the pools?" I eyed Freesia. "Where does that all fit in your vast amounts of knowledge? Why kill us if they need brides?"

Freesia crossed her arms on her chest, a different emotion flitting across her face for a split second before it settled back into smug superiority. "Maybe they don't need as many wives this year. Or they only want the best and strongest."

One of the brown-haired girls next to me started crying.

"Hey now, we made it here," I tried to reassure her, not sure how to handle tears. In the mud quarter, you learned real quick that no one cared if you cried. Crying only made you thirsty, and water was scarce. "We'll watch out for each other from now on. Won't we?" I glared up at the girls assembled, daring them to say otherwise. Murmurs of yesses and an occasional 'of course' mumbled toward me.

"I'm Mari," I announced to everyone. "I will not bother with second names because we're here and don't need them unless we run into a double name. That's Leilani from the bread quarter, and that's Azalea from the art quarter." I gestured to each, and they smiled and made a welcoming gesture when I said their name. I turned to the girls who had to be sisters. Their hair was light brown.

"Heather Stone—er, Heather, of the stone quarter," the one on the left sniffed, then elbowed her sister.

I wondered what it would be like to always have someone else there to lean on—a sibling to share every fear and joy with you.

"Hyacinthe, also of stone," the one on the right said.

I gave them wide, fake smiles. "Well, we all know Freesia, I take it." I rolled my eyes at Freesia's haughty nod. "How about the rest of you?"

A girl whose hair was light brown stood nervously, shooting wary glances at Freesia. Her eyes were green, and she looked similar enough to Freesia that I could guess where this was going.

"Ivy. Stone quarter."

Freesia rolled her eyes and gestured at the next girl with ashy hair, mixed with tones of brown and copper. She had a straight, flat nose that reminded me of my mother, and gave an embarrassed wave to Leilani. "Wisteria, also from the bread quarter."

That left one more girl with brown hair. "Oleria." She glared at Freesia. "Stone."

I liked how she glared at Freesia. The girl either had existing beef or just good instincts.

Five girls from the stone quarter, two from bread, one from art, and just me from the mud. Nah, this game wasn't rigged at all.

I stood and clapped my hands together. "Well, now that's over, let's strategize the best way to not all die horrific deaths."

FOUR

"I'd like to hear about the dragon. No one talks about it. Has it always been there?" Leilani clutched a pillow to her chest as if that could protect her from everything in the world.

Freesia's building indignation deflated a bit at this. We all glanced around the room at each other.

Azalea raised a tentative hand. "We study the dragon for our art. That naturally leads to talking about it. I could share a bit, I guess."

We closed our girl circle a little tighter around her, and I gave her a confident nod.

"Well, it starts with our records of the dome, I suppose. A long time ago the royal family contracted us to design it, though my father says the exact records are gone, so it's hard to say exactly when."

My brow furrowed. What if every other quarter had adult men except mine? Did all the other girls have fathers?

No. That was impossible. We couldn't be the only quarter

with no true families. That was just ... unthinkable. I put the thought out of my head.

"We designed the dome, and the families from the stone quarter got to work figuring out how to get the materials needed. They rumored it to have taken over a hundred years to build!" Azalea said with a flourish.

The girls all went wide-eyed at the thought.

Azalea continued, "One reason it took so long was because of the dragon. It kept disrupting progress and killing the workers, as well as destroying materials. Eventually, they figured out how to craft dragonsbane. Construction pushed forward due to sheer need: more people would die if it wasn't built. The workers went at it day and night without stopping."

Hyacinth clapped her hands like a ninny. "I don't care about the dome. Tell me about the dragon!"

Azalea paused, considering. "We get a lot of commissions from the noble quarter, and many of them want art with the dragon. To do this properly, the fireguards gave us access to some of their drawings and accounts. From everything they've seen, the dragon is pure gold with scales that glint red in the sun's light. His eyes are black like pitch, and his teeth are razor sharp. His wings are mostly gold, but it fades to black at the tips, which are also sharp like his claws."

"And he breathes fire?" Heather added, picking up where her sister had left off.

"Of course. It breathes red and orange flames hotter than any fire we can conjure. That's why we had to find special materials from the earth that could withstand it. Steel mixed with iron, and as much stone as we could get away with. Stone chars, but won't burn."

"How do you build something in the air out of stone? Won't it be too heavy and fall?" Ivy sat with her chin in her hands, lying down on her belly.

Azalea's back straightened, proud. "It can be done, but carefully."

"Where did the dragon come from?" I asked. "Why has it claimed our city as its home? Will it eventually die?"

Azalea sighed. "Dragons live hundreds of years. We don't know why this one came, or chose us … but … there are rumors." Her voice lowered as we all imperceptibly leaned toward her. "Rumors about a judgment passed on the city, and that the dragon is our punishment."

I leaned back, my hands on my knees. "Until when? For what?"

Freesia snorted, and I ignored her. Azalea blinked. "What do you mean?"

I huffed. "Well, is it an unending punishment until the end of time? That seems unfair. The people who did the bad thing are likely dead. Why punish all of us forever?"

Freesia picked a piece of imaginary lint off her white shift. "If it's a curse, most curses have ways to break it."

For once, I agreed with her. "Right. So what's the bad thing, and how do we make up for it?" I turned toward Azalea. "Do your fireguard records say anything about that?"

She thought hard. "I don't think so.…"

Freesia scoffed and swiped a pillow from Wisteria. The smaller girl made a small noise of protest but found another one rather than fight the larger girl. "If something bad happened, the royal family would hardly want anyone to know about it, would they? They wouldn't just hand that information out. Knowledge is power," she finished succinctly like it was a stone tenet that every child learned at the knee of their mother. Or father, in her case.

Privately, I agreed. Knowledge of the fireguards and their habits could mean the difference between an entire loaf of bread or crumbs, or clean drinking water versus whatever dirty swills were left. It was critical to know which mothers would share leftovers and which would give you a smack for asking.

Yes, knowledge was indeed power.

"Enough talk about dark deeds. If there was anything to be done about it, don't you think the royal family would?" Freesia shook her long hair over her shoulder. "I mean, it isn't like they want the dragon to be here."

I wasn't so sure about that. The queen looked like someone who would delight in having one as a pet if she could manage it.

"So, it's been here at least a hundred years?" I asked for clarification. No one in the mud quarter could read, let alone know the history of our city.

Azalea shrugged. "I guess. We're only allowed to look at the parts of the records that mention the dragon. My father remembers it, and his father remembered it. From there? Who can say?"

The king and queen, apparently, I thought with bad grace. Why keep information like that hidden? What was the point? Unless it was like Azalea said, and everyone was trying to hide something: something big, something like the reason the dragon was here in the first place, and how to kill it or make it go away.

I decided that would be my mission. I was in the best position of anyone in the city to figure out this mystery. I'd find out the reason the dragon was here, and fight to expose it and have the city work together to get rid of it, or, barring that, kill it.

Marigold Mudthrice: the dragon killer.

I liked the sound of that.

"Enough about dragons. What's going to happen to us?" Wisteria hugged herself with her arms, her chin tucked into her knees.

Freesia looked ready to burst, so I leaped in right away to goad her into giving up her information.

"I've heard nothing about it in the mud quarter," I admitted, knowing there was no way she'd miss a chance to lord her knowledge over me. Manipulation was my second name. After all, the fireguards who distributed food sometimes gave you more if you did it just right. "We only know they took the girls away, and no one heard from them again," I finished dramatically, making my eyes wide with fear.

Hyacinth and Heather clutched each other, but Freesia snorted. "It's not that big of a deal. The girls are first sorted and cleaned, then comes our physical examination." She paused, frowning. "That will probably happen first. After that, the girls may show any talents they have for their prospective husbands since certain men want certain traits. There are tests of physicality, wits, learning, etc...." she trailed off, waving her fingers in the air dismissively.

The girls seemed less alarmed at the news that we would simply be on display like prized peacocks, but I hadn't forgotten the deaths.

My eyes narrowed. These 'trials' set the girls from my quarter up to fail. We had none of those things available to us. Why even bother bringing us? It made little sense.

"Don't look so upset, Muddy. I mean, Mari," Freesia cooed, giving me a wicked smile. "I'm sure there's something you're good at. Father said mud girls are good for one thing, after all. Is it true they brand you like cattle?"

Azalea blushed, but a few of the girls' eyes were wide with innocence.

"What's that?" Wisteria asked, her voice hushed. "What's the one thing they're good for?"

Freesia halted, her barb not having nearly the damage she

wanted if half of them didn't even understand it. The other girls shook their heads, uncomprehending as well.

But I knew what she meant, and I was furious.

Rather than punch her in the face, I stalked to the large wooden doors, grunting as I pulled one open. Dragon's above, these things were heavy.

"Where do you think you're going?" Freesia called out snootily. "We're not allowed to leave."

I put all my weight against the door and it slowly bulged outwards. "Either I get out for a walk or I break your nose," I gasped, slipping between the small crack that appeared in the door. The last thing I saw was Freesia's affronted face, and the look of fear on the other girls'. They probably thought they'd never see me again; I'd get caught and be another dead girl.

And maybe I would. But I wasn't used to being cooped up anywhere for long. Even a suite as large as that was still a tool to contain us. It was just a fancy cage. In the mud district, I was used to sleeping under the great dome, the air hot but the ground cool against my skin. The dragon came and went as he liked, and at night the glow from his mouth was like a giant night light for the entire kingdom, and the sparks that flew from his snout like little fireflies.

I missed it. I missed being free.

I eased the door closed, shutting off the chattering protests behind me. There were no guards! They truly thought us cowed, then.

With the silk sandals they gave me on my feet, I was a silent wraith in the night. My injured foot barely twinged now, so I knew the injury wasn't serious. Plus, the prima had put some sort of poultice on it that stopped the bleeding and made the pain go away.

Perhaps they didn't mean to kill all of us. Just the dumb, useless ones.

That didn't bode well for Hyacinthe and Heather, I thought, then immediately felt bad. They couldn't help being here anymore than I could. And at least they had each other, which was more than I had. I wondered what life would have been like if my brother had been a girl, or if he hadn't been forced to the Seat when he was five. Would we have been friends? Enemies who fought over scraps of food? I'd drive myself mad considering all the different possibilities.

I stalked along the corridor, wondering if there was a way to get down to the gardens myself. That would be a fun place to explore, wouldn't it? I rounded the corner, lost in my own thoughts, and ran headfirst into a wall of muscle.

CHAPTER
FIVE

"Well, hello there."

I nearly had a heart attack as a man rounded the corner at the same moment, slamming into me.

I stopped in my tracks and gawked. *The handsome fireguard!* He was practically indecent in just light black pants, boots, and a white shirt with billowing sleeves that fell open down his chest to reveal lithe muscles.

Zariah, he'd said his name was.

I'd never seen him without his helmet, but those silver and green eyes I would know anywhere. And that smile, which simultaneously made me feel safe and irritated with its smugness. Why was he here now, and dressed like that? Was he off-duty? Did fireguards live here when not actively on call? The gold threads around his collar looked far too fine for someone with black hair to be wearing.

I smacked him on the shoulder, more so to calm my nerves than anything else. "You scared me!" I chastised him in a harsh whisper.

He flinched when I hit him, staring at me in shock before grinning like mad.

Dear lord, that smile.

"Have we met?" He asked point blank.

My eyes roved over his face, trying to memorize every detail at once. His hair was black like mine, but the texture was different. Instead of my frizzy mass, his hair curled everywhere, hanging off his head in little ringlets where it was long enough, and curling around his neck and ears where it wasn't. His nose was proud and straight; his cheekbones were prominent but not sharp. His lips were full and right now parted with slight shock upon seeing me.

Did he not remember me from the girls? Had I imagined the small spark between us? I couldn't answer him; only gawk in confusion.

"I ... what are you doing here?" He continued. "Aren't the girls supposed to be in their quarters?" His voice was just as I knew it: sensual and dark, but with an edge of confusion and fear I was unused to.

"I was tired of the squawking in our wing. You can't imagine. It's like living with a flock of terrified, hungry geese."

His eyebrow rose. "You're right. I can't imagine," he repeated non-committedly, his eyes raking up and down my form.

Oh, right. I'd stormed out wearing only the thin shift the primas dressed us in. At least I had shoes this time. Self-consciously, I crossed my arms over my chest.

Heavy footsteps sounded from down the end of the hallway. I turned toward the sound, unable to keep the fear from showing on my face. Would I be in trouble for being out? They'd take me somewhere and kill me, and no one would hear from me again. I'd simply disappear, like the girls who fell or the ones who drowned—

A hand wrapped around my waist and another clamped down on my mouth, and he dragged me into a darkened alcove behind one of the massive marble pillars.

"Ssh," he whispered slowly, voice caressing my neck and shoulders. My body pressed tightly up against his, our shared heat palpable with both of us in such states of undress. My heart beat rapidly in my chest, and my pulse raced.

Lumbering footsteps clanked down the hallway, announcing at least two guards. They mumbled among themselves, but too quietly for me to make out what they were talking about. Something about the dragon.

We waited a long while for their footsteps to retreat. When they did, Zariah continued to hold me to him.

"Were you looking for me? That is brave. No one has tried to do that before." he said, sounding pleased about the prospect. The hand on my waist slowly drifted across my belly, tracing my hip through the thin shift. His head descended to nuzzle my neck and shoulder. It tickled, but I'd be damned if I would move now.

"No, but it's good to see you again," I answered.

His brow furrowed at that, confused. But then a soft touch, wet and heated, replaced the sensation of his skin on mine.

His lips.

I'm sure I stopped breathing as his lips dragged down my shoulder, then back up and lingering at the side of my neck.

His hand at my hip ghosted lower, and lower, and I found myself not caring as his tongue tasted my skin, languidly leaving a glistening trail on the back of my neck. This wasn't the same as what the men in the mud quarter tried to do. They were fast and rough—this was slow and gentle.

And I liked it.

I sucked in a breath as the hand questing lower found the

edge of my shift and lifted, his fingers skimming the hot, naked flesh of my thighs. My hips. My stomach.

He paused and circled my belly button, then spread his fingers wide as if to touch as much of me as he could.

Higher.

Goosebumps erupted on my skin as he skimmed my ribs, feeling every indentation and bone that stuck out from a lifetime of poor nutrition and partial starvation. He moved on quickly and for that I was grateful.

His fingers skimmed the underside of one breast, palming it in his hand without actually grasping it. I pushed my body back against him as if that would spur him forward to touch what needed to be touched.

Zariah chuckled darkly in my ear.

"So trusting. Why?"

"I'm not," I bit back. I could feel the vibrations from his voice against my flesh. I couldn't help it; I shivered with anticipation and need. He kept one hand tantalizingly close to my breast, and the other went to my hips and pulled me tighter against his pelvis. I felt him behind me, hard as a rock.

I wanted to tell him how I trusted him because of what he'd done as a fireguard. That he'd tried to save us when he could.

Words wouldn't come. All I could focus on was the hand on my breast, and how he moved behind me, hips gently moving against my backside.

A second hand went under my dress at the same moment he bit down on the back of my neck.

I moaned even though it hurt a little. What was it about a bit of pain that heightened the pleasure?

"Good girl," he praised, licking where he'd bitten. "You like it rough. You long to be owned, don't you? To have someone take care of you for the rest of your days? That's why you're here with the others, after all."

Yes. *Yes.*

The second hand hovered around my core. I stiffened slightly, unsure of what he was going to do. Two fingers grasped my nipple and pinched at the same moment his other hand dipped inside of me.

My knees buckled, and he held me up.

"I dare you to scream," he taunted me, rolling my right nipple between his fingers like a bit of clay. In my core, one finger stroked a sinfully slow path in and out of my heat. I couldn't explain it, but I needed more there.

"Make me," I bit back, exhilarated and not caring what the consequences of our actions were.

His grip on my breast became possessive and borderline painful.

I loved it.

"Don't tempt me, flower. You don't know what you're playing with." He added another finger inside me, no doubt trying to discourage me. I ground down on his hand harder.

"Fire. Flames. That's what they call you. And for me it doesn't matter, does it? All flowers die in the end," I answered in between gasps.

He let go of me, dropping me back to the ground. I was so shocked by the loss of his hands on my most intimate parts that all I could do was stare dumbly at him.

"Not you," he swore, his eyes ablaze. "I will see to it." He glanced down the hallway, then back at me. "When the others are abed, I will come for you. Would you like that?"

My mouth went dry. *Remember your mother. You want to end up like her after how far you've made it?* Yet for some reason, what came out of my mouth was "y-yes. After they're asleep."

He twirled his fingers at me. A clear dismissal. Feeling a bit like a misbehaving child caught stealing a sweet, I quickly puttered back to the 'flower' wing. I was thankful not to encounter any guards and sighed with relief when I recognized our door. Adrenaline made it easier to pull it open and sneak inside.

The common area lay empty and dark. I made it back to the room I shared with Azalea and Leilani. "Where have you been?" Azalea whispered at me, eyes sharp with suspicion.

I already looked flushed and bothered, so I played into it.

"I uh ... got lost when I stormed out," I admitted sheepishly, not needing to fake the red stain on my cheeks and neck.

Leilani sat up in bed, her eyes crusted with sleep. "Oh. Hey Mari." She laid back down and promptly started snoring again.

Azalea rolled her eyes and went back to her book. Wondering where she got it, I glanced around our room, noticing there were indeed books and other trinkets on the various shelves and on top of the tables.

Huh.

Not that I could read any of them.

I put it all out of my mind and at least pretended to go to sleep. My brain still spun in circles; my body abuzz with all the sensations Zariah had drawn from me.

What if I could marry *him* instead of the prince?

The thought felt as forbidden as his touch. And why not? The prince would not choose a mud girl; everyone knew that. Surely I was good enough for a lowly fireguard, wasn't I?

I closed my eyes, images of myself dancing in one of the colorful prima's purple robes frolicking around in my head. Sleep snuck up on me before I knew it.

I woke to a hand on my mouth and silver-green eyes staring down at me. My hands flew to my face, but Zariah smirked. Confident I wouldn't scream, he moved his hands under my chin and pulled me up to his lips. My eyes shot to the beds to my left, but both Azalea and Leilani were still and silent.

Zariah's kiss was ravishing and possessive, and as vicious and blistering as he was kind and considerate on the streets. It was a side of him I didn't know existed, but I was quickly becoming addicted to it. He bit down on my lower lip, and I opened my mouth wide in surprise. His tongue stroked in eagerly at the opportunity, probing deeply inside of me just as his fingers had hours ago.

When he finally released me, I tried in vain to catch my breath. "I thought we were going to your ... er, somewhere else," I whispered lamely. He hadn't exactly promised that we'd go to his chambers, had he? Surely, this was just as dangerous though, if not more so? What if they caught him in here, deflowering one of the prince's little blooms?

Zariah buried his head in my chest. "Here is safer. They don't watch you like they do me. Besides, everyone thinks I'm up on the wall."

He was shirking his duty for me? The very thought sent a hot bolt of need through my veins.

Leilani made a grunt of unconscious protest in her sleep, rolling over so that she was facing me.

As much as I was into Zariah, this couldn't happen here. Plus, I didn't want to get myself entangled in any situation where I'd suddenly get with child. I would learn from my mother's example. I gently pushed him off. "Find somewhere else then if we can't go to your quarters, but it can't be here."

His eyebrows nearly went to his forehead in disbelief. "You're saying no?" His voice rose to an incredulous pitch, and I smacked his arm to remind him to *shut up*.

"I'm saying we're both idiots. Find somewhere else. Don't come here again in the night, and—"

The dragon suddenly roared, drowning out what I planned to say next. He was so loud and so close that the castle walls shook. Leilani and Azalea bolted awake, and I grabbed Zariah and rolled with him off my bed.

"Get under the bed," I whisper-yelled at him, shoving him at the small space and hopping back onto the mattress to find Leilani wide eyed and staring at me.

The dragon roared again and must have been spewing flames as an orange glow filtered in through our open door. Azalea and Leilani scrambled out of bed to race toward the balcony. Sighing in relief, I went behind them. Surely, as a guard, Zariah was smart and stealthy enough to get out of the room while we were all preoccupied.

SIX

We sprinted toward the balcony, all of us looking like ghosts with our white shifts and pale faces.

Heat billowed into the sitting area from the open balcony, and Ivy was the first to dart outside. I wanted to see as well, but survival instinct kept me inside. I remembered how thin the dome was closest toward the castle.

"IVY! COME BACK!" I shot a glance at Freesia, who seemed to know oh-so-much about everything. There was a flash of fear in her eyes, and she was staying away from the balcony. I took a step toward the balcony and called out. "Ivy! I don't think—"

Oleria grabbed me and yanked me back as a blast of fire hit the balcony so quickly all we could do was scream and dive away. Heat scorched my skin, even as I rolled and put a couch between myself and the flames.

"T-thanks," I muttered quickly to Oleria, who gave me a knowing nod.

Just as quickly as the fire came, it was gone. I darted up, terrified. "IVY!"

No answer.

I took two steps toward the balcony.

"Don't." Leilani put a hand on my arm, stopping me. "It's still too hot. Just give it a minute. Make sure it's gone away."

It made sense, but Ivy was out there, actively dead or dying. The dragon roared again, but this time it was faint and distant. From the corner of my eye, I spied the heavy door to our suite open and close.

At least Zariah got out.

I hurried onto the balcony, the others behind me but keeping a healthy distance. Dawn was just peeking out over the horizon, the pink link filtering through the dome to announce the next day's arrival. I grit my teeth and looked around. The white marble floor and pillars were remarkably untouched by the fire, but the heat burned through the soles of my shoes. Ignoring the pain (which was significant to my injured foot), I made my steps as quick and light as possible as I scanned the balcony.

There! Halfway down the steps, crouched between the balcony's railing was a charred body, devoid of hair or any other distinguishing characteristic. I turned away, my stomach lurching at the sight.

"Is she alright?" Heather called from the living area.

The sound of flesh hitting flesh followed, along with Freesia's snide tone. "Of course she isn't alright! She took dragon fire to the face!"

I rounded the corner just in time to watch Wisteria land a vicious punch to Freesia's jaw. My lips parted in shock, but silently I cheered. I shook my head to get the image of Ivy's charred body out of my mind. She'd been crouching behind the railing, which meant she'd had enough time to realize death was coming for her.

"Stop! Stop it!" I yelled at all of them. Wisteria flexed the hand she hit Freesia with a few times, then scowled and went to her bedroom.

Freesia was still rubbing her jaw as I numbly sank into a cushion. The bottoms of my feet hurt, but the numbness of my mind overruled any physical pain. "When a dragon gets aggressive like that, you *hide*," Freesia announced to us all. "It's looking for someone to roast or munch on!"

I stood at that, the pain in my feet only egging me on. I took two steps toward Freesia and grabbed her by the neckline of her thin shift, balling it in my fist. She was taller than me, but for a split second, she cowered as I held her, Wisteria's punch already beginning to bruise on her skin.

"You knew all that and let her run out there?" Anger made my voice a low growl.

The flash of fear in her eyes felt good, but she quickly replaced it with indifference. Freesia remembered she was taller than me and swatted my hands away. She pushed me hard in the chest and sent me flying into Leilani.

I knocked the smaller girl to the ground, and she let out a cry of pain. I rolled off her and immediately helped her to her feet. "Leilani! I'm so sorry. Are you alright?"

The smaller girl's split lip spoke for itself. Ok. Now I was furious.

I whirled back around to face Freesia, who had the nerve to smirk at me. "This is a competition, mud girl."

I was going to beat her face bloody, and show this stupid pampered stone girl what happened when you flapped your mouth on the mud streets.

Before I could so much as raise a fist, a heavy bang sounded on our door. Everyone jumped except for Freesia and me, still locked in a stare down.

The door opened, and the queen stood before us, her expression put upon in her finery as she gazed upon our terrified, exhausted faces. Oleria poked her head out of the room, eyes wide at seeing the queen.

"I see you're all up and about. Wonderful." Her eyes darted between us, brow furrowing. "There are eight of you. Where's the ninth?"

Mutely, I pointed out toward the balcony. The horror on our faces must have said the rest.

The queen smoothed down the purple silk of her gown and tilted her head toward her fireguards. Two peeled off and went onto the balcony. I stared at her dress, covered in silver with bright gems on the bottom to give the illusion the hem was covered in sparkling drops of water in the morning's sunrise.

So much expense. For whom?

"Come. It is time for your inspection," she intoned, gesturing at us to fall into line like a bunch of children. Which we did. Freesia's nose lifted in the air with superiority, gloating over the fact she'd been correct about what would happen next.

The queen clapped her hands twice and grinned, the two remaining fireguards opening the heavy doors for us. I hoped Zariah had gotten away ok and didn't get into any trouble because of me.

And another girl was dead. Not just another girl. Ivy. She had a name.

Would the rest of us make it out of here alive? It didn't seem so. Then again, why kill us if we could be useful as wives to other nobles? Something about this entire premise didn't sit well with me, but I couldn't put my finger on what it was. Not yet.

The queen didn't speak as she led us down the corridor, down a set of spiral stone steps, and through another hallway, taking lefts and rights that left me completely turned around.

There's no way we'd be able to get back to our rooms without help.

Finally, we descended the final staircase. Here, the white marble gave way to a dark, foreboding stone. The air was musty and wet, and the light faded. It was dark, and getting harder to see. Slimy growths crawled along the stone walls and under our feet.

"Watch your footing. Wouldn't want to start the day with a snapped neck."

Every girl slowed their steps. No one wanted to see a second death today. Well, *I* didn't. The fireguards probably thought it was all entertaining.

The bottom of the steps opened up into what I could only describe as a dungeon. It was a large room with a raised platform in the middle. It was made of wood, but on top was a smooth, flat stone. Standing next to it was a man in stiff white robes, as well as a prima in her flowing purple. The prima looked as unflappable and expressionless as the others had in the bathing chamber. For a moment I thought the man had black hair like me, but as I stared, I realized that wasn't quite right—it was just a dark brown like Heather and Hyacinthe's. Regardless, it was oily, and tied back in a knot behind his head. He also had hair on his chin like the king had. He and the prima didn't look any happier to be there than we were.

Surely, they were joking. With the excess of fur and fabrics upstairs, they couldn't at least put something down between us and the cold stone slab?

No, this wasn't a coincidence. This was a power play by the queen to remind us of our place, and to make us afraid.

The queen gave us a sickening smile. "Come now. Don't waste the day. The prima and my noble will inspect you to ensure you are free of diseases and worthy of my son." She pointed at Leilani. "You, dear. Go on."

Trigger warning begins here.

I cringed for my friend and reached out to give her hand a squeeze as she walked by. Slowly, she climbed up onto the platform, and the man and woman moved to stand in front of her.

"Lie down," the prima commanded. "Noble Vession is here to ensure we do a proper inspection. He speaks for the nobles and makes most of the matches."

The girls straightened up at this, and I resisted the urge to roll my eyes. I was more concerned for Leilani, whose fear was palpable as the prima reached for the bottom of her dress the moment she laid down.

Leilani let out a small gasp as the prima unapologetically hiked her dress up past her hips, baring her naked bottom before all of us. Then she was laying down.

That was bad enough. Then the prima put her hands on Leilani's bare knees and wrenched them apart, her most private areas on full display for the two strangers standing over her.

At least we couldn't see that part, though it must be little comfort. I refused to look away, as did the others. It was awful, but we needed to know what we were going to face. We were next.

It wasn't hard to deduce what was going on by the pained expression on Leilani's face as tears leaked from the corners of her eyes. She bore it bravely, her fingers gripping the edges of the stone so hard the white of her knuckles shone. Was this sacrifice still worth the reward? Would all the girls in the quarters be as eager to come to the Seat if they knew what inner horrors awaited them? Probably. My mother would always be bitter her chance had been taken from her; it didn't matter what she would have had to endure. A moment of discomfort was well worth a guaranteed lifetime of food and shelter.

Freesia swallowed heavily next to me. "My father said the exam was only cursory and limited to our outside skin."

The queen's eyes snapped to her with vicious delight. "Oh, but surely you realized we must take *extra* care of those vying for my son's hand? The royal line is at stake after all."

Freesia had nothing to say to that, nor did I.

Apparently Azalea did, though. "Is it true that sometimes your ... your *purity* breaks doing other things? I heard a girl say it can happen, and you'd never know."

The queen's smile didn't budge. "For ladies of proper breeding, this won't be an issue." Her silver gaze flashed to me, and the corner of her lip upturned in a smirk.

Oh, that bitch. She was counting on the fact I'd lived a hard life to disqualify me. And then what? Kill me? Feed me to the dragon? Send me off to wed some other noble? And, I didn't even really understand what they were talking about. Our purity? What the hell was that and how could we unknowingly break it? My mind sped to last night with Zariah, and panic flared through my veins. My rational brain fought for control. *How would you know any of that took place from looking between my legs?*

I looked away, unable to take the grimace of pain on Leilani's face.

Finally, the prima declared her 'pure' and allowed Leilani to roll off the platform. She walked back to us with silent tears streaming down her face.

The queen gleefully pointed at Azalea, and the process continued.

I refused to look any more, instead staring directly at the ground. Each girl went their turn in succession. After Azalea, Freesia's turn came. She met it with a face so white I thought she'd pass out halfway to the table. Then the queen picked Heather and Hyacinth, who each sobbed so loudly and screamed in such pain that I thought the queen would surely put an end to all of it.

She didn't.

Oleria bore hers with no tears or expression at all, to where I wondered if she was alright. Then the queen's finger roved between me and Wisteria.

"You," the queen pointed at Wisteria, but gave me a smirk.

Oh boy. She was saving the best for last.

Wisteria's hands clenched into fists at her sides and they stayed that way through her entire examination. At the end, the prima withdrew and told her to sit up, then addressed the queen.

"This one is spoiled."

Wisteria's face broke, twisting into despair and confusion. Vession grabbed her by her hair and yanked her up, scowling. "Who was it, eh? Did some fireguard pay you for the privilege?"

"NO!" she screamed, her hands going to her hair to pry his fingers off. "He didn't pay me, he just shoved me down in a back alley and *took*—"

End of trigger warning

"That's enough," the queen whispered, her deadly tone carrying across the large room. "Get her out of here. She is not worthy of my son."

Fireguards must have filed in behind us without my notice, as two came forward, each of them taking an arm and dragging Wisteria between them toward the steps.

"NO! PLEASE! IT WASN'T MY FAULT!"

She tried to rip away and reach us, but the guards were bigger and stronger. Her screams carried up the stone steps, eventually fading.

We all watched her go with wide, terrified eyes.

The queen's gaze landed on me.

Before she could order me up to the table, clanging footsteps banged down the stone staircase to reveal the fireguard's captain, slightly out of breath.

"Your highness, I apologize for interrupting. The prince has finally returned from his inspection of the wall."

Trumpets called from a distance, and the queen smiled, gesturing dismissively to us. "Give them proper clothes immediately. I won't have my son see them so debased." Her gaze turned directly to me. "We aren't done."

I couldn't hide my mild flinch. The queen turned on her skirts and left, ascending the spiral staircase quickly.

Vession clapped his hands, and the fireguards left. Several minutes later, they returned, each bearing beautiful robes in different colors.

"These will be your day-to-day clothes for your rooms," Vession began. His voice was as oily as his hair. If he offered me an apple in the street, I'd be quick to run away. "You'll have a court dresser who will consider how best to dress you. We will make custom gowns for each of you."

Every girl perked up at this, and I resisted the urge to scowl. We'd (well, everyone but me) just been defiled and humiliated, and they had dragged one of us to an unknown fate. But mention a pretty dress and silks? Smiles all around.

A pattern soon emerged as the fireguards stepped forward with their bundles. I tried to search their faces for Zariah, but didn't see him. The stone girls all received a slate gray robe that none-the-less shimmered silver where the light touched it, complete with matching sandals. Azalea got a gorgeous light blue that went well with her coloring, and Leilani got a golden robe that likely represented bread and butter.

Scarcely daring to hope, a fireguard approached me. He handed me the bundle, and I glanced down.

Mud brown.

It didn't shimmer. It didn't glow. It was as ugly and plain as I was.

I fought down my disappointment. I'd known this was coming. I really wasn't supposed to be here, but having physical proof still hurt.

I didn't like the judging looks being shot by the other girls. It was as if I deserved such an ugly robe for being spared the torture they'd just endured. I put the brown robe over my white shift and slid the new sandals onto my feet without complaint. Clothes were clothes.

I could see it was on the tip of Freesia's tongue to argue that I hadn't been examined, but I suppose even bullies had their limits. She shot me one glare, but it lacked her usual venom. Freesia, along with the other girls, just looked vacant and sad.

"Follow," Vession intoned. The prima walked just behind his right shoulder. We fell in line behind her and ascended back up the steps, down the halls, and then finally through the ornate iron doors that opened to the throne room. I'm sure normally we'd be gawking at the walls and finery once more, but there was a tightness to our group that hadn't been present before.

In some way, most of the girls had been innocent when they'd first arrived, only to leave it all behind on that cold, dungeon floor. I smoothed down the rough fabric of my robe, which stuck out awkwardly where the other robes didn't, but I'd definitely take an ugly robe over being examined. My hands shook through it all, belying just how unnerved I was with my narrow escape from assault. I didn't deserve anything less or more than the other girls, but I would take what precious, lucky breaks I could.

Just breathe. You're fine.

I just hoped the queen forgot about it.

We filed into the throne room, every eye turning to us. The gazes weren't kind.

I stared, open mouthed, at the high ceiling, the marble pillars, and the sheer amount of color. The ceiling was open to the sky, the dome acting as the only roof. It must be thinner here, though, because it wasn't as dim as it was in the mud quarter.

The floor shined so much I could see my reflection. Everything about this palace was so *clean* that it only made me feel dirtier. Then again, the dirt was safe, wasn't it? All of this polished marble and spotless possessions made me feel like it was a cover up for the true filth that lay hidden underneath it all.

Nobles lined the side of the hall, and a large purple velvet rug ran down the center and up to the thrones.

The *thrones*.

They were solid gold or looked to be. They were currently vacant. The king stood on the steps, most likely awaiting his son. With his black hair and beard peppered with gray, he looked old enough to be the queen's father. The queen seemed slightly out of breath, tucking a few errant strands of hair behind her ears. Her youthful face was flushed with pleasure.

The trumpets blared a majestic call, startling all of us. We all turned as one as the heavy iron doors parted to reveal the man who would choose one of us to be his wife.

A familiar man walked out first, and I smiled as I recognized Zariah. He was out of his fireguard uniform today, instead dressed like the king himself in a matching tunic of purple with gold embroidered at the edges. Velvet breeches were tucked into soft black boots, and they had pinned a silver sash to his shoulders.

They really go all out for their guards, I thought.

I watched vaguely as Zariah mounted the platform and

walked toward the royal family. I hadn't realized he was so well connected. Was he a captain or his son? That would explain why he got away with being able to help us. I glanced back at the door, craning my neck to see where the prince was. He'd be just behind his guard, wouldn't he?

There was no one else coming. In fact, the fireguards closed the door, and it shut with a heavy bang.

I snapped my gaze back to Zariah, the fireguard who'd tormented me the entire way here, yet had tried to save as many of us as he could. He was also the man who'd kissed me senseless and grazed his fingertips where no one had ever touched me before.

He endured a firm handshake and bear hug from the king, then allowed the queen to kiss him on each cheek.

My breathing hitched, finally putting it all together. Why would they lower themselves to kiss a lowly fireguard?

Because he wasn't a fireguard. The queen was his mother, and the king was his father.

And he was the prince.

CHAPTER
SEVEN

"Prince Zion has returned with perfect timing, as usual." The queen addressed the assembled nobles, a wide, self-satisfied smile on her face. With one sweeping gesture, she showed the seven of us standing below her.

I couldn't stop staring at Zariah—no, Zion—trying to catch his eye. And for what purpose? He'd *lied* to me to take advantage of me! He'd even given me a fake fucking name!

My throat felt tight as I viciously fought back tears. I had to toughen up, or I wouldn't survive. I wouldn't fall for it next time. This was what happened when you let your guard down; this was what had happened to my mother. I was only lucky I'd been firm enough to push him away before he'd gotten what he'd truly wanted.

"This year's crop of flowers had their first inspection. As we celebrate the festival of the flames this week, our first ball will kick off their trial. Tomorrow night, they will show their talents for you. On the third and final night, they will be free to walk among you." She paused, smirking. "Well, those left, of course. The festival will culminate where we celebrate the new marriages and unions made from the games."

I elbowed Oleria next to me. "This is a freaking holiday?" I grumbled underneath my breath.

She nodded dully. "Marriage season. It begins with the Festival of the Flames. All the matches and marriages happen then. It ends in a month after all the new wives are confirmed to be with child."

My stomach rolled.

The nobles smiled along with the queen like they were all in on her little jest. Except we were the joke, not her.

"But before all of that, the prince's arrival interrupted something very important."

My insides froze, and every girl standing near me went stiff. Vession and the prima approached the thrones, stopping at the very bottom. Fireguards brought in a small wooden table and placed it before them.

"All of our new flowers endured their suitability test except one. To kick off the festival, I offer the last inspection to all of you for entertainment."

The crowd broke into loud muttering and excited whispers. Sweat broke out along my forehead.

The queen strode to her throne, gracefully flaring out her dress before sitting down. The king looked annoyed, his lips thinning into a single line. He said nothing, however, even as the same two fireguards grabbed me by my upper arms and dragged me forward.

My eyes shot to Zion in terror.

Something that could have been guilt or shame rippled through his gaze. For a moment he looked like he wanted to stand, but a sharp hiss from the queen had him slamming back into his seat with a grimace. He didn't sit like his parents to watch the show, but neither did he raise a hand or his voice to stop it from proceeding. He just sat there, a blank expression on his face as his fingers dug into the armrests of his throne. Why? Why did he just fucking sit there?

I was numb until my back slammed against the table. That's when I lost my mind. I growled and twisted like an angry cat, refusing to lie there and take it like all the other girls had. If they were going to do this, and in front of an audience no less, then they were going to earn it.

"Oh dear," the queen intoned, voice dripping with false concern. "Perhaps we should just throw this one out. How uncouth."

I went limp. I'd be damned if I gave her a reason to throw me out. Vession pushed me down with two hands on my chest. Each fireguard took one of my legs and tried to wrench them open. I kicked hard, feeling vicious satisfaction when I caught one under the cheek with a vicious kick even if it was on my injured foot.

The sight of blood on his face warmed my heart.

Before I knew what had happened, a hand went around my throat, gentle but firm. In confusion, I glanced up, seeing nothing but dark curls and those green and silver eyes. He ran a finger down my face, starting from my forehead, trailing down my nose, my lips, chin, then neck and chest. My body went fuzzy and warm, everything tingling as my eyes went in and out of focus. I couldn't concentrate on his face above me as my body began to go limp. And the kicker was that I didn't entirely mind it. What magick was this?

"Ssh. Just relax. It'll be over soon."

My legs dropped to the table, completely slack. I knew there was a reason I shouldn't relax, but I couldn't remember what it was. I yawned. Everything was fine, wasn't it?

A cold hand ran up the inside of my thigh, then wrenched them open.

Then the world exploded.

The castle shook and everyone fell to the ground as the dragon above screamed in anger, heat pooling down from the ceiling in waves as the dragon blasted at the dome overhead with his fire over and over again. His roars of fury were so loud I thought my eardrums were bursting—nothing existed except heat and noise.

The hands holding me down were gone. I must have rolled off the table at some point, because the marble under me was cool. I pressed my body against it, desperate to escape the heat. I was sure I was screaming like everyone else, but we could hear nothing over the dragon. We could feel nothing over the dragon. I tried to breathe and couldn't. The air was too hot. The dome protected us from the physical flames, but not from the sheer *heat*.

Hands grabbed me and hauled me up. They cradled me against a body that was hot—far too hot to be walking and moving the way this person was. Shapes and colors whizzed by, but slowly the heat dissipated as they carried me away from it. Blessedly cool air filled my lungs, and I coughed and hacked, unable to calm myself to breathe properly.

Some fucking holiday, I thought.

"Easy now. Easy."

My back hit a soft bed, with silk sheets and soft satin pillows. A hand was on my brow, moving down to press on my chest. The muscles beneath his fingers went loose and warm, relaxing under his touch. I took a full breath in, and fell asleep.

I opened my eyes.

Him. Zari—Zion. The prince.

I cried. Tears of betrayal, despair, and frustration poured down my cheeks. I gulped down breath after breath, but I couldn't stop sobbing. It was as if I'd gone my whole life without crying, and now the dam had burst free, bringing with it every hardship I'd ever faced in my life.

And Zion was getting to see it all.

That only made me cry harder.

"Relax. I got you out. It's fine."

I took a few more shuddering breaths, willing myself to be calm enough to speak. "The other girls," I choked out. "What about them?"

He hesitated, obviously seeing how important this was to me.

I scowled. "Don't you dare lie to me! Again!"

His brows furrowed in anger, but he answered. "The fire-guards guard their charges. If there were any near the girls, they would have risked their lives to protect them. You are all under the queen's protection from outside forces."

I snorted, unable to help it. "And who protects us from her?"

He ran a hand through his hair, clearly rattled. "That was ... unfortunate. I'm sorry. She's never done that before."

Zion stood, pacing around the small room. I slowly sat up, noting the lavish bed and the stone walls. I balled the fabric of the sheets into my fists, trying to make sense of it all. A window across the room showed only empty sky.

Open sky.

"I need you to stay here while I take care of a few things. I will make excuses for you. I'll say you're injured and can't move. I can't explain anything, but you need to stay here."

The intensity in Zion's eyes was alarming, but I didn't care for him or his warnings. My body shook as I realized he had trapped me in his personal tower, so high up that there wouldn't be any protection if the dragon flamed the area near me. I'd be a crispy, charred bit of black ash like Ivy.

The plan was so obvious I started laughing. Hysterical loud guffaws left my mouth, even as tears ran down my face. I couldn't control the tremors of my body.

Zion was leaving me here as dragon bait.

He was trying to talk to me. He was yelling, maybe. I didn't hear any of it. I was so lost in my emotions nothing could touch me. I was out of control and—

Zion hovered over me and sat on my hips, pinning me to the bed. One large hand wrapped around my throat and simply held there, firm. That warm, fuzzy tingling feeling spread through my body again.

All the noise stopped. My thoughts focused. I could breathe. I could think.

"How do you feel?" he asked, his voice strangely detached and clinical.

I hesitated in answering, because I didn't want to admit it. "Contained," I managed. "Safe."

He leaned down and nuzzled into my neck with a pleased growl. I bucked against him, remembering I was pissed at him.

"You lied to me! Get off!"

His hand left my neck, and I pushed away the odd sense of loss.

Zion refused to move, instead glaring down at me with narrowed eyes. "Lied to you? You practically threw yourself at me in the corridor that night! Besides, I didn't hear you complaining." He smirked, and my gaze drew to his mouth. I couldn't help but remember how it taste when we'd kissed, or—

The room rattled and shook, but no roar or wave of heat was forthcoming. Zion sighed and rolled off the bed. "Stay here. I will return. Do not leave this tower. The guards at the bottom will forcibly bring you back if needed."

And with that, Prince Zion abandoned me in his tower, shutting the iron door behind him.

I threw the covers off and dove out of bed, resisting the urge to scream. That scoundrel! That lying sack of—I paused, truly appreciating where I was for a moment. *The prince's private tower.* My earlier thoughts of seeking knowledge and solving the curse popped back into my head, claiming that this was a wonderful opportunity to *snoop*. It wasn't like the prince had forbidden me from going through his things, and what did he expect me to do stuck here—potentially all day? I owed it to my own survival—and begrudgingly, the other girls' survival —to find out what I could.

I started with a small table across the room that was serving as a desk. Paperwork scattered the top of it, and never had I felt as lacking as I did in that moment.

I bet Freesia could read. And Azalea, with her histories from the fireguards. Even frightened Heather and Hyacinthe probably knew their letters. The answer to the curse and the dragon could sit right in front of me, and I wouldn't know it.

It was tempting to rip everything to shreds, but even I admitted that was petty. I turned from the desk and instead crossed to the large wooden cabinet.

Inside was a rainbow of fabrics. Long tunics hung in every shade imaginable, organized by color. Gold and silver tassels winked at me from the darkness, as well as jewels and gold that were inlaid into the fabric itself. The smell of smoke and ashes met my nose.

Then again, everything this high up smelled like the dragon. I shivered as I remembered the heat and the screams. I really hoped the other girls were alright. I wouldn't be too upset if it had boiled the queen alive, but I wouldn't hold my breath.

I shut the cabinet doors, not interested in clothes. Long tapered candles lined the walls, currently unlit since it was approaching midday. I spied an apple and a hunk of cheese on a small table in the middle of the room, and seized it eagerly.

I didn't feel a smidge of guilt as I scarfed it down. They had yet to feed any of us since we came, after all.

I stopped chewing at a knock on the door, bits of apple sticking out of my cheek. I swallowed.

"It's me. I've brought you something to eat."

Zion. Back so soon?

Reluctantly, I opened the door and there he stood in all his fireguard finery minus the helmet, holding out a tray with chicken and rice.

"Sorry it took a bit, but it should still be warm. I had to ... switch shifts."

A bit? He must have run to not only fetch me food so quickly, but also change into his armor. Then again, he'd likely made a servant get it. Regardless, his apologetic attitude wouldn't make up for lying to me earlier.

I made Zion watch in uncomfortable silence as I ate, not caring a wit if he felt awkward or not. This was my first meal since they had taken me from the streets of the mud quarter, and it was *hot*. Hot food was a luxury. I was used to hard bread and cold cheese and dried meats. This meat was warm and moist, and without helping it, I groaned aloud as the meat practically melted off the bone and into my mouth.

I expected a rude comment from him, but he only gave me a genuine smile as if seeing me happy made him happy.

My eyes narrowed.

That wasn't the Zion I was familiar with. Then again, it *was* in line with the fireguard who'd tried his best to save as many of us as he could.

Zariah.

Was that the difference? Did Zion feel as though he had to act a certain way as a prince, and then another as a fireguard? Or was it the other way around? Perhaps the selfish jerk *was* his real self, and the fireguard persona was a lie.

My head hurt, so I took another bite of chicken. And I ate all the juicy yellow vegetables and the warm bread with real butter. I barely tasted the sweet juice as I drank it too fast, worried he would take it away before I could have my fill.

"Easy now. I can get you more if you'd like."

I dropped the drumstick I'd been holding, gazing at him dumbstruck.

"There's *more?*" I asked, incredulous.

He laughed nervously, putting a hand behind his head. When he realized I was serious, he cleared his throat. "Yes. Well. Alright. I'll get more."

I barely noticed his departure as I wiped the rest of the plate clean, even taking advantage of his absence to lick the plate like a dog. Even the drippings from the meat sent my taste buds exploding with flavor. I'd be damned if I wasted a drop of the best meal I'd ever had. I barely glanced up when Zion returned and swapped out my empty plate for the full one.

I was halfway through that plate before I slowed down, pausing enough to study him more. What was it about the fire-guard uniform that transformed him? His eyes were the same green and silver, but he looked at me differently than he had with his prince persona.

"I'm going to take you back now. You need to be fitted for your dress for the final evening and clothes for your talent portion." He smiled down at me as though that were some-thing to be excited about.

"If I survive, I suppose," I quipped back smartly, feeling more myself with a full belly.

Zion smirked. "From what I saw of our journey here, you will have no trouble with anything thrown at you. Getting here is where most girls fail."

My eye twitched. "You assume I have some sort of talent to display. Unlike the other girls, I grew up … differently. I can't even read—"

I stopped myself there, not sure why I was about to reveal a weakness to someone I didn't fully trust.

"Surely, you're good at something," he pressed with a touch of arrogance I recognized from his prince persona.

I rolled my eyes, resting my head on the table between my arms. "Only thing I'm good at is fighting off the other kids. I usually got to the food wagons first. The bigger girls would try to steal my food once I left, but they could rarely catch me."

One eye rose. "So you're a good fighter?"

I snorted. "I wouldn't call it fighting, not like what you do with swords and training and all of that. It's more like street tussling with dirty tricks and hair pulling and teeth kicking."

"Try me."

Zion took his armor off, setting the heavy breastplate on his chair along with his arm cuffs and knee guards. The metal shone like liquid fire on the floor, and he slowly turned to face me.

Too slowly.

I dove for his legs, and he toppled over me, surprised by the sudden attack. His chin hit the tabletop, gashing it open. Desperately, he rolled on his back, but I already had a hand on his scabbard and pulled a short sword free, shoving it forward and resting the blade against his neck a second later.

"Dragonfire. You're fast," he panted, not even moving to staunch the blood flowing down his chin.

He grabbed the back of my neck and did that weird trick where he made all my muscles go loose and fuzzy.

I dropped the sword on his chest and he rolled off, smirking. The moment he broke contact with me, I could move again. Huffing, I sat back down to finish the rest of my chicken.

"Careful, you have your dressing fitting later." He stood gingerly, one hand pressed to the wound on his chin.

I narrowed my eyes at him. "What's that supposed to mean?"

He frowned. "Not sure, really. It's just something my mother always said when she ate."

"The queen," I stressed, unable to believe that horrible woman birthed someone who wasn't completely evil.

"She has ... nicer moments," he insisted, still more concerned about the gash than me. "We really have to get going. I'll need to take care of this before anyone sees."

He put his sword back in his scabbard and pulled the door open, grabbing a bundled shirt from the floor and pressing it to his face.

"Why? Don't want anyone to know a girl messed up that pretty face of yours?" I taunted him.

He shot me a dopey grin. "You think my face is pretty?"

I sputtered in indignation, and he laughed. I raced ahead down the stairs, my face burning. I heard him descend behind me.

"If you must know," he began, still chortling, "I simply don't want you to be whipped for besting a fireguard in hand-to-hand combat, let alone me. So if anyone asks, I tripped on the stairs."

I blinked at him.

Zion overtook me in the hallway. "Do you remember how to get back?"

He was kidding, right?

"It's not that bad," he continued. "You'll get it, eventually."

Yeah. Sure. I tried to keep track as we turned left, then right, then right again, then down a winding staircase that messed up my sense of direction, then another hall, then more turns, and another staircase. I gave up after that, and instead focused on the paintings that lined the walls. This side of the castle was mostly landscapes, and seemed older than the flower suites or the throne room, oddly enough. The scent of ashes and smoke lingered constantly here, a reminder that this wing was the closest to the dragon. Like the rest of the palace, it was white and clean and too sterile for my liking. It felt like my very presence was enough to dirty the pristine environment around me.

Eventually, I recognized my corridor along with the heavy doors to the flower suite. They were currently wide open with servants and strange men and women coming and going.

"I see they've already started. I'll leave you to it." Zion nudged me forward. I almost considered asking why he'd told me a different name, but it seemed obvious: he wanted to keep his personas separate. I understood that.

Zion turned to go, then paused, his expression thoughtful. "You really should show your fighting style. It's unique and you're quick."

He gave me a small smile that felt only for me, then he stomped away, his heavy armor and boots clunking after him.

CHAPTER
EIGHT

I took a deep breath, steeled myself, and walked into the suite.

"THERE SHE IS! Porter! She's here!" A hand landed lightly at my elbow as a short man in flowing robes quickly took charge of me, guiding me forward onto a makeshift pedestal surrounded by servants holding mirrors. All around me were the other girls in similar states. They pointed and cried out when they saw me.

"Mari! We were so worried!" Leilani shouted at me from across the room. A servant pulled at her hem and poked her to bring her attention back to standing still.

"Yes! Especially after Oleria," Azalea added.

I wanted to ask what she meant, but the short man at my side demanded my full attention. He had to be a noble, and a very ... fancy one. His hair was a bright yellow, combed through with gold dust. His robes were bronze and shimmered just as much as he did. His large eyes were a light gold color I'd never seen before. Or was he simply trying to look like the dragon? The thought that someone would spend time and effort on something so ... frivolous was mind-blowing.

"My name is Elio, and I will design your dress for the big night," he gushed out with enough enthusiasm for the both of us. Or so I figured.

He fingered my ugly brown robe distastefully, shooting looks at what the other girls were wearing. "Yeah ... sorry you got put with me. I'm the mud girl," I informed him quickly, wanting to get his disappointment over with. I doubted the queen would let him make anything nice for the girl from the mud quarter.

His eyes grew cold, and his gaze sharpened. "Nonsense. There is nothing wrong with dirt. Jewels come from the dirt, don't they? They must pry the most precious materials in the world from the earth's grasp."

His grip on the fabric between his fingers tightened. "No, this won't do. My dear, we will ensure you *shine*."

I barely kept from rolling my eyes at him. "The stone girls will wear jewels. I'm not one of them."

Elio let go of my robe and rubbed his hands together with excitement. "No, but there is one gem. They don't mine it because they can't find it. It's the one precious resource that hasn't surfaced in hundreds of years, and those from the mud quarter used to mine it exclusively."

I leaned in, curious. I'd thought Shava was pulling my leg when she'd said our people used to be miners. What did he know?

"Oh no, my dear. We won't ruin the surprise. I'm taking your measurements, and that will be that. You'll see it the day of and get no other hints beforehand!" He trilled in delight, then accosted me all over with a long piece of string, muttering and calling out numbers to a servant who dutifully marked them down on a piece of parchment.

My mood soured. Even the servants here knew how to read and keep sums.

"Lift your feet, dear."

Begrudgingly, I lifted my leg and let him trace the shape of my foot against yet another sheet of parchment. He tutted at my injured heel, but said nothing else.

"What garments would you like for your talent display?" he asked suddenly.

I blanched, then remembered what Zion had suggested. Surely that had been a joke, though. I couldn't seriously fight. Could I?

I thought carefully, then turned to Elios. "Clothes for fighting. Worn leather boots or soft fabric that won't be tight. I'd like fitted pants at the waist, but flare them out a little from there, so they don't restrict my movements. Have the fabric stop at my calves."

He stared at me for a full second, then his face exploded in a wide grin. He snapped at his assistant. "Well? What are you waiting for? Write what she says!" The servant stared at me, mouth hanging open slightly, then shook her head and dutifully took down what I said.

"For my shirt, something like the fireguards wear, but lighter in the chest. I want it to protect me, but also to be flexible. I need a full range of movement in my arms." I tried to think if there was anything else. "And something to tie my hair back with."

Elion was grinning like a lunatic. "Anything else?"

I shook my head.

"Very good, very good. I cannot wait to see your talent, Miss Marigold Mudthrice." Finished, he shoved all his parchments and tools at his two servants, who scampered away with them. For a moment I thought he would follow, then he paused, turning back to me.

He leaned in close, brushing my ear with his lips. "You are stronger than you know. You are more beautiful than you will allow yourself to accept. The dragon is rising."

Before I could turn and demand he explain himself, he fled the room. In all the commotion, no one had noticed our strange interaction. At least I was now free to wander to the other girls.

I went to Leilani first. Her stylist was a red-haired noble-woman in a sweeping silver gown, whose lined face only made her look more distinguished.

"Definitely something as pale as possible to bring out her eyes and the color of her hair. How high of a heel can you handle?"

At Leilani's panicked look, the stylist merely huffed and made a tick on her parchment.

I leaned in. "Azalea said something about Oleria. What's up?"

Leilani kept her body and head still as servants measured her from head to toe, moving only her lips. "When the dragon attacked the dome, she was closest to the middle. The heat left burns all over her body even though there was no fire. The primas took her to recover. That's all we know."

Well, that was reassuring. At least she hadn't died.

"Is she still expected to compete?" I asked, curious.

Leilani shrugged, earning her a small slap from the servant measuring between her shoulders.

"What clothes do you require for your talent this evening?"

Leilani bit her lip, thinking. "Are you familiar with the traditional garb from the bread quarter?"

Her stylist blinked slowly as if the question were an insult.

"Er, right. Well, I need a traditional dress from my quarter, down to my knees, embroidered in my house colors of yellow and blue. And—"

My eyes glazed over slightly as Leilani ordered a very specific set of garments. I only recognized half of the words she said and had no clue what her talent was based on what she described. Her stylist kept up, eyes shining with interest the longer Leilani's list of demands grew.

A little stunned, I wandered over toward the stone sisters, Heather and Hyacinthe.

"Something matching," they were telling their stylist, a young girl who seemed eager to please as she nodded quickly at everything they said. "As long as it's pretty, and keep the sleeves short. We'll be using our hands. Well, I will be, at any rate," Heather finished, shooting her sister a rare grin.

I glanced over to Freesia, who had servants and stylists dancing around her as though she were already queen.

One by one, the girls finished, and the mob of people coming in and out of our chambers diminished. Finally, it was just the six of us, since Oleria was with the primas. I tried not to think about what happened to her. The next time I was alone with Zion, I'd ask if he knew anything else.

We'd barely been alone for a moment before Freesia turned on me, her face twisting with jealousy. "You were gone all night with the prince! Did he finish his 'examination' in private?"

A few of the girls looked outraged on my behalf, but most shot me knowing looks as well. I grit my teeth. "I spent most of it unconscious, actually. Is Oleria alright?"

Freesia waved my concerns away, but Leilani intercepted her before she could get too wound up. "Come off it, Freesia. At least only two people saw our privates. The prince was about to show Mari's to the entire court."

I frowned, brow furrowing. He'd certainly been about to, hadn't he? He'd even done that fuzzy muscle thing to make it easier to do so. I mentally reminded myself to kick Zion in the nuts when I saw him next. Or Zariah. Whoever the fuck he was pretending to be.

"I guess there are a few drawbacks to living in the Seat, aren't there?" I asked the group at large, sitting down on one of the low couches. Down in the quarters, we'd always dreamed of living high on the Seat with all its wealth and riches. We'd never considered what it might be like to live that much closer to the dragon.

"I don't know why no one kills it. Maybe that could be *your* talent, mud girl: dying despite all odds."

I rolled my eyes at Freesia, not even bothered by her vitriol. "The next time I'm in the prince's bed, I will ask."

Her face went red like I knew it would, and she stomped off to her room. Azalea, Leilani, and the stone sisters stayed.

"I think it must have been horrible, almost being examined like that in front of everyone, and in front of the king and queen!" Azalea whispered in horror, covering her eyes with her hands.

I thought back to that moment, frowning. Zion had done something with his hands to me—twice. If I closed my eyes, I could still feel it, the strange sensation that started at my neck and went down my forearm, trailing down my chest to rest in between my breasts. The sensation left behind had been nothing but warmth and comfort, and to my utter embarrassment, need. Whatever it was, it had left me utterly boneless and vulnerable.

I couldn't afford to be vulnerable.

"The prince is an ass, like most princes are, I imagine," I said instead, trying to shake off the feeling. "His tower was just a single room, high up." My gaze wandered away, remembering the smell of fire and brimstone in the air. "It has to be high up, because all you could smell was smoke and ash. I was half-convinced I was being set up as dragon bait."

I gave a wry grin, but no one else was smiling. Even Freesia was gazing at me with a mild look of horror.

"But, uh, I'm here," I finished lamely. "What are all your talents? We should practice."

I wasn't sure if it had anything to do with losing Ivy yesterday and almost losing Wisteria (and me, apparently), but no one protested this idea. We all went our separate ways, huddling into corners or going away to practice in our rooms.

Freesia was oddly quiet, watching with sharp eyes but saying nothing. I wasn't going to do anything to disturb the quiet since it allowed me to think.

Why had Zion taken me to his rooms? Why had he saved me at all? Was it because we'd formed some kind of bond on our way up to the Seat, or because he was trying to save us all? It was the only thing that made sense, but I didn't understand what would make him decide to talk to me out of all the other girls. As far as I was aware, he didn't give any personal attention to anyone else.

He definitely was interested in me. Now, whether it was lust or something more? Well, that remained to be seen. If I won this competition, I would earn the right to stand by his side permanently. I'd be in a perfect position to demand someone read me all the fireguard scrolls, and I'd discover the dragon's weakness. I'd kill it and finally end its reign of terror. I paused, realizing that this could be about more than me surviving, more than the other girls surviving. If I won this thing, I could improve the lives of *everyone in the mud district.*

Whether Zion had feelings for me or I him, I would be in the best position to kill the dragon if I was his wife. Killing the dragon meant I could research these claims of my people mining, and give them purpose again. That made the way forward clear: I had to win this stupid competition despite the queen's best efforts at subterfuge. I'd survive, win, and help my people. As queen, I could feed and clothe them. I'd bring them all up to the Seat, and the girls could go with the boys to learn how to read and do sums. I would leave no kids to fight over scraps in the streets.

The image of the little girl who'd stood crying next to me at my reaping filled my mind. She wouldn't have to grow up like I did, taking care of a mother who slowly withered from the inside out. I would make sure that girl had a future.

After I ended the reign of flames and killed the dragon, of course.

I grabbed a nearby apple from a food tray and took a deep bite. Juice flew from my chin. Plotting to save the world was hungry work.

CHAPTER
NINE

I 'd been dreading this, but it was the next necessary step to advance in these 'games.'

They led us all into the grand ballroom where the royal family was already seated on their thrones on a raised dais. Zion was in his princely demeanor today, dressed in a formal military jacket with woven threads of red and gold that looked like liquid fire going up his shoulders.

Always fire. Always flowers.

The king had the same jacket, but the entire piece was nothing but woven thread meant to represent flames. While the effect worked on Zion, it looked garish on the aging king. The queen sat serenely by his side in a dress of pure silver that wrinkled and creased when she moved. She eyed all of us with thinly veiled disdain in her tight smile until her eyes landed on me.

Vession led us proudly into a straight line and motioned for us to all sit on the bottom step of the dais.

Like we were all exotic pets.

I couldn't help but notice how everyone stared at me. The

queen glared openly, twisting her head and whispering franti-cally into the king's ear, who frowned. Zion stared.

Not that I blamed them.

Elio had covered me head to toe in a glittering jewel I'd never seen before—one that shined so brightly that the other girls only stared in jealousy as he wrapped the heavy skirt and bodice around me. He said I only got away with it because he was borrowing the jewels from deep within the royal vaults: something the queen had allowed them to do without real-izing this gem was in there as well.

"That's not fair! Why can't we wear such jewels?" Freesia had argued when I'd emerged from my room fully dressed. The other designers weren't happy as they'd clearly been outdone, but they answered nonetheless.

"It is the mud girl's birthright," they murmured and went back to dressing their own girls.

The stones ranged from the size of my head to no bigger than my pinky nail. They flashed a pure white around me, and in that dress, I felt beautiful for the first time in my life.

"They're called diamonds," Elio had whispered into my ear, "and your people used to be king of them."

I had so many questions, but we were immediately whisked off to the ballroom.

Elio had kept my hair up high in a tight braid and out of my face. I'd submitted to a bit of makeup, though I wore flat black boots on my feet. The other girls were radiant as well, but they all acted like I'd stolen something from them with my special dress.

Freesia looked captivating in a white gown that was covered in moonstones and quartz that flashed different colors as the lights hit it. Her dress was lined with silver edging, and she matched the queen so perfectly with their silver outfits and white hair that I knew it had to be intentional.

They dressed Heather and Hyacinth in purple silk with flowing gauze trains and cowls that ghosted over their shoulders. They covered their dresses in amethyst and black lace; I thought their designer had done a fair job making them complement each other while still marking them as individuals. Heather's hair was down and curled, making her look more like an innocent child than she already appeared. Hyacinth's hair was half-up, half-down, making her look slightly older and more sophisticated. They both wore silver jewelry and sandals.

Azalea was a vision in a white dress, setting off her red hair brilliantly. The dress was simple, but had the effect of enhancing her natural beauty—her face was bare of the makeup caked on the other girls.

Leilani looked magickal. Her stylist had put her in a dress made of flowers. I yearned to touch one to see if it was real or made of silk, but resisted. The colors were all pretty pastels, ranging from soft pinks to yellows and oranges. The same shades offset her blue eyes, and she wore simple slippers and ribbons in her hair.

Oleria was nowhere to be seen. She must be too injured to keep competing.

I ignored the stares and kept my gaze straight ahead as Vession had instructed.

"The contestant from the art district will go first."

Vession bowed and backed away to stand next to our row. Azalea shakily stood, and mentally I sent her a wave of support. What would she do? Paint? Draw?

She made her way toward a small table off to the side, and a guard carrying a silk screen approached from the wings. The guard unfolded it with one shake of his wrist and shielded Azalea from the front.

Muttering broke out among the crowd. What *was* she

doing? A second guard came with a second screen and shielded her back. Azalea was still visible from the side so we could see what she was doing, but not the results.

"Cosmetics?" scoffed Freesia, putting a hand daintily to her chest. "What a waste. She should have painted a rock or something."

None of us had anything to offer. The ballroom went quiet as she worked. I'd thought Azalea would have painted as well and maybe she was. Makeup and paint both used brushes; the only difference was the canvas.

Ten minutes passed, and the crowd was growing restless, muttering darkly among themselves. The queen rapped her nails on the edge of her throne impatiently, her lips pursed into a thin line. Those of us still sitting on the steps wiggled a bit, trying to relieve our cramping bottoms.

We all jumped as Azalea threw down the brushes and cosmetics with a *clank*. She reached down into a small basket and withdrew a long, white wig, flipping it easily onto her head and making a few small adjustments.

"I'm ready," she intoned with confidence, and the fire-guards stepped forward and removed the screens simultaneously, stepping out of the way with a flourish.

The crowd gasped. The queen stood up from her throne, eyes sharp. My jaw dropped, and the surrounding girls gawked and elbowed each other, forgetting for a moment we were supposed to all be terrified and competing against each other.

Azalea stood before us, transformed into an exact twin of the queen, minus the silver eyes.

I stared. How had she done that with just *makeup* and a wig? It almost seemed magickal!

"What sorcery is this?" the queen hissed, anger flushing across her pale skin.

Azalea flinched, then rushed forward with a wet rag.

"No sorcery! Look!" She dragged the rag across her nose, wiping off a large smear of cosmetics. Her own larger, more pronounced nose stared back at us, shattering the illusion.

"Here, I will show you!" she continued, rushing back to the cosmetics and picking up a few items. She rushed over to the queen and started working on her nose again.

"It's all about shading and painting. It's a visual trick," she explained desperately, drawing dark lines on either side of her nose, then blending them out. We all watched in fascination as her larger nose disappeared under the paint, and she carefully sculpted the queen's nose back onto her face.

The queen sat back on her throne, suitably impressed. "What skill," she mused quietly. "I did not know such feats were possible."

Azalea stepped back, nervously clutching her materials.

"Well done, daughter of the artisan quarter."

The queen clapped, nodding her head. As if the queen's actions were a blessing, the crowd rushed to add their own applause, thunderous and enthusiastic.

Azalea flushed, then moved to wipe her face. The queen stopped her with one motion of her arm.

"Leave it while you're here, as a reminder to everyone of your skill."

Azalea nodded, then came and squeezed down next to me on the steps. I stared at her hard as she sat down, feeling for a moment as though I were next to the queen's younger sister. I shook my head, turning to watch the fireguards quickly clear away the materials.

Who was next?

The queen gestured her hand carelessly. "You two. The twins."

I used her distraction to glance up at Zion. His face was an impassive mask, so different from the open emotions he displayed when he paraded around as Zariah. I glanced up at the ceiling, which was free of the dragon's dark shadow. Perhaps he was gone today.

Heather and Hyacinthe went green as they stood and shakily made their way toward the middle of the ballroom. Neither of them dared to correct the queen about them being twins. As if that even mattered. Hyacinth was slightly taller than Heather, whose hair was a slightly darker shade of brown than her older sister's. They clutched each other's hands hard, and mine twitched in reflex. It would be nice to have someone I could safely show my fear to, instead of having to maintain an unaffected mask at all times.

Two fireguards approached, one carrying what looked like a string box and the other a small table.

Hyacinth took the strange box from him and arranged it just-so on the table. It was a rectangle covered in strings, with chipped gold embellishments along the top. It looked old. Heather stood slightly in front of her, looking ready to puke.

But then Hyacinth withdrew two small metal hammers from within the instrument and gave a few taps. Haunting, beautiful sounds filled the space, echoing off the pillars and floating toward the ceiling.

Music.

The muttering stopped, and the hall went deadly silent.

Hyacinth took a deep breath and looked to her sister, who nodded weakly.

The song itself was charming and beautiful with Heather's voice singing a pretty melody that was a warm compliment to the instrument's notes. Yet, Hyacinth and Heather were clearly terrified, which made for a difficult show. They would have been better off playing in a corner somewhere as background music and not as the main event. Even Zion looked bored, his head leaning against his hand propped up on the armrest of his throne. His eyes drifted shut.

I half-suspected the queen to end it early, but she simply sat listening, neither hating it nor enjoying it. When it ended, the two girls bowed, and the queen nodded slightly in their direction. The fireguards took the table and the instrument away, and they scurried back over and squeezed in on the end after Azalea.

"I forgot the words!" Heather mouthed to me, horrified, but looking relieved that the entire ordeal was over.

I didn't need to look at the queen to know who would be next. They would design the order to humiliate me. Leilani would be next. The queen would call up Fressia after her and then have me go last, just so she could prove how lacking I was compared to such perfection.

I wiped my sweaty palms against the cool marble floor underneath me. I hoped my plan worked.

"The bread district girl," the queen drawled next, not even bothering to name Leilani. The queen wasn't even pretending not to have favorites. Then again, why would she? She was the queen.

Leilani popped up brightly, ignoring the insult. Her skirts and ribbons tumbled around her like a summer sprite, her blonde hair curling and shining. Her white teeth flashed as she smiled at everyone, gazing at the crowd with contemplation. No fireguards came to give her materials, so she obviously would not bake. The crowd seemed as mystified as I was.

"Will you come dance with me?" She touched the arm of a young nobleman in a black velvet tunic. The man blushed at her attention and shot an anxious look at an older man next to him, possibly his father.

"I don't know if—"

"Don't worry, you can come too!" Before either could

protest, Leilani pulled both men out of the crowd, then another woman, who was likely the older man's wife and the younger man's mother.

"I'm going to teach you a folk dance of the bread quarter. It's very fun!"

I covered my mouth at the look of horror on the faces of the nobles, but the nervous glances they shot toward the queen told me they wouldn't dare refuse. And Leilani knew it.

"Stand next to me and the men across from us, like this."

Leilani positioned everyone, then took a few steps forward toward the young man, holding out her hand flat. Instinctively, the man took a step forward to meet her, his hand matching hers.

Leilani beamed. "That's it!"

The older couple repeated it, then followed as Leilani stepped back and gestured for the younger man to do so as well.

"Great! Now, just—"

I watched with amusement as Leilani patiently taught a simple, yet graceful little folk dance, complete with twirls and even a small lift at the end. The nobles with her looked flustered, but determined.

"Now, let's try that faster!"

The older woman let out a startled giggle as her husband lifted her into the air and spun her around, her dark locks flying. Sped up, the dance looked much more fun.

Above us, the same instrument Hyacinth had played earlier now emitted a lively little tune as a noble musician joined in. Leilani beamed at him and started clapping to the beat. The crowd slowly joined in one by one, and Leilani turned toward her partner, grinning madly.

"Ready?"

He couldn't take his eyes off her. "Yes."

They spun around the floor, doing the dance at over double the speed they'd just done. His parents watched one circuit, then joined in with determination. Whoops and catcalls floated out from the audience to cheer them on, and even the king was tapping his foot along with the beat, leaning forward eagerly in his seat. Zion watched stoically, but I could have sworn the corner of his mouth twitched with a smile.

The queen rolled her eyes.

Pride rose in my chest. Leilani had charmed everyone in the court with nothing other than herself.

"Come on! Everyone!"

The crowd of nobles rushed forward, finding partners and clumsily attempting the dance for their own. It was simple enough that most picked it up in a few rounds, and soon the hall filled with lively laughter and swirling skirts.

"Will you dance with me, my queen?" The king rose from his seat and was holding out his hand to the queen.

"Mindless peasant stomping," she muttered under her breath and continued to stare forward.

The king huffed, then descended the steps to offer Freesia his hand. Stunned and going pale, she let the king swing her out to the floor. I was in such shock watching that I didn't notice Zion until he tapped me on the shoulder. I jumped, putting my hand to my chest.

"Zion! I—"

"Dance with me."

He didn't give me a chance to refuse, tugging me to my feet and practically dragging out onto the floor.

I did not know what I was doing, stumbling along as the dance forced me to lean on Zion or risk falling. My feet stepped on his toes at least a few times. But after a few minutes when no one stopped us or insisted he quit touching me, I noticed the smiles and laughter of the surrounding couples.

Leilani's dress floated around her as she moved gracefully with her chosen partner, who was red in the face and probably half in love with her by now. Freesia wasn't doing much better, trying, and failing, not to stare at the king as they danced together. My steps became less stilted as I relaxed into Zion's left hand around my waist, his right fingers entwined with mine.

This was ... fun.

"Faster!" cried Leilani, and the musicians complied. The steps were pretty basic, which was absolutely necessary as the speed increased. I gave a small yelp but held onto Zion for dear life as we jumped and stepped forward, back, only to do it all over again. A grin split my face as Zion skipped the jump and picked me up instead, twirling me around in the air and sending my skirts whirling around me like I was a true princess. The diamonds scattered the light and bathed everyone nearby in its reflection. I laughed with the sheer joy of it all, never in my life having taken part in something so frivolous.

I gave Zion's hand a squeeze, suddenly thankful for the opportunity to be here. He grinned at me, then pulled me close against his chest, stopping our movements. The other dancers continued to move around as if we were the center of the universe. My breath caught as those silver eyes tinged with green caught mine.

Time slowed.

He leaned forward, his lips inches from mine.

"Stop!"

I crashed into Zion as I leaned forward and he didn't, my nose colliding hard with his chest. He caught me with one hand and pushed me back on my feet, his gaze angry and fixed toward the queen. I didn't need to look to imagine the angry expression on her face. I should have known anything that made me happy would make her furious. Especially when it involved her son.

"You keep getting me in trouble," I muttered.

His face pinched. "She has overstepped her boundaries. I am supposed to be running these trials, not her."

I snorted uncharitably, remembering the cruel and invasive 'exam' I had barely escaped from. "Then why don't you? Unless you find her cruelty amusing?"

He leveled a glare at me, equal to his mother's. "I must obey her."

It was on the tip of my tongue to ask why, but I didn't get the chance.

"Everyone will cease these foolish antics. I want to see Freesia perform," the queen ordered, sitting down imperiously on her throne. The king kissed Freesia's hand and gave it a pat, urging her forward. The rest of the nobles and girls drifted back to their spots like mice scattering when the pantry door opened.

"I am supposed to be running the games," Zion angrily repeated as we parted.

I whipped my head back toward him. "Then run them," I grumbled quietly before taking my seat on the steps. Leilani reluctantly bid goodbye to her dance partner, and the nobles gathered back on their side of the hall. Leilani's face was flushed, but oddly pleased as she sat down on the end of the line. She'd performed well.

Freesia stayed in the center, still looking a bit rattled after dancing with the king. Oddly, the queen didn't seem angry at her for *that*.

Whatever.

She opened her mouth and with no kind of accompaniment sang.

CHAPTER

TEN

My mouth dropped open. Heather's voice had been pleasant to hear, but she had absolutely nothing on Freesia. Her voice was simply ... otherworldly. She reached notes I didn't think were possible and all with a tone and sound so pure it didn't seem real. She didn't even sing words, but just let her voice soar up and down. The king stared along with most of the court, while the queen leaned back in her throne, smirking as she rapped her red nails on the edge of her arm rest.

Zion's attention was rapt on Freesia as well.

I didn't enjoy the music as much after that.

Why bother going through with all of this nonsense if the queen already knew who she wanted? Was Zion content to let his mother pick his wife for him? He could insist he was in charge all he wanted, but everyone knew who really held the strings.

My heart ached at how useless it all was. We'd had custom outfits made for this event, and the nobles stood in their finest. There was a mountain of food spread around the edges of the hall that no one touched. It would have been enough to feed everyone in the mud quarter for a week.

The waste made me sick.

Focus on your task; get close to the prince, find out the truth about the dragon and kill it.

My nerves settled, and the nausea faded. I could do this. I had to do this. Otherwise, I was just Marigold Mudthrice, another dirty girl born on the third street of the mud quarter.

After what seemed an eternity, the last note from Freesia's vocal cords hovered in the air for a moment, her eyes closed as the sound dissolved into silence.

I jerked as thunderous applause erupted, first from the queen, then the king, Zion, and the rest of the nobles that were gathered. Numbly, I brought my hands together as the other girls cheered as well. Freesia may be a frigid bitch, but that bitch could sing.

Moisture gathered on my palms as I realized I was next. My 'talent' would seem common and dirty after such a magnificent display. I shot a look at the queen, who was already smirking at me.

Speaking of bitches ...

My throat moved as I swallowed heavily.

"I cannot wait to see what our final girl has for us."

I stood automatically as the queen's voice picked at me, barely noticing Leilani's whispered 'good luck' as my feet carried me to stand in front of the throne. Elio had planned for this. I grabbed at the three ties holding my dress up; one at my neck, one at my waist, and one on my back. I pulled them hard, and the dress fell to my feet in a glittering pool.

The crowd gasped at the cheap trick, but I didn't pay them any attention. The fighting leathers that had been under the dress this entire time felt strong and flexible as I took a deep breath and closed my eyes.

"Well?" the queen demanded, tapping one fingernail against the wood of her armrest again. It seemed to be a habit for her.

"For my talent, I would like to fight a fireguard."

The queen laughed, tension bleeding from her body as she assured herself this was a silly, pointless task. "How predictable. Very well. Why not make it more ... *interesting?*"

She leaned in from her throne toward me, doing her damnedest to intimidate me.

I refused to back down. "How so?"

The queen put a dramatic hand to her breast. "In the past we've had girls ... try to run away. None have truly been fighters. If you are sincere in this 'talent' of yours, then let us seal the match with blood. That way, I assure my court you won't try to cry or faint your way out of it. It will be a blood match. If my fireguard wins, you are disqualified."

How inspiring. "And if I win?"

A slow, sick smile spread across her face, as though such a thing were laughable. "I suppose I'd have to relinquish my crown if such a thing were to happen."

I raised an eyebrow. "Is the fight to the death, then?" How utterly predictably of her.

The queen tittered, trying to sound like a bird. To me, she sounded like a cawing crow. "How barbaric. First blood will suffice."

My hands tightened into fists at my side. *Yeah, first blood, which may or may not be a deadly blow.* If the guard killed me, then she wasn't at fault because *she* hadn't directly ordered it. It would be impossible to prove otherwise.

That was alright. I had a plan.

"Fine," I agreed.

The queen stood. "Step forward."

I approached the dais as she regally descended, the train of her silver dress trailing behind her in a swatch of glittering fabric. She held out a hand, but I refused to take it. She rolled her eyes in disgust. "Karthus, if you would?"

The captain of the fireguards stepped forward from his post near the dais, eyeing me with distaste. I glared back, refusing to forget how he and his men had stood aside as two of the girls drowned in the bathhouses.

Bastard.

He drew a dagger from his belt and I flinched back, but he seized my wrist in an iron grip. "What are you doing?" I yelled.

"The only reason I willingly shed my blood is so yours can bleed out on the marble floor," she threatened, her voice nothing more than a low whisper. "The blood magick will ensure you can't back out of this, and neither will I."

Blood magick? The queen could do *magick*? I didn't have any more time to absorb such startling news. The captain made a swift cut across my entire palm, and I reached up with my other hand and gave him a rude gesture. He ignored me and instead gave the queen the tiniest of pricks in the middle of her hand.

"To the first blood!"

The crowd echoed the sentiment, and the strange ritual was over. The captain daintily cleaned the queen's nonexistent wound and made a grand show of binding it. He ignored me once again.

I curled my injured palm into a fist. Fine, I'd bleed all over the floor then. I should have rubbed my blood on her dress. The captain turned to face me, putting away his dagger and reaching for his sword.

I smiled, which was the last thing the queen expected me to do while facing down her captain. I directed it straight at Zion, who frowned.

"I wish to fight the fireguard, Zariah."

Silence.

The queen blinked as though she were sure she misheard me. Her gaze flicked to the king and Zion, who had both gone white.

"*What* did you say?" the queen sneered at me. Zion (or should I say Zariah) purposefully avoided my eyes. The captain of the fireguards gripped his sword harder.

It only strengthened my resolve. "My talent is fighting. To showcase it, I would like to challenge the fireguard Zariah."

I expected Zion to step forward from his throne, but he didn't. The royal family was stiff in their seats, shocked as though I'd just proclaimed I'd eat a small baby in front of them.

"There is no such person," the queen breathed out, trying for her usual imperious tone, but her voice wobbled.

Every sense of mine sharpened. Were they going to deny it? Was this ... fake name of his a carefully guarded secret?

"He doesn't have a choice; it's sealed in blood," grunted the captain."If he doesn't fight, the deal voids and she wins."

The king chuckled. "And you remember what you promised should you lose," he needled the queen, whose eyes narrowed.

Overhead, there was a large thump, showing the dragon had just landed on the dome above the roof. Did it find it hilarious to keep interrupting the court? I would if I were a dragon.

"Everyone out," screeched the queen.

For a moment, no one moved.

Karthus stepped forward, and the line of fireguards stepped with him. "You heard the queen!" he roared. "OUT!"

There was a small stampede as the nobles rushed to be the first out the doors. It would have been comical if my life hadn't been on the line.

"You all as well," snapped the queen at the girls. I stayed

rooted to the spot as they were all shuffled out by fireguards. Leilani and Azalea gave me hopeful, yet sad, looks.

It was clear they thought this was the last time they'd see me. It wasn't an unreasonable assumption.

"I won't even ask how you know about him. You want to fight Zariah so badly?"

With the room empty of her court, the queen stood, no longer needing to hide her hatred or venom.

Zion stood with her, putting a hand out. "Mother, let me handle this—"

"*Sit down.* This little trollop does not know what she's asking for. Let's show her."

An invisible force slammed Zion's body back into his chair. He winced, then stood again.

"No!" he ordered. "I'm the one supposed to be running these games. I order you to stop! You will not do this."

The queen whipped around, fury etched in the wrinkles around her eyes and forehead. The wrinkles weren't visible normally, but I was so close that I could count every crevice and imperfection.

"You do not rule here. Down!"

Zion stumbled and fell. It was as if his body wouldn't listen to his brain. He tried to leap toward me, but only fell on his face. "NO!"

"Hold him!"

Fireguards stepped forward immediately to subdue Zion. The king stood with a red face, but the queen whirled to him next. "Do you have a problem with how I manage this kingdom?"

Come on, I willed him. *You're the king. Stand up to her.*

I didn't know what Zion was trying to save me from, but it had to be bad if the queen was so insistent about it. My heart sank as the king bit his lip, then shook his head.

The queen turned to Karthus. "Take her up to meet Zariah."

Karthus didn't look pleased at all by this, but with a gesture of his fingers, two fireguards stepped up and grabbed my elbows, hauling me through the ballroom. Confusion overwhelmed me more than anything. Why couldn't we have the fight here? Where were we going? Was she simply going to have me killed with no one here to witness the fight? It made sense if she didn't want anyone to see me whip the prince's ass …

"Hey! Let go! I can walk!" I insisted, but as per usual, they ignored me.

The queen strode ahead of us, the king at her heels and Zion writhing and fighting the guards that held him. Instead of going down the main hallway, once we cleared the doors of the ballroom, we took an abrupt left up a narrow, steep, winding stone staircase. We climbed for ages until I was half-thankful for the guards who dragged me. Was this the queen's strategy? Keep me bleeding and exhausted so I couldn't possibly win my fight?

No … that couldn't be right. She'd want the entire court to witness my humiliation. Why send them away?

Up, up, up …

Sunlight flooded my vision as we emerged at the top, golds and oranges highlighting everything on the floor as the sun filtered through the dome that protected the kingdom from the dragon. My mouth dropped open. I'd never imagined that I'd ever get this close. The dragon above us crawled over it like a giant lizard, trying to reach us and unable to because of the magick and metal separating us. Fire poured from his mouth and he roared in anger. The heat was intense.

"My queen, I do not recommend this," Karthus grit out.

"Noted." The queen sniffed. She turned to me. "I thought I

was clever in forcing a blood deal on you. You thought you were clever by naming the soldier." A nasty smile twisted her lips. "You want to fight him, and thanks to the magick you must. Goodbye, you little mud slut."

Confusion flooded my veins, quickly replaced by panic as Karthus himself grabbed me and hauled me up a set of wooden stairs. I followed them with my eyes, noting how they ended at a small trapdoor in the dome.

Oh fuck. No.

Zion screamed behind me. As if the dragon could feel his mood, it bellowed and raged above us, spitting fire everywhere and clawing at the dome like it could shred it with its claws.

"Hurry now, I think Zariah's hungry," the queen offered nonchalantly, picking at her nails.

My eyes widened. What kind of sick joke was this? Zion's protests fell deaf upon my ears. The dragon's roars were the only thing I could hear, and the heat from his fire was the only thing I could feel. I didn't even struggle as Karthus hauled me to the top of the stairs, opened the hatch, and pushed me through, slamming it shut behind him.

Blinding light forced me to shut my eyes even though I knew it was a death sentence. Was the sun supposed to be so bright? I'd never seen it without the dome layered between, and it was hot and bright and it hurt.

Too bad. I'd have to open my eyes or die. I regained my senses enough to whirl around, but the hatch was closed and an ominous click followed. I wrapped my fingers around the lip and tugged at it with all my strength, but it wouldn't budge.

I whirled around, the dragon only feet from me.

He was enormous. Gargantuan.

My world filled with gold scales and heat. He had eyes of fire and gold and black pupils slit like a cat. He hunched down on all fours to get a better look at me, then he launched himself at me, jaws opening and revealing razor-sharp teeth.

I didn't bother screaming. It wouldn't do anything. I closed my eyes.

I expected the pain of sharp teeth to tear my skin from my body and cut me in half. I expected to feel the hot gush of my blood as it left my body in torrents.

I cracked one eye open, flinching and falling backwards on my ass as the dragon's snout was an inch from my face. He *sniffed* me.

A growl rumbled in his throat. Would he roast me to death with its fire?

"I'd prefer if you'd just eat me. That seems a better way to go than burning," I suggested mildly, my voice shaking horrifically.

The dragon cocked his head at me like a confused dog would. I would have snorted in laughter if I wasn't pissing myself in terror.

"N-nice dragon," I soothed shakily, holding my hand out palm up. The cut from the fireguard captain had at least stopped bleeding, but blood still crusted over my hand. The dragon sniffed at it, growling again.

I drew it back, not wanting to taunt it into eating me.

I wished I had a weapon or something. He was just staring at me, his great gold belly just there within reach. Or should I stab it in the eye? Large, vicious looking spikes protected the neck area, so that was a no-go.

I spared a glance away from the massive beast in front of me and noticed the dead, dried-out carcass of an animal beside me. A large, splintered leg bone lay tangled up in bleached fur and scraps of guts. It was tempting to dive for it, but I inched slowly, oh so slowly, the five feet it took to my left. The dragon watched me with interest, but didn't appear angry or threatened. He folded his wings against his body and settled in to observe.

Right. It wasn't my fault if the beast was stupid, was it?

Flies scattered as I approached the corpse, and I steeled myself against the sight of maggots buried in the rotting flesh. I reached in and snapped the bone in half, whipping around to point the broken, jagged edge at the dragon's nose.

If I could just jab it in an eye, maybe it would get distracted enough that I could stab it—

I stopped cold. The eyes that held mine weren't that of a savage beast. There was an intelligence there—a sense of recognition that stopped me in my tracks. This close, I could see the eyes weren't completely gold; their innermost rings were flecked with green and silver.

"What are you waiting for? Kill her!"

The queen's voice screeched up to us, muffled slightly by the dome, but still heard all the same. The dragon twitched his head toward her, then back to me, again sniffing. Like lightning, one clawed hand shot out and pinned me to the hot surface of the platform. My weapon skittered across the dome, falling down in the depths of the kingdom somewhere. Dimly, Zion was yelling. The sun blinded my eyes, blocked only by the silhouette of the monster who held me down. His clawed hand seized my neck and squeezed.

His snout nudged my chest and I reacted on instinct, punching it as hard as I could.

He shrieked in anger. The sharp edge of the claws around my lips went limp as the heavy weight of the dragon disappeared, and soft lips descended onto mine.

CHAPTER
ELEVEN

ragons don't kiss.

D That was the first thought that ran through my head. The second was how hot his lips felt against mine. My eyes shot open and smooth skin and black curls greeted me. What? Where was the dragon? Had Zion gotten the trap door open after all?

I tried to push him away—we had to run, not kiss! My palm met hot flesh as I pushed him away, and I flinched backwards. Zion made a guttural sound in his throat, and I realized with a jerk he was filthy and *naked*. Wild eyes tinged with green flickered between silver and gold.

I glanced beneath my feet, seeing the *real* Zion put a guard on the ground with a vicious right hook. If Zion was below me ... then who the fuck was this? It certainly looked like Zion, but with a feral, starved looked in his eyes.

Zariah is hungry.... That's what the queen had said, hadn't she?

Oh shit. Oh fuck.

They were goddamn twins. Zion and Zariah were two separate people. And Zariah was also the dragon.

I bolted for the door and Zariah screamed at me; the roar coming from his throat all wrong for a human to make. He took a step toward me and then fell over, his skin rippling as gold scales pushed their way through again. His eyes flickered black and gold, then silver and green.

"Fucking OPEN!" I screamed at the hatch, and somehow it did. Perhaps in his haste to descend, Karthus hadn't locked it properly behind him, or I hadn't tugged on it the right way in my earlier panic. My upper body fell through the hole just enough for me to see what happened next.

"Karthus," the queen intoned at her captain, glaring at me as if all of this was my fault. Without hesitation, Karthus withdrew his sword in one hand and a dagger in the other. He stepped up to the two soldiers who'd been holding Zion (the one he'd punched had gotten up and grabbed him again), and stabbed both in the heart simultaneously.

A high-pitched gasp left me as the soldiers fell, their twin looks of shock and betrayal something I would never forget. Blood poured through their hands as they clutched at their wounds, too little too late.

It only took them seconds to bleed out and die.

The queen met my eyes with venom in her gaze. "Kill her."

Karthus sprung at me, and I shot back up through the hatch, slamming it after me. Between the man with a sword and the dragon, I would gladly choose the dragon. I ran straight toward Zariah/the dragon/whatever the fuck he was, stumbling as Karthus easily opened the hatch and lunged toward me with his sword in the air. Out of the two beasts near me, the dragon had proved himself the least likely to kill me.

I screamed and Zariah jerked, then my world exploded in a haze of heat and scales. The dragon bellowed his fury at

Karthus, who backpedaled so fast it would have been comical had I not been half-convinced I was going to die. Something hard and sharp seized me in a vice grip and suddenly I was floating—no, I was flying. The hatch opened and Zion sprung out, screaming and waving his arms frantically. The dragon—Zariah?—paid no attention, beating his wings hard and leaving the dome and kingdom far below us.

"Don't drop me, don't drop me ..." I pleaded out loud, but could barely hear myself over the thump of his wings as I dangled in his claws. Terror shot through my veins as I rose higher and higher and realized I'd never been outside the dome's protection in my life.

Sooner than I thought possible, we landed, and the hard grip around my middle loosened. I sucked in a deep breath and clung to a large rock, realizing we were in a rocky overhang that led into a dark cave. The dragon took a big step toward me, then turned back into Zariah, naked and dirty.

"Zariah, I—"

He rushed me blindly and tackled me between the rock and the ground. I grunted in pain as my back hit the rock, thankful I hadn't cracked my head on it. Before I could squeak in protest, Zariah's nose nuzzled in my neck, sniffing me as his fingers buried into my hair and twisted.

"Did he touch you? Did he taste you?"

Zariah's voice was rough and gravelly, almost unrecognizable from the smart-aleck fireguard I knew. I drew my knee up to my chest and kicked him as hard as I could.

He gave a comical 'oomph' as he fell backwards, and I frantically looked around for an escape. We were so high up I got dizzy, taking a stumbling step toward the edge. Nothing but black, charred earth was visible as far as my eye could see. The landscape was a disgusting, ugly eyesore devoid of any beauty or life. This was what I'd been so eager to see? The only untouched portion was the kingdom back to the east, wrapped up in the protective dome and high walls.

There was nowhere to go even if I could get down. I was trapped.

I didn't mean to lean so far forwards toward the edge, but I'd never been so high before; it was higher than even the cliff to get to the seat. Panic took hold of my body and suddenly I was falling, my feet and arms scrabbling uselessly at the hardened, black earth. There were no trees, no vegetation to grab onto. Nothing but pain and heat and darkness. I didn't even scream as I fell, the ground rushing up to meet me.

A strange whooshing filled my ears and the dragon dove underneath me, flaring his wings as I dropped onto his back with a hard thump. I gripped onto his neck spikes like a lifeline as Zariah tried to pump his wings and gain altitude. It was too little, too late, and together we slammed into the ground. I was thrown from his back and hit the hardened ground viciously. Pain exploded through my body as a I rolled, finally coming to rest a short distance away from him.

I sat up slowly as I gasped in air, making sure I still had my body parts and that nothing was broken. I felt like the food cart had hit me, but the pain would pass. I turned toward the giant mass of scales next to me. The dragon—Zariah—wasn't moving.

Tentatively, I took a few steps toward him. "Hey," I said softly, as though I were talking to a wild animal. "You ok?"

The dragon made a low groaning sound in his throat and rolled toward me. Scales rippled and limbs sucked inwards, and in seconds, Zariah collapsed in front of me on his back. I hovered over him, holding my breath as I tracked the rise and fall of his chest. Good. He was alive.

But still naked.

A bruise was already forming on his chest from where I

kicked him, and I felt a little bad about it. There was obviously more at play here than a man trying to press his advantage. I just wish I understood any of it.

"Zariah? Are you ok?"

I tentatively pushed and poked at all his limbs, getting no reaction until I prodded a lump near his shoulder bone. Zariah hissed at me, his eyes cracking open and glazed with pain.

"Broke something here, I think. It's swelling," I remarked calmly. I scampered to his other side on my hands and knees. I felt around his hairline, finding another large bump on the side of his head. Silver eyes shifted to gold and back as I tentatively touched around the edges with my fingertips.

"Yeah, that's probably going to sting," I agreed. I shifted behind him and put his head in my lap. It was softer than the hard, charred black ground, anyway. The sun was setting, and already the wind held a chill that was slicing through my fighting leathers. It could have been worse: at least I wasn't in a silk dress. Had the ball really taken most of the day? My stomach growled.

"I'm assuming we shouldn't stay here," I asked the empty air.

Zariah shifted under me, then went limp.

"Wonderful," I remarked to no one.

For a while we simply sat there, my focus primarily on ensuring he was just resting and not actively dying on me.

Sssssssst.

I jumped as a hissing noise came from my right. It was getting hard to see in the semi-darkness, but I didn't miss the glint of the hard exoskeleton of *something* that slithered out from under the rock.

Sssssst!

It looked like an ugly little monster with eight legs and a hard outer body. It had a tail that reared over its head with a sharp little jabber on the end. I didn't want to find out what it felt like.

"Alright, we gotta go."

I stood and shifted Zariah, getting in front of him and bracing my legs under me. Seizing my strength, I hefted him up so that he sprawled across my back, his weight as evenly distributed as I could make it. My legs trembled for a moment, but then I adjusted. I may be skinny and underfed, but I was strong.

I glanced back down, seeing the little monsters had gathered. Four of them had slithered out from under the rocks and hardened earth, and they were all hissing at me.

"Yeah. Thanks, but no thanks."

I started trudging back toward the large cliff that rose in front of us like a mountain, but realized I was at a loss. There was no way I'd be able to climb with an unconscious prince/dragon man on my back.

I sat Zariah down on a rock carefully, slumped against the side of the cliff. "Wake up, Zariah." I shook him slightly, but his head only lolled to the side.

Ssssst.

Sssssst.

Ssssst.

The little monsters were coming out from everywhere and circling us. A bolt of fear shot straight into my stomach, and I forced myself to take a deep breath. I would not enjoy this, but it was necessary.

SLAP.

"ZARIAH! WAKE UP!" I shook the sting out of my hand as a red mark appeared on the side of his face, but he barely cracked his eyes open at me.

SSSSSSTTTTTT.

Fear spread through my body like a poison. I yelped and

jumped up on the rock next to him, trying in vain to keep all our arms and legs off the ground. Could they smell fear? I huddled close to Zariah, trying to present a smaller target.

I nearly cried with relief when his eyes snapped open, his nostrils flared wide. With a shriek of pain, he shifted, one massive dragon claw stamping down and squishing two of the little monsters. The others made disturbing shrieking sounds and scuttled away. I didn't even mind that he'd thrown me a few feet away as his larger dragon body took over.

"T-thanks. I guess we can't stay here," I managed, standing up and resting one hand out on his massive head. The scaled skin was warm and comforting.

He swung his head around and looked at me with concerned golden eyes.

"Yeah, I know you're hurt. Can you get us back up? We can rest then, and I promise I won't do any more cliff diving."

The sound he made could have been a disgruntled, barely amused huff, but maybe I was just imagining it. Regardless, he jerked his head to the side in a very human motion that was clearly an invitation to climb aboard.

"Right. Ok. Get on the dragon."

With very little grace, I climbed up onto his back, trying to be careful of his wings and settling myself in between them on his back, and close enough to his neck that I could hang on to the thick spikes around his throat. The moment my fingers closed tightly around them, Zariah leaped straight up onto the side of the cliff. I shrieked a bit as I went completely vertical, clutching onto his horn spikes and digging my heels into his sides like my life depended on it.

Which it did.

Roughly and laboriously, he climbed the mountain, each move difficult for him as he huffed and puffed. Eventually, we made it back to the top. I slid off him quickly, and he collapsed onto all fours, his belly on the ground.

"Can I do anything for you?" I asked him sincerely. He'd gotten hurt diving after me and preventing me from becoming a splat on the hard ground below, so I felt responsible. I swear I didn't imagine the sarcastic look he shot at me. Dragons couldn't be sarcastic, could they?

"Right. I'll just ... be in the cave, then."

It only took a few steps inside before the darkness swallowed me. I wished for a candle or ... something. I turned around and nearly had a heart attack as a giant dragon head filled the entryway.

"Warn a girl next time, will you?" I huffed.

He nudged me to the side of the cave with his snout and then blew out a small stream of fire.

"HEY! I—"

I shut my mouth as fire erupted in a small fire pit dug into the center of the cave. Moonlight shone through the top smoke hole.

"Oh. Thanks."

I sat in front of the fire, trying to get the cold out of my bones. It wasn't nearly as freezing inside the kingdom. Was it because of the walls and the dome? It had to be. I wasn't used to this ... wind. Even though I was out of it now, the chill had settled in my bones and wouldn't leave.

"A-any b-blankets?" I joked wearily, my teeth chattering. The fire was a good start, at least.

The dragon pushed itself further into the cave, filling most of the small space with his head and one arm. He scooted toward me and the fire on his belly, then wrapped an arm around me and tucked me into his chest.

I resisted at first, then realized how gloriously warm his scales were. And laying on his arm was far more comfortable than the floor of my hut had ever been. Between that and the fire, my eyes grew heavy. A sense of safety I didn't know existed settled around my shoulders. Nothing was going to fuck with a dragon, after all.

Reveling in my newfound sense of freedom and protection, I drifted off quickly to sleep.

My eyes fluttered open, the smell of smoke and charred wood filling my nose. I was so warm and covered, glorious heat wrapped all around me. I sat up and yawned, pushing away the arms that held me. Had I ever slept so well in my life?

Wait.

Arms?

Hands seized me and dragged me back down against a warm body, snuggling me like I was a giant pillow.

"Uh, Zariah?"

He growled, irritable in his sleep, and squeezed me tighter. I would have laughed at how adorable it was, but there was the fact that he was still naked.

"Let me go. Please."

I pushed him away again, and his eyes opened. Seeing the tension on my face, he immediately dropped me, pushing away and turning his back to me at an attempt at modesty.

"Sorry, I—"

"You're apologizing to me?" His voice rose with incredulity as he craned his neck over his shoulder to look at me.

I blinked. So he was sane now? Good to know. "Well, you got hurt saving me from falling. I feel bad about that."

Zariah rolled his eyes. "There's a basket behind you with some pants. If you don't mind?"

I narrowed my eyes, then reached behind me. Sure enough, there was a basket with some old clothes. I snatched a pair of pants and threw them at his head. He snatched them out of the air before they hit.

"Unless you prefer I keep them off?"

I choked as he gave me a smoldering look, and throwing my hands in the air in surrender, I turned around. I was dying to ask about him and his twin, Zion. Now that I knew they were two separate people, it made so much more sense. Who had I actually met that night in the corridor of the palace? My sinking heart told me it hadn't been Zariah, had it? It was Zion. At least that explained why he'd seemed so confused to see me.

"So ... twins," I said in the empty silence of the cave. I snuck a peek over my shoulder and saw Zariah had put the pants on. It did nothing to hide the chiseled abdominal muscles and or his shapely arms and calves, but that was alright.

Don't drool, Mari. Men are bad ... remember?

Zariah's silver eyes flashed gold, his face twisting with anger. "Zion has touched you. I can smell him on you."

Oh. Uh.

"To be fair, I thought he was you," I countered irritably, hoping it was enough to soothe him.

It wasn't. In fact, it enraged him more.

"He took advantage of you? I'll kill him! I'll—"

I put a hand on his arm to calm him as scales rippled underneath his skin. He didn't need to go all dragon on me just yet. "Calm down. He didn't know I thought he was you. How could he know? Fucking twins ..."

His skin heated under my fingertips, to where I could barely stand it. He wasn't calming down. I was so confused. Where was my kind fireguard?

"Oh, for the sake of the gods," I muttered and wrapped my arms around his neck and kissed him.

He went ramrod still, then relaxed against me. He'd barely gotten to press his lips to mine on the roof, and I'd been unprepared.

But now?

Zariah took his time, deepening the kiss and pulling me tight against his body. His tongue slid in between my lips and I let it, curious how he differed from his brother. Zion's kisses had been teasing and possessive; Zariah's were tender yet deep. It was as though our very souls were rising to meet each other for the first time.

Need built in my core and sent my stomach flipping. I pressed myself tighter against him, feeling his need as well. His hands cupped my face, one sliding south down my body as the other held me in place by my jaw.

I snaked my hand down to grip his length, and his entire body went taut. "Why does the entire kingdom think there is only one prince when there are clearly two?"

His hand went around my throat, squeezing just as hard as I was around his cock. "You just saw me transform into a dragon and back, and that's your first question?"

I squeezed harder. So did he.

We were at a stalemate.

My eyes fluttered shut. The pressure of his hand around my throat felt soothing and calm; it was as though I didn't have to decide or worry about surviving while he held me like that. I slid my fingers up across his tip, and he groaned.

"Never mind, I can guess," I continued. "One of you plays the prince while the other is off playing the dragon. Am I far off the mark?"

My hand kept sliding up and down his length as if it had a mind of its own. His hand tightened painfully around my throat, and I stopped.

"I'd say you're right on it," he grunted. "Most people aren't silly enough to poke a dragon."

I let go of him, and he released me. I slid back to the other side of the cave until my back hit the stone wall.

"Your mother tried to feed me to you."

Zariah winced. "She ... has never coped well with all of this."

I scowled, pulling my knees to my chest and resting my arms and head on top. "And what exactly is *all this*?"

Zariah sighed and sat down, unconsciously letting his arms hang down over his propped knee. "It's a curse, Mari. We've had it since we were born. Zion was born first, and when I came out ... I ... well, it was a shock to everyone. So that's how we play our parts."

My arms crossed over my chest. Azalea had been right about the dragon being a curse! "Pity you didn't scorch your mother from the womb out."

He glared at me, and I glared back. "Don't be ridiculous. We didn't start turning into dragons until *after* we came out of her womb."

I rolled my eyes at his non-answer. "So, Zion gets to be the official prince since he was born first. And you get ... what? To play guard?"

He refused to rise to my bait. "One of us has to be the dragon. If we don't, we lose control over the transformation. We lose our minds. It's for everyone's safety that we take strict shifts. We've done it since we were infants. Zion and I switch in and out when needed."

My jaw dropped. I couldn't imagine a baby just being ... left out here in the open. Then again, I could imagine the queen doing it.

"Why were you cursed?" I asked. Hadn't Azalea mentioned the curse had lasted a hundred years? Zion and Zariah were my age. The wall was much, much older than that!

"It's a punishment," he shot back, surly.

My eyes rolled to the back of my head. "And here I thought it was a birthday present."

He huffed in acknowledgement, but went silent. I wasn't about to get any more information out of him. My stomach rumbled loudly in the cave, and I put my arms over it, hunching in on myself.

Zariah frowned. "I need to get you back."

I barked out a laugh. "You're *joking*. Your mother just tried to make me dragon kibble. There's no way she's taking me back."

He arched a dark eyebrow. "You survived the dragon. She won't have a choice. To do otherwise would thumb your nose at the gods. You'll be fine. Besides, everyone will see you triumphantly returning on my back. Quite a feather in your cap, really—a splendid performance. It's the best talent of all, really."

I growled at his smug grin. "It isn't funny. Your brother—at least I think it was him and not you—said he *had* to obey your mother. Are you the same way?"

His nostrils flared in irritation, but he didn't deny it.

I laughed. "What's to stop her from ordering you to murder me then? Why didn't you eat me on the roof? She'd been pretty clear about that."

Zariah sighed. "She does control us. I can't really explain why: it just *is*. It's a good thing when you think about it; she can make sure we don't go on a rampage and destroy the entire kingdom. As for not eating you? Well, she must have made a blood pact with you. I can smell it in your veins. She won't be able to make anyone else hurt you. She must do it herself."

My jaw dropped. "I'm supposed to be happy because your mother has to kill me herself?"

His eyes closed, and after a moment, he shifted back into his dragon form. I yelped as golden scales filled the small cave, scampering on my bum toward the mouth of the cave. Zariah gave a small huff of heat at me as if my fear was amusing. I raised a fist threateningly at his nose. I'd punch his snout again if I had to.

He grumbled, then lowered his head and neck down to the ground. The meaning was clear: get on.

"I will go back, but only if you promise to tell me everything about this curse in less than two days," I added, knowing he'd stall if I didn't put an expiration date on it.

The dragon growled but nodded his massive head.

Fine, then.

I slid onto the base of his neck, sliding down as he stood until it wedged me on his back between his wing joints. I took a hold of the spikes around his neck and took a deep breath.

It didn't keep me from screaming as he dove off the cliff's edge.

My knuckles were white as I held his spikes in a death grip, wanting to close my eyes but unable to look away as the ground rushed up at us. But soon enough, Zariah's wings flared, and he flattened out. We stopped falling and instead we were gliding down to the massive dome across the horizon.

The sun burned against my skin, but I relished every sensation. Even though the surrounding landscape was nothing but a charred, blackened crisp, joy flooded my body at *feeling* the sun. I'd never known what it felt like, having grown up under the dome's protection my entire life. It felt warm, and ... nice.

WHUMPF.

We landed hard on the left side of the dome where I knew my mud district was. What was my mother doing right now? Was she getting enough food? I hoped someone would share now that I was gone and unable to elbow an extra loaf of bread for us. That fire guard had said he would help.

Zariah skittered along the dome's surface on all fours, heading toward the same platform I'd been ceremoniously shoved through yesterday. He bent his head and neck down so I could easily jump down.

"Thanks."

I blinked in the brightness, wondering if it was a sunny day or if this was just what it was like to be under its gaze. I admired the blue hues in the sky and the fluffy looking clouds.

"Have you ever flown through one?" I wondered out loud.

Dragons couldn't grin, could they? Zariah flashed his fangs at me and nodded his head up and down. I don't know why, but the thought of this massive beast frolicking through the soft, white clouds above me made me smile.

Zariah gave a comforting rumble, nudging me gently in the chest with his nose toward the latched door.

"Yeah, I know. Return as the dragon whisperer or whatever. You will come to me tonight to talk?"

He tilted his head to the side, looking sad.

"Zion, then?"

He gave a curt nod before flying away. His wings nearly clipped me as he took off in a huff.

I hefted the latch (which was unlocked) and descended the stairs, pulling it shut behind me. I jumped down, noting with bitterness that I was alone. Someone must have cleaned, because the floor was spotless despite two fireguards bleeding out on it. Now, where to go first? Should I make a grand disturbance in the main audience hall or go back to my rooms with the other girls?

Choices, choices ...

A big scene would piss the queen off, and while that would be enjoyable for me, I didn't need to taunt her into killing me outright. I needed to have my conversation with one of the dragon boys and figure out what was going on with this curse. Obviously, killing the dragon was no longer an option. Breaking the curse, however, was. If I found a way, the royal family would be indebted to me. I would force them to improve conditions in the mud district and actually feed my people. From what I'd seen of the Seat and the plump people who made up court, they could afford it.

Back to my rooms it was.

Assuming I could find them.

"There you are."

I jumped a foot in the air and swore as Zion rounded the corner, leaning against the wall and crossing his arms over his chest. His eyes narrowed, lips pursed in irritation.

"What, can you two talk telepathically or something?" I grumbled.

The furrow in his brow only deepened.

"Great. Not only are there *two* of you, but you can also talk about me to each other in secret. Just wonderful."

One dark eyebrow raised, so similar to his brother's that my teeth ground together. "Look a little happier. You've just tamed a dragon, after all." He reached out to put a hand on my shoulder.

I fisted my hands at my sides, trying to remain calm. Zion pushed all my buttons in a way Zariah didn't.

I shoved him away. "Don't touch me."

Silver eyes glittered at me. "That's not what you said that night I—"

"You asshole. I thought you were your brother."

His face shuttered, flashing for a moment with dismay before smoothing back out. "Don't worry, I'm under strict instructions not to touch you. Zariah insists we ... give you time."

His shoulders were stiff as he jerked his head at me, indicating I should follow.

"I wish to return to my rooms," I said clearly. He didn't answer, but as we navigated this staircase and crossed through that hallway, I recognized where I was. Zion paused in front of the large double doors of the girls' suite and gave a mocking bow.

"You or your brother owe me answers today or tomorrow," I reminded him.

He leaned in, and my back hit the door. He braced one arm over my head and against the door, and the other trapped me on my left side.

I refused to shirk or cower. I glared at him.

"Or what?" he challenged, his voice a dark purr.

I lashed out and punched him in his stomach, just like he was one of the boys trying to nick my hunk of cheese. Zion made a funny sound as he doubled over, and I used his distraction to turn the door handle and slip inside.

"Mari?!"

"Oh gods above, seriously?"

"She isn't dead! The dragon didn't eat her!"

"Pity."

I ignored Freesia's remark with a grin, opening my arms as Leilani rushed in for a hug. Azalea followed behind her, tears running down her face. With a pang in my heart, I realized that was all of us.

"Where are Heather and Hyacinthe?" I asked quietly.

Leilani pulled away, wiping her nose on the sleeve of her dress. "The queen dismissed them from the competition. Don't worry though!" She rushed to reassure me as my face twisted in horror at all the things the queen could have done to them.

"The moment the queen announced they were out, two nobles proposed to them. It thrilled them to continue living in the Seat. Their families will come to the wedding, and—"

"Enough. You'll make me sick." Freesia sat on the edge of a couch, flipping her braid over her shoulder.

I was simply relieved they hadn't been killed.

"You're just jealous you didn't tame a dragon!" Leilani shot back, giving me an excited look. "Tell us everything! How did you manage it? We all saw you returning through the window, riding on its back! Will it do what you want? Will it breathe fire if you ask? Oooh, how exciting! You won't have to do the physical test for sure now!"

Azalea led me over to the cluster of couches, pushing me down to sit in the one opposite of Freesia. The blonde girl sniffed at us, but I noticed she didn't turn away or go to her room.

She wanted to know how I'd tamed the dragon just as much as the rest of them.

"I can't really get into specifics, other than to say he likes me."

Freesia scoffed, rolling her eyes. "I heard the guards say the queen tried to execute you, but it didn't work."

She sounded so put out I laughed in her face. "No, it didn't," I confirmed, then went silent. "Oh! Berries!" I rushed from my seat toward the table set in the center, full of berries and meat. Azalea blushed. "We were too worried about you to eat—" She shot a glare at Freesia, "Well, *some* of us were."

"Don't hold up on my account. I plan to eat half myself," I

announced and picked up a delicate, porcelain plate and heaped it with food.

Taming dragons was hard work, after all.

I listened politely as Azalea and Leilani chatted around me, their world once again happy and orderly, knowing I was safe and back with them. Freesia kept to herself, but shot me wary glances now and then. None of us were stupid, but we all dealt with our fear in different ways.

Freesia now knew I was a threat.

As I ate, I couldn't stop thinking about Zariah and Zion's upcoming 'talk' with me. Screw that. I couldn't stop thinking about how warm it had been sleeping against Zariah's scales, and how good it had felt to have his arms wrapped around me. I wanted to feel the sun on my skin again, and the wind flying through my hair as I soared through the skies like a wild bird.

"It's such a shame we didn't get to see you fight.... I was so looking forward to it," Leilani commented offhandedly, her lips forming into a pout as she finished a piece of ham.

I flashed my teeth at them all. "Oh, don't worry, I'm just getting started."

THIRTEEN

Everyone eventually ended up in bed, but sleep was the last thing on my mind. I waited anxiously for Azalea and Leilani's breaths to even out. Once they did, I slipped silently from bed and padded across our suite on silent feet. My fingers trailed on the cold metal of the doorknob.

"I knew it. You've been sneaking out to see the prince."

I whipped around in a defensive position, but it was only Freesia, her arms wrapped around her thin nightgown as she glared at me.

"It isn't fair. If you think being a whore is how you're gonna win—"

"Oh shut up. You want to see the prince so badly? Come with me." I don't know what made me say that, but it effectively ended her tirade. Freesia gawked at me, her lips parted in shock. She blinked rapidly, giving herself a once over.

"I'm not dressed appropriately! My hair is a mess! It'll take me forever to put my makeup on!"

I rolled my eyes and opened the door.

"If you go out, I'll tell the fireguards!" she whispered harshly.

A laugh bubbled its way out of my throat. "Right. And then I'll set the dragon on them. Who do you think will win that fight?"

Her face went white, and without looking back, I slammed the door in her face. The look of fear twisting her dainty features was one I'd enjoy for a while.

"Can I be of help?"

I jumped for the second time in five minutes as a fireguard appeared out of nowhere, leering down at me.

"Sweet Mother, were you hiding in the shadows, waiting to pounce?" I asked incredulously.

The fireguard looked ready to hit me, then froze when he saw my face. "You ... the dragon girl..."

I was done with everyone's shit. Just yesterday, I thought I was about to become dragon fodder. Now everyone was afraid of me. A new surge of confidence went through my veins. It was amazing how your perspective on life changed when you didn't, in fact, die.

"Yes, *me*. Kindly escort me to the prince's tower. We have some urgent business."

The man was young with dirty blonde hair, and dark eyes. His helmet obscured his other features.

"I need ... I need to tell the queen you're back."

The poor man seemed in a daze. Had the queen told everyone I'd died or something? That would be like her.

"Yes, very well, do what you need to do, but after you escort me." I crossed my arms over my chest and tapped my foot impatiently.

"No need, fireguard. I could smell the mud all the way down the hall."

I whipped around as the queen stood behind us, her onyx jewelry glittering off the torches lining the halls.

The fireguard bowed. "My apologies."

The queen sniffed. "Dismissed."

We stood in tense silence as my only witness marched away. My anxiety grew as she turned, giving me her full attention.

"Not dead."

My eyes narrowed. "Not quite."

"And?" she asked impatiently.

I had no response. "And what?" I asked.

Her jeweled shoes tapped impatiently against the marble floors. I couldn't help but wonder how long just one gem on one shoe would feed my entire street.

"Will you expose the secret? Can I bribe you for your silence? Should I simply kill you?"

My hackles raised, and I took a half step back.

The queen laughed, the sound laced with hysteria. "Can't exactly do that, can we? The entire kingdom saw you ride him back in, didn't they? You're a clever little bitch."

I had nothing to do with that, but I bit my tongue.

"How about we simply stay out of each other's way?" I suggested firmly, forcing myself to make eye contact with her.

She bared her teeth at me. "I want what is best for my son."

My eyebrow raised. "I want what's best for my people."

The queen flinched as if I'd struck her, then drew herself up to her full height, arms crossed over her chest. "So. *So.*"

There was a moment of tense silence.

"I suppose you think this means you win, doesn't it?" she snarled.

I barked out a laugh. "You make me seem like this great manipulator, like a genius mastermind who had a plan. Let me remind you that your fireguards dragged me here kicking and screaming. I wasn't the one who threw me up to the dragon, either."

Rage filled me on Zariah's behalf. I knew how he'd tried to save the girls on the journey up here. His mother hadn't cared a wit about putting another death at his feet. "How does Zariah even put up with you?"

The queen narrowed her eyes. "He would never reveal himself to you. It's too dangerous. Did you fuck the dragon then, to get him to do it? Behind our backs?"

I wouldn't let her crude words throw me. "Zariah has been a perfect gentleman, dragon bits aside." Which was more than I could say for Zion.

The queen lunged forward, grabbing me by my dirty clothes and hauling me up to her face. For such a tiny woman, she was deceptively strong. Her floral perfume invaded my senses this close, my eyes watering as I coughed and choked. Why was it so strong?

"I'll say this once. My sons may amuse themselves with you, but eventually they will tire of you. Or better yet, you'll drive them too far and they'll kill you. There's a reason we guard their secret the way we do. And when you die, I will throw a feast that will last a week, and round up twenty virgins from the mud quarter to offer to the dragon and the gods as a sacrifice. How does that sound?"

I didn't expect the backhand to my face as she let go of me. My lips parted in shock, but I refused to grab my face or show any more signs of pain. I glared at her despite my stinging cheek, wishing looks could kill. She didn't care about laying more lives down at the feet of her sons. She didn't care at all.

"I remember the blood oath. Do you?" She hissed at me, producing a knife from inside of her dress and pushing the blade against my throat. Her other hand fisted in my shift, pulling me toward her.

"Dearest? There you are! I've been searching the corridors. Is it another night terror?"

I blinked in shock as the king walked toward us, a benevolent smile on his face and in burgundy sleeping robes.

The queen's entire demeanor shifted into one of sickly sweetness. In a flash, the knife was gone and her posture shifted as though we had merely just shared an embrace. "My love! Of course ... let's get you back inside."

I grimaced. How could he not hear how sickly sweet and false the queen tone was? His gaze shifted to me, widening to an expression of delight.

"Ah! Mari! How good to see you. Trouble sleeping?"

I side eyed the queen. "Something like that."

"I had the same problem when I first came here. Walk with me?"

I tried not to run to the king's side, away from his murderous queen.

"Five minutes then. You know I can't abide going to bed without you," the queen simpered. "I hope my son eats you," she viciously spat at me as I passed her, before turning on her heel and stalking off down the hallway.

"Which one?" I shot back, unable to help myself.

The queen stopped short, her back muscles tightening, but only for a moment. She shook herself and kept walking, eventually disappearing around the corner and down the hall.

"She's going to kill you," the king said nonchalantly, leading me down the hall. All traces of senility were gone from his voice.

I struggled to keep up with his longer strides. He took us to a large stone window that overlooked the city.

"I think she's trying to kill all of us. I'm just getting special attention," I wryly shot back.

The king raised a thick, dark eyebrow at me.

"Are you from the mud quarter?" I asked, burning with curiosity to confirm my theory. The king braced his arms against the stone ledge of the window, leaning out into the open air.

"We're all from the mud quarter deep down," he grumbled roughly. "I had a sister like you once. She was beautiful. Fierce."

I didn't like the sadness in his eyes. "What happened to her?" I asked.

He chuckled darkly, withdrawing a small flask from his hip and taking a large gulp. "The same thing that happens to any flower after it's plucked, Mari."

The stone was cold and rough under my hands. I relished the harsh scrape of the edges against my skin. "Why are you telling me this?"

He set the flask on the ledge. "Flowers aren't the only ones used and discarded. I thought I could save my sister. I thought I could help the mud people. Don't waste your time and energy like I did."

The king turned to me, his eyes tired. He looked so *old* in this moment. "The queen controls everything. She will *always* control everything. She wants to use you like she used me. There will be *more* dragons that she can control if you let her get away with it. The best thing you can do is–"

"That is enough."

The king jerked so hard he knocked his flask over, sending it clanking and tumbling out the window. The queen appeared with her lips pursed, holding her hand out to the king. He took it wordlessly, his eyes on the ground.

"Goodnight, mud rat."

The king shot me a compassionate look, and I fled down the hallway toward Zion's tower. I could see it out one window in the hall, so I felt reasonably confident about finding my way back there.

As I walked, my head was full of questions. How had the queen used the king, and how would she use me in the same way? Shouldn't the queen be relieved I already knew her sons' secrets? Did she really expect the two brothers to share a wife in between taking turns as a dragon, and for the poor woman to never notice? It was absurd.

Me. For me to never notice.

I was the poor woman.

A growl rumbled in my chest. I wasn't a poor woman. I needed to find out what this curse was, and how to stop it. I wouldn't end up like the king, sad and powerless and full of regrets.

"Zariah told me you'd seek me out. He didn't say you'd be angry." Zion stepped out from around the corner, wrapped in an elegant nightgown studded with emeralds. His excess irritated me. Had he been following me this entire time?

"Your place. Now," I demanded.

"Ooh, eager to get me alone. I see how it is." He looped an arm through mine and I allowed it. The scent of ash clung to him, and the arm around mine shook slightly.

"Are you alright?" I wondered out loud.

He grimaced. "As you said: my place, now."

I tried to memorize the twisting passages and how many turns we took. If needed, I wanted to get to his quarters on my own. *Just keep going up. That should do that trick,* I thought.

Sooner than I expected, we climbed a spiral set of stairs that led to a familiar door at the top of a similar tower. It was hard to explain, but being this close to the edges of the dome made me feel more secure, not less.

Probably because the raging dragon man likes you.

"In."

I didn't comment on his rudeness as he held the door. I did, however, jump as he slammed it behind me. A heraldry banner hanging on the wall fell with a crash. I bent down and picked it up, running my fingers over the soft velvet. It was red and blue: the entwined emblems were unfamiliar to me. Frowning, I laid it on the bed.

"I am relieved Zariah didn't harm you," Zion began, his voice stiff and formal. "He can be wild."

That was rich. Zariah was the kind one. Zion was the one trying to press his advantage at every turn. I sat down on the bed, running my hands through the mess that was now my hair.

"I'm sure," I wryly remarked, roughly braiding it to give it and myself some semblance of control and order.

"Mari. Please believe me. Neither he nor I want you to come to any harm."

I shot him a suspicious glance. "How did he tell you anything? Isn't he still out there being a dragon?" I gestured carelessly with my hands to the window and the outside world. I didn't actually believe they could communicate telepathically. That was ridiculous.

"Like you said. We can communicate to each other in our minds, but only when one of us is in our dragon form," he admitted, seeing my determination.

My jaw dropped.

"What happens if both of you are a dragon at once?" I asked.

Zion rubbed his face, already getting frustrated with my questions. "I don't know! Mother has always made sure we haven't by ordering us to never shift together. She said it could be disastrous. It's part of the cur—"

He cut himself off abruptly, glaring at the ground.

"Curse. You're under a curse. I already knew that. Zariah told me," I taunted. "He said you'd explain more."

An odd tremor went through Zion, but he shook it off and crossed the room to sit beside me on the bed. "I'd rather not. I'd rather distract myself. What do you think?"

He leaned in close, one hand resting on my thigh.

I smacked it hard, and he withdrew it with a wince.

"You're disgusting and pushy, literally, the opposite of your brother."

Zion's eyes widened. "He did have you! I knew it! Well, I was the first one to put my fingers—"

"Finish that sentence and I will break them," I threatened. "Now tell me about the curse."

His face twisted with irritation, and he sighed. "What's to tell? It's a curse to punish us for something my parents did. I didn't exactly ask for details."

My lips parted in exasperated shock. "You turn into a fire-breathing dragon and never thought to ask why?"

His face flushed with embarrassment. "I have my royal duties and only shift when I absolutely must now and then. Zariah spends the most time as the dragon." Seeing my angry expression, he continued, "Zariah enjoys being the dragon! Claims he's 'one with the beast' or whatever that means."

He glared at me. I glared at him.

Figures I'd be stuck getting explanations from the stubborn brother.

I stuck my finger in his chest. "Listen here. While I'm stuck in this castle with guards and even your mother too wary to kick me out or immediately kill me, I'm going to get answers. I'm going to find out who cast this curse, why, and how to break it. We're going to bring down the dome, and I'm going to help those from the mud quarter restore their lives and honor. Got it?"

Because if I didn't, all of this was a waste. This all couldn't be a waste. *I* wasn't a waste.

His jaw dropped slightly, and then he smirked, only just holding in a laugh. "Sure." Zion leaned back on the bed, his hands behind his head. "I will enjoy watching you try."

I stood, resisting the urge to smack him.

"I suppose I can handle being the dragon for a few hours tomorrow so you can get your precious answers and leave me alone," he drawled. "Sure you don't want a goodnight kiss?"

My hand was flying up toward him before I could even think about it, but he caught my wrist. "Careful. I like a bit of a fight."

I wrenched my hand away, glaring.

"RRRRRWWWWWRRRR!"

I jumped badly as the dragon (no, Zariah) roared from somewhere above us, sounding pissed as hell. The accompanying rush of fire followed, and the tower swayed and shook with the force. The castle stones rumbled and vibrated.

Zion didn't look surprised at all. "He's in a bit of a temper. Guess you'll have to stay here for the night."

My eyes narrowed. "Really?"

Zariah roared again from somewhere above us, rampaging on as the noise and shaking continued.

Zion rolled his eyes. "Maybe it has something to do with the annoying girl and her annoying questions and demanding nature."

"Or," I shot back, "it has something to do with the spoiled brat who can't keep his hands or his cock to himself."

Zion raised an eyebrow. "I haven't shown you my cock yet."

Without waiting for a response from me, he turned around and shucked his shirt off, uncaring as it landed on the floor. He stripped his boots off next and then moved to his pants.

"What are you doing?!" I cried out, caught between the

horror he was stripping and a mild fascination of wanting to know if he was identical to his brother in *every* way.

The pants went next, and I grit my teeth and turned around.

"I'm going to bed. Just because you have to stay doesn't mean I'm giving up my bed. It's big enough for the both of us."

The one bed trick. Did he think I was an idiot? That might work on any of the other girls back in the suite, but not me.

"I'll head back. Zariah won't hurt me."

Crossing the room, I grasped the door handle at the same time Zion shouted.

"DON'T!"

Too late. My hand met the scalding hot metal of the door handle, searing my flesh. I gasped in pain, but refused to give in. I fought through the white-hot agony and opened the door.

"MARI! NO!"

A wave of blistering heat covered me, so thick and potent I couldn't breathe. The floor came up to meet me and the heat cut off as Zion rushed to catch me, one hand around my waist, and pulled me back. His door slammed shut, a barrier between me and the heat.

"You stupid, stupid girl …" he mumbled, but I didn't care. The heat was gone. "No, don't touch it."

He kneeled down on the floor, putting my head in his lap. His naked lap. I tried to roll away, but the pain in my hand made it hard to think, let alone move.

"Too late to get prudish. You're the idiot who opened the door when I told you it was impossible to pass. I wasn't trying to be a dick on purpose. This time."

Was that a joke? I'd laugh if I didn't feel like I was going to die from the pain in my hand.

"Easy, there. We're cut off from the castle for the night, so no poultices or ice or anything helpful."

I cried then. Big, silent tears that snaked down my cheeks and rolled to the floor.

Outside, Zariah the dragon raged on.

"Great, now he's pissed you're hurt." Zion sighed. "What are we going to do with you?"

He carefully picked up my injured hand, wincing at what he saw. I didn't have the courage to look at it, so I steadfastly stared at the opposite wall. His face lowered toward my burned palm, so close his nose was almost touching. I tensed and tried to pull away, but he held me in place.

"Stop. I just want to see."

Ha. Fat chance.

He hovered there for a moment, so still that I wondered what in the hells he was doing. Then his head lowered the rest of the way, and I felt something wet meet my flesh. I yanked my hand back hard, uncaring of the extra white-hot flare of agony that went through my hand.

"Did you just *lick* it!?" I cried out, and then froze. The throbbing in my hand wasn't as bad. I gathered my courage and looked at it, wincing at the shiny red skin already covered in boils. Except for a few inches right in the middle, where the skin looked pristine and new—right where Zion had licked me.

My chest seized at the impossibility.

"Do it again," I demanded, shoving my hand back in Zion's face.

He blinked rapidly, his neck red in embarrassment. "I'm sorry, I didn't know what came over me, I—what? You want me to do it again?"

"Look!" I thrust my hand under his nose, willing him to understand. "It did something! Just shut up and lick me! Please!"

I wasn't above begging. Not when the wound hurt so badly and his tongue had felt like the sweetest relief ...

Zion took one look at the distress on my face and grabbed my palm with both of his. Without hesitation, he brought his lips to my burn, and I moaned as cool, sweet relief soared through the damaged flesh.

My eyes drifted closed in ecstasy as his tongue dragged across my hand, leaving a trail of dizzying numbness in its wake.

"Mari. Mari? Are you alright?"

I gave a slight grunt, not wanting to be bothered. My hand felt so good, and a strange feeling was buzzing just underneath my veins. I didn't want to stop it. It was similar to what Zion had done to my body before, but more localized. It was the sweetest drug....

"Mari."

My eyes cracked open to slits, just enough to take in the sight of Zion, his lips kissing my healed hand as hooded eyes stared directly into mine.

"Ok ..." I slurred at him.

When he wasn't being a prat, his small smile was just as dazzling as Zariah's.

"Ok what?" he asked, nuzzling my hand against his face.

"Not a total cock," I whispered, yawning and closing my eyes again.

"You and your obsession with my cock," he muttered back, amusement tinging his voice.

I ignored him even as he lifted me into the air and set me back down on a wonderful, luxurious softness, and I fell asleep.

FOURTEEN

I woke slowly, my hand itchy. I scratched at it, then remembered I'd horribly burned it and scratching would only make it worse.

Yet no pain came.

My eyes snapped open, and I stared down at the perfectly healed flesh. My mind caught up with the rest of me, including the heated reminder of how Zion had licked it healed.

What?

Speaking of, the asshole in question was nowhere to be found. That was likely for the best since I didn't know how I'd react if I'd woken up to him spooning me or anything else quite ridiculous. He made me just as hot and bothered as his brother, but he was a complete dick about it.

Though he had healed my hand.

I carefully got out of bed, my nose wrinkling at the state of my filthy clothes, which were the same ones I'd had on when Zariah had taken me. I would need a bath and to change as soon as possible.

Approaching the door with caution, I picked up a cloak on a nearby chair and used it to grasp the handle. It was cool. I opened it and chanced a peek down the staircase.

Dragon fire blackened it, but it was otherwise intact. Stone would do that, I supposed. A layer of grime and soot gathered on my boots as I descended the winding staircase. My stomach grumbled, and I wondered what time it was. If breakfast was still on in our rooms, I'd snag something to eat first, then shower and change my clothes.

I was still mulling over my schedule for the day when I pushed open the door to my suites. I expected to hear the chattering of the other three girls, or at least for one of them to scold me for leaving in the middle of the night again. Surely, Freesia wouldn't miss a chance to rub my mistakes in my face.

And yet, there was silence.

"Leilani? Azalea?" I raced to our rooms, but the four extra beds were empty and tidied.

"FREESIA!" I raced to the other side of the suite, but Freesia's bed was just as neat and unused as the others.

My heart sank in my chest. I checked the bathroom, the balcony and even looked in the closets and under my bed.

They were gone.

"No, no, no ..." I'd give anything to see even Freesia's smug face again. This couldn't be happening. This was all my fault! I shouldn't have threatened the queen—clearly, this was her retribution for being an upstart. She'd taken all my friends in the middle of the night and had them killed! What if I had been there as well? Would I have died too? I—

"Ah, I thought you might be here."

I whipped around, only half-surprised to see a twin standing behind me. "Why are you so goddamn *quiet?*" I demanded. Were they constantly stalking me?

His silver-green eyes twinkled at me with a genuine, fearless smile. Zariah, then.

"Dragon powers." He shrugged and put his arms around me.

Automatically, I relaxed against him, taking in his scent as he nuzzled against me. He was so different from Zion; it was jarring.

"Zariah, where are the others? I think your mother might have—"

"Zion ended the contest early this morning. It's for the best, all things considered."

All things considered?

"But where are they? What has your mother done with them? She hasn't ... She hasn't ..." I couldn't finish the rest, not able to bear the thought of Leilani or Azalea's white faces as fireguards led them to their deaths. I doubted the queen would harm her precious mini-me Freesia.

Zariah's grip on me tightened. "They're fine, Mari. I told Zion to ensure they were taken care of. Now that the competition is over, they are free to be courted by the other nobles. They'll be set for life."

My fingers dug into his forearm as though through him I could keep a grip on reality. "Oh, right. Sorry."

He gazed down at me fondly, wiping away a tear with his thumb. "These rooms are yours now. Was Zion able to answer your questions?"

That chased away the lingering sorrow and panic, quickly warping them both into anger.

"No," I said, letting my frustration seep into my voice. "He was as helpful as the fireguards who watched those girls drown in the bathing halls."

Zariah let go of me, flinching backwards as if I'd struck

him. I didn't feel a twinge of remorse. He'd stood there just like the rest of them.

"Mari, please understand. My mother is the queen and runs every aspect of the kingdom. She had explicit instructions that—"

"Why?" I interrupted, my voice sharp.

Zariah gaped at me. "Why what?"

Was it really such a mystery to everyone in this perfect little city on the top of the hill, with enough food and water that they questioned nothing around them?

"*Why* don't you simply refuse? Why don't you stand in opposition to her? These ... games have been going on for decades, haven't they? And Zion made the ridiculous claim that he is supposed to run them!"

Zariah sat down on a couch. I noticed numbly they had laid a breakfast spread out, but less than before.

Since my friends were gone.

Zariah snagged a pastry and took a bite, thinking. "It's hard to explain. As far as I know, fireguards have gone into the other quarters and rounded up eligible girls to parade in the Seat for over a hundred years. You'll see your friends at the closing ceremonies feast this week. It's a win-win."

They kept saying that. So much so, I wondered who they were trying to convince.

"And standing up to your mother?" I asked, interested in his reasoning for that.

Zariah winced. "There's just something in me that forces a pause when I think of challenging her. It's connected to my inner dragon, but my human brain can't figure it out. I would like to take her down a peg sometimes, but my instincts always warn me away."

Another non-answer. I threw my hands in the air. "What *can* you tell me?"

Zariah plucked another pastry from the table; this one had strawberries and cream on top. He offered it to me.

The urge to smash it into his face was strong, but I resisted. Plus, my stomach grumbled. I swiped it from his hand and sat down across from him, trying not to shove it down my throat in one go. I reached for another, hating how good it tasted. They did not give us sweets in the mud quarter. Just bread, cheese, and dried meats.

As I ate, I turned over everything in my mind. The more I thought about the 'choosing' and the discrepancy between the low quarters and the Seat, the more disturbing it all seemed. There was plenty of food up here. Why not bring more to the mud quarter? Why make us fight and elbow each other for scraps?

Well, it made most girls eager to be taken to the Seat, that was for sure.

Yeah, as if the royal family starved the mud quarter so we'd want to marry into the Seat ...

The pastry fell from my hand to the floor. Zariah frowned. "Are you—"

"Why do the nobles in the Seat want girls from the mud quarter so badly? And the other quarters as well?" I asked. "Why us? Why not marry their own women? Why are all our men taken to become fireguards? They took less from every other quarter. What's wrong with the boys and girls in the Seat that they need us?"

Zariah blinked at me as if he'd never thought about it.

"Well?" I prodded, sure I was onto something.

"I ... I don't know, actually. I always thought it was nice we were giving others a chance—"

"You thought your mother was being charitable?" I choked out, scarcely believing anyone could be so dumb. Or so sheltered.

"Well ... no," Zariah admitted. "Now that you point it out, it begs the question of where the offspring of the nobles are. I can't ... I can't recall ever seeing any."

Now it was my turn to gawk. "You grew up in this palace with no other children or playmates other than your brother?"

Zariah leaned back in his chair, his face darkening. "Well, we could turn into dragons any time someone told us no until my mother stepped in. It wasn't safe for us to be around other people, let alone other children."

I felt a stab of sympathy at that. "But back to the nobles. Why do they need us?" Any possibility I could come up with wasn't good. Not at all.

Zariah looked just as disturbed as I did. Good, at least he realized the severity of the situation. "I'm not sure, but I think I know where we can go to get answers."

I perked up. "The archives? Azalea had mentioned something about them."

Zariah rolled his eyes. "The girl from the art quarter should know better than to mention those. We try to keep them hush-hush."

Another red flag waved frantically at me. "Why?" I questioned.

He frowned. "I don't know. It's just something—"

"You've always been told," I finished for him, already guessing the answer.

Zariah stood, reaching for me. "Let's remedy it then. I'll take you now. Together, we'll find the answers and we'll make it right."

For one wonderful, terrible moment, I almost believed him. My cynicism crashed back down to reality quickly. I would learn nothing good from the archives. If they were kept hidden from everyone, something was deeply wrong.

"Zion never mentioned the archives," I threw out moodily.

Zariah chuckled. "Odd. He's the bookish sort, much more than I am. I'd rather be out flying."

I shook my head. Flying. "Interesting. If you were to ask me, his only interests have been aggressively trying to get under my pants."

I'd meant it as a joke: a little light-hearted jape to ease the rising tension between us. Instead, it exploded in front of my eyes like a blast of dragon fire. Zariah's face shifted, incensed. His voice was a deadly whisper. "If he did anything against your will—"

"Zariah!"

"—throat, for ever daring to touch you like that against your will, and then I'll drape his body—"

"ZARIAH!"

His skin flushed red, eyes oscillating between his silver-green and the gold of his dragon form. Nothing I was doing was getting through to him. I stood and went to him, wrapping my arms around his neck and squeezed, intent on holding him to me so at the very least, he couldn't storm off and murder his twin on my behalf.

Though the very thought of Zariah feral for me had my blood hot and boiling.

"Zariah, it wasn't like that. He—"

I got nothing else out as he attacked my mouth, savaging me with his lips and teeth while his hands held my face and neck. I didn't realize my feet were moving until the back of my knees hit the couch behind me. I fell into it and Zariah tumbled into me, not missing a beat as his body pressed mine into the soft cushions.

Sharp teeth bit down on my bottom lip, pulling it until I felt a delightful sting. He continued his fiery trail down my neck and collarbone, biting at the column of my throat and sliding down the rest of my body. His hands slipped under my pants and sat on top of my hip bones, squeezing.

"You're mine. No one is to touch you. Not without your permission and mine."

Cool air hit my private parts as he ripped the pants down my ankles, tossing them carelessly over his shoulder.

"Zariah—"

A hand went to my throat, squeezing. Not painful, but enough to stop me in my tracks. He was a predator who had caught his willing prey. Extremely willing

His other hand gently parted my thighs, his palm softly stroking just above the apex. My hips rose on their own accord, trying to create more pressure and friction between me and his hand.

"Do you want me to stop?" he practically purred, his nose and lips kissing a path down my navel.

I couldn't even think straight, let alone speak. One finger gently swiped at my wetness, and I whined with need.

He chuckled darkly, and the pressure on my throat eased. "More?"

I wanted more.

"But first, I need to tell my dear brother to keep his hands off what doesn't belong to him," Zariah growled, and it took a moment for his words to catch up to my brain as he stood and made his way toward the door.

"What? No! Zariah! Zion did nothing, I promise. It was a joke. A horrible, tasteless, stupid joke! He stopped when I said no!"

Zariah stopped short of the door, his shoulders tense.

I put my arms around him though I knew that I likely wouldn't be able to physically stop him if he was determined.

Zariah relaxed into me, then turned in my arms. "My apologies. I am mostly one with my dragon side, but I wasn't expecting the odd possessive rush. Usually Zion is the one who goes all dragon rage on people. He resists it, so it makes it worse in the end."

I nodded dumbly. Sure, whatever. It was easier to focus on his arms around me, and how nice he smelled—of ashes and smoke, of singed wood and cedar.

"So, want to go to the archives?" he asked.

CHAPTER FIFTEEN

W hat a dumb question. Of *course* I wanted to go.
He seized the new topic with enthusiasm. "I
can take you there." He looked around, locating my
breeches and tossing them to me.

I blinked at the sudden change of subject and mood. Zariah
was going to give me whiplash. "I want to find information
about your curse."

His nose twitched, then grabbed my hand after I'd put my
pants back on. "The archives. Let's go."

Down the corridor we went, taking a right, and then
another right. These hallways were long, and it felt like we
were going clear to the opposite end of the castle. When we
finally reached the end of the third long corridor, Zariah didn't
even pause before the massive grand staircase, he just started
taking the steps two at a time.

I yanked my hand out of his grasp, bending over with my
hands on my knees. "Give me a second, you beast!" I wheezed,
half joking, half serious.

He flashed a mischievous grin that I swore held a hint of a

fang. "And here I thought you were in the best shape out of all the contestants."

I ignored the stitch in my side and stood up straight, crossing my arms over my chest. "I am."

One dark eyebrow raised. "There's street fit and then there's dragon fit. Come."

I ignored him and sucked it up, taking the stairs as fast as I dared. Up and up and up ... I pumped my arms to give me momentum, and didn't hide how hard I was breathing. It was a challenge to conquer: a task to manage. I didn't take breaks on the landings and pushed on. When I finally crested the last step and reached the top, Zariah and a massive door that stretched to the ceiling met me.

And the fireguards.

"Are books and scrolls usually guarded so heavily?" I asked dubiously. The guards had no reaction to Zariah, but eyed me with open curiosity.

"Let us through. I'm taking her in. And if she ever wishes to come alone, you're to grant her entrance."

I envied the way he gave orders so casually. There was no question in his mind that they would obey him. What a way to live life.

It took six guards working together, with three on each side, to open the massive doors. Once they parted, my jaw dropped.

Books. Shelves. As far as my eye could see, at least five levels spread out in a space bigger than the entire mud quarter.

The door closed behind us with a heavy thunk, but I barely noticed.

And the glass. The walls and ceiling were entirely made of glass, letting in so much light it nearly blinded me. It was much more intense than when I'd been shoved outside the dome for the first time. How could anyone see with so much light?

Then I realized why it was so bright. "Zariah, we can't be here. The dragon—er, Zion—*there's no dome!*"

I only caught a flash of Zariah's smirk before he led me over to the far side of the room, which was pure glass cut into perfect squares with white paneling in between each sheet.

"It's safe. Look."

I pressed my hand up against it, frowning at the odd tingle that raced up my spine when the pads of my fingers met the smooth surface. The view would have been spectacular if I wasn't terrified. The desert and the mountains stretched out in all directions, even if it was a black wasteland. To our right, the dome's edge shimmered at us. My eyes squinted shut, the sun so bright off the dome's reflective surface that it hurt.

"How long did it take to build?" I asked, wondering how many people died before the kingdom was safe.

Zariah sighed. "It took a full generation. But they did not build it to keep the kingdom safe. It was built before we were cursed to turn into dragons."

My brow furrowed. "What? But why—"

"Hundreds of years ago, we were a rich trade nation. Every kingdom braved the desert to reach us for our precious gems. Gold, diamonds, sapphires, rubies ... we had it all in our mines. And the other kingdoms would pay handsomely."

I still didn't see what that had to do with the dome, but I waited patiently.

"Then one of my ancestors decided our riches made us vulnerable—that eventually another kingdom would get sick of paying exorbitant sums for our jewels and that they'd try to take them. Diamonds aren't available anywhere else, as far as I'm aware. He was also paranoid that his own advisors and workers weren't being honest in the gem count. They accused people of stealing and keeping gems for themselves or smuggling them out of the country on a secret gem market. From what I can put together from the writings of the time, they did not build the dome and its surrounding walls to keep the kingdom safe." He paused, his face suddenly serious. "They built it to keep everyone in."

I blinked. "But then the dragon thing—"

"Just the icing on the pastry." He put one hand above mine on the glass, and his body leaned in behind me, pushing me up against the glass.

I found I didn't entirely mind. "I hate history. It's sad and full of mistakes."

I couldn't think when he was pressing up against me like that, each of his hands taking one of mine and spreading it up on the glass. His head ducked down to mine, his teeth scraping against the back of my neck. Surely he wouldn't—

RRRRAAAAWWWWRRRR!

I jerked back in fear as the dragon—no, *Zion*—landed on the dome only a few feet from us, massive claws digging into old grooves and even creating new ones as he roared his fury at us. His massive head gazed at us in irritation, anger welled in his black and gold eyes. Before Zariah or I could react, a wall of fire erupted straight at us. Someone was screaming, and I realized it was me.

FWOOSH.

The fire pummeled the windows. I expected heat. Fire. Flames and agony. I grit my teeth and turned away, Zariah's arms holding me steadily in place. Wasn't he going to shield himself? Wasn't he going to run?

Wasn't it supposed to hurt?

Zariah's laugh jolted me enough that I opened my eyes. The glass stayed intact in front of us, whole and not singed or melted. Zion still stood on the dome, his neck spikes raised like the hackles on a dog as he breathed fire at us over and over again.

I was too shocked to speak. What magickal glass was this? Why didn't we use it instead of the dome?

Zion gave up on his ineffectual flames and rushed us with his entire body, slamming it into the windows over and over with his wings flared to keep him in the air. Zariah kept laughing as the walls shook, but there was nothing funny about the bruises and blood forming on the skin between Zion's scales.

"Stop it! This isn't funny! He's hurting himself!"

I ran from the windows without looking, ducking behind shelves and getting lost in the rows.

"Mari! Wait!"

No. *No.*

Hot, angry tears gathered at the corner of my eyes. Why had I thought Zariah would be any different from Zion? They were both asses in their own way. Did Zariah even want to show me the library or was taunting his brother his only goal?

My stomach flipped over and over, bile rising in my throat. I found a shadowed desk in an alcove and dove under it, pulling my knees to my chest.

I wasn't a commodity to be plucked from my home and paraded around the nobles, only to be given to the highest bidder. I wasn't a piece of flesh to be toyed with, existing only to make other people jealous.

I was Marigold Mudthrice. I was born in the mud district in the third row, and I was done with riddles and boys with their smirks and smug looks.

"Coming out?"

The bored voice was far enough away that I scowled.

"I could sniff you out, but that's no fun. Zion's flown away if that's what you're worried about."

There was a pause.

"I've pulled out a few of the scrolls that talk about building the dome. Would you like to see them?"

Manipulative. Self-serving. Effective.

I crawled out of the desk space and brushed myself off. Fists clenched, I slowly made my way back out of the stacks, and back toward the center of the room. Zion was gone. Zariah waited impatiently, tapping his foot and gesturing to a pile of parchment he'd put on a long table.

"If you look here, I think—"

WHAM.

The moment I was close enough, I punched him in the nose as hard as I could. His eyes flashed with shock, then dilated as they shifted dizzyingly between gold and silver, and back again. Blood dripped from his nose, but I don't think he noticed.

Zariah just gawked at me.

"You don't use me to taunt the bloodthirsty dragon who is also your twin brother."

He opened his mouth to argue, but I raised my fist again threateningly. Zariah slammed his mouth shut.

"No more vague answers. Tell me what is actually going on. Then you will describe these parchments. I can't read."

Zariah blinked rapidly, then flushed red from his ears down to his chest. With one hand, he pinched his nose shut, trying to stop the flow of blood.

"Sit."

I glared at him.

"Please," he tried again.

I relented.

He pulled out a handkerchief and stuck it to his nose, sitting across from me. His face looked suddenly tired and worn.

"It isn't my fault my brother refuses to accept the beast raging inside of him. It makes the dragon harder to control. But I ... I will refrain from ... taunting him." He frowned. "That's why he can be violent and angry."

I snorted. "And you're not?"

He matched my glare. "I didn't eat you, did I?"

I rolled my eyes and picked a parchment at random. "This one. What does it say?"

Zariah dabbed at his nose and sniffed, making sure there was no blood on his fingers before gingerly picking up the aged parchment. "It's a history of the kings of the past, and their great deeds. It's how I figured out when the dome was built—"

"Not interested. What else?" I demanded since I'd had enough of men going on and on about how wonderful they were.

Zariah eyed me, but set down the paper and picked up another one. "This details the trade agreements between Cantrada and us, back when we were trade partners. It's actually quite interesting." He pushed the large book toward me, but I noticed something wedged in the pages toward the back.

"What is this?" I carefully pulled it out. Zariah held out his hands, and I reluctantly handed it over.

"Hmm. Just a ledger book. Quite boring. Who dug up what on what day, how much it weighed ... trivial day-to-day minutiae that no one cares about."

I snatched it from him. "Maybe a prince or a king wouldn't care, but I'm neither."

The fluid strokes of the letters swam in front of me like mystical symbols. I knew a few numbers, which I recognized after squinting at the fancy script for a few moments.

"There are very large numbers here. What do the numbers mean?" I pointed at a few lines, curious.

Zariah frowned, leaning over my shoulder. I ignored his

smoky scent and tried to focus. "Just saying which slaves brought in which amounts of specific gems."

Everything in my body and my mind came to a screeching halt. "Slaves? What slaves?"

Zariah jerked back suddenly, his face blanching before it resumed its calm facade. "I misspoke. I meant workers."

I slammed the book shut. "You want to get punched in the nose again?"

He closed his mouth, winced, then answered. "They weren't slaves. It's just ... they worked in the mines. Usually slaves do that or the punished criminals from what I gathered from the books. Political prisoners. I apologize. No one in this kingdom has ever been a slave. We are all equals."

Yeah, right. And my mother got the same amount of food every week that the queen did.

My disbelief must have shown on my face because Zariah leaned forward, intent on arguing. "Mari, you must believe me. My father, the king, was only a fireguard from the mud district before he married my mother! He was raised up and—"

I held up a hand. "Excuse me?" Rage built as I remembered how the queen had looked down on me for my birth while her own husband was no better than me. That absolute bitch. Maybe it also explained his meekness and why the queen rode roughshod over him. Why didn't he use his power to help his people?

It's curious, isn't it? Why marry a dirty mud district boy? Why not another noble? Something is wrong. Something is wrong.

And whatever it was, it was clear either Zariah didn't know about it or wouldn't be telling me soon. I took a deep breath and changed the subject. "Where are the mines? I know there are some underneath the stone district."

Zariah pushed away the history books and grabbed a few more, flipping through them quickly before landing on an extremely large book. He blew the dust off and opened it up. A gorgeously illustrated map unfolded in front of my eyes.

"Here. This is us." He pointed to the red star on the right page in the middle. "There are a few small local mines here, and here." I followed the trail his finger made over where I knew the stone quarter was.

He frowned. I watched his eyes dart here and there, but I didn't miss it when they lingered on a small group of mountains just to the west of the city.

"There. It is large and has a sketch of an opening. Are those mines?"

Zariah frowned. "Yes ... I believe so. I never noticed before. The entrance must be hidden from view."

He studied the map some more, then abandoned it as he stood and disappeared behind the shelves.

"Zariah?"

I waited with ill patience as he rustled in the stacks, clearly searching for books if the thumps and mumbling were anything to go by.

"Ah ha!"

He came around the corner with three thick, dusty volumes in his hands. He dropped them hard on the table and I jumped, wrinkling my nose at the small cloud of dust that exploded in front of my face.

"More records of the sla—workers. The workers."

As he read, I was deep in thought. "I assume we stopped mining when the wall was built? That's what I heard."

Zariah hummed in agreement, still deep in his book. Did he even realize how privileged he was with his reading and his fed family? I thought of Azalea and Leilani, and how sad they were to leave their families. I'd been sad, but we understood in the mud quarter that leaving was a good thing: there was more food, opportunity, and jobs elsewhere.

Wait.

Jobs.

Everyone in the kingdom had jobs. The stone quarter, the bread quarter, the art quarter ... even the nobles in the Seat did *something.*

But the mud quarter didn't. We were beggars and thieves. We had no education. We couldn't read, and there was no land to plant crops and no mines underneath our homes to maintain. We had no purpose.

My blood went cold.

Maybe we had no purpose because the only purpose we had was taken from us.

"Zariah. When do you switch with Zion?"

He paused from his reading, an excited gleam in his eye. "Can't get enough of the dragon?"

I kept my face stone cold. "I want to visit the mines." I pulled the book over to me, stabbing my finger right on the illustration so my meaning was clear. "These mines. And I want to go as soon as possible."

Zariah closed the book on me, grinning. "Of course. You're my princess now. Our princess, that is. We can do whatever you want."

I narrowed my eyes. "Is that why Zion canceled the games?"

Zariah clapped his hands twice, then wriggled his fingers in the air in what I supposed was a celebratory manner. "You won. Woo-hoo."

I didn't feel like a winner.

"You're going to marry me?" I stuttered out, recognizing he was trying to change topics again, but it was a hell of a topic change.

The same hands waved dismissively at me. "Marry, mate, live with, ravish ... it's all the same."

I scowled, resisting the urge to pummel him. "Just come get me when it's time to go. Can you handle that?"

The smirk he sent me made me feel as if somehow I'd gotten the raw end of this deal, yet again.

Hours later, I was still thinking about the archives even as I took a bath without a prima or a fireguard trying to drown me.

The smaller, shallow tub with its hot water felt marvelous. I was a new woman. Unlike the bathing pools where I nearly drowned, the water only came up to my chest. I don't know how the primas knew to come in and set it all up for me, but the likely answer was Zariah.

As soon as they poured the water in the tub, I dismissed all of them. Apparently, I had that power now.

Me ... someday queen. It was ridiculous. Obscene. And perhaps ... an opportunity. If I was queen one day, I could help my people in the mud quarter. I could make us all equal. I would end the fighting for bread, the starving, the fear in the streets that made all of us enemies instead of concentrating on *why* we were all so poor to begin with, and where to shift the blame for that.

The king's sad face invaded my happy vision, and I brushed it away. I would succeed where he failed. He hadn't done it right. I would.

The clear water was soon brown and black, but I didn't care. It was the most luxurious thing I'd ever experienced. My heart ached as I imagined my mother getting a hot bath. Her joints had been bothering her lately, and I bet the small bags of herbs and flowers that the primas had added to my water would help her.

I just wanted to help everyone.

And I'd start by going to the mines. I didn't know how it would confirm or deny my suspicions, but I had to try. It was a piece of this ever growing puzzle.

When I got out of the bath, new clothes were strewn on my bed. To my relief, no gaudy dresses were in sight. Instead, a simple linen tunic with black pants waited for me, along with a belt and practical boots.

Praise the gods.

As I dressed, the smell of chicken caught my nose, and I drifted out to my common area like a moth drawn to the flame. The door to the suite clicked closed just as I rounded the corner, so I'd barely missed whoever had brought my meal.

My jaw dropped. A sumptuous feast of chicken and lamb awaited me, along with a colorful rice dish with powerful seasonings if the smell was anything to go by. Green vegetables were mixed in, but I ignored them in favor of the meat.

I never got meat. Not until here.

I groaned with appreciation at the first bite and didn't hold back as I devoured the chicken and lamb in short order. The rice was next, and I downed the wine and the other carafe of a tart juice I'd never had before. I supposed I hadn't technically eaten since before the queen's little talent show a few days ago.

I wasn't a stranger to hunger.

A knock on the door startled me, but it was only Zariah. Or at least I thought it was.

"Have you eaten? Have you bathed? I want to ensure they have properly cared for you before we set out."

Definitely Zariah. His nose was a little black and blue, but otherwise still in perfect shape. Shame. Perhaps I'd have to constantly leave marks on one of them to definitively tell them apart.

I didn't pause from chewing my last bite of rice, stretching my hands out to show everything I'd eaten. After swallowing, I picked up a hunk of buttered bread and held it out to him. "Want some?"

"Sure."

He took the bread and tore a hunk off with his teeth, clearly relishing the fluffy, soft texture just as much as I had. "Fresh from the bakery. It's always best fresh."

I wouldn't know, so I kept quiet. Bread was bread, wasn't it?

"Is Zion still outside, then?" I asked, unsure how it all worked.

Zariah smirked. "We're going to sneak by him. He's pissed off from earlier and having trouble reigning himself in. He'll likely stay far to the south, away from us. That will give us an opening to fly out to the old mines and back with him not being the wiser."

Two major things seemed off with that.

"I thought you both couldn't be dragons," I argued, sure that I'd heard one of them say something about that.

Zariah scowled. "It's something Mother has always insisted on, but I tried it earlier in secret and nothing happened. She must not have ever specifically ordered us *not* to. She claims it has something to do with the curse and magick, but I know it's bullshit. She just wants to know one heir is safe and sound inside her castle. Can't have us fighting each other and dying. That'd be embarrassing to announce to court."

The bitterness in his voice was telling.

"Alright," I allowed. "But you're acting like this should be a secret. Are we not allowed in the mines?"

His smile was too easy this time. "You're our princess. You're allowed to do what you want."

"Except tell Zion what we're doing," I guessed, proved correct when Zarish flushed red. "I thought you didn't like Zion," he argued. "I thought you hated him."

My eyes narrowed. "I find it hard to trust either of you lately with how little information you have given me and how willingly you will obey your mother. Are we going or not?"

I tucked another piece of bread in my pocket, then thought better of it and shoved it into my mouth.

Zariah clucked his tongue in annoyance.

"Ready," I declared, my mouth still full.

It was time to solve a mystery.

SIXTEEN

I was sure someone would see Zariah and me sneak back through the hallways and up to the hatch. I paused at the bottom of the ladder, remembering the spot I'd seen two of the Fireguards murdered for being unlucky enough to see both princes human at the same time.

The blood was gone, but the memory lingered.

"Coming?" Zariah called ahead of me, shedding his pants and clothes as he climbed, letting them fall carelessly to the floor. By the time I reached the top of the stairs, he was naked and climbing through the hatch.

He offered his hand gallantly, and I took it, accepting his help in stepping over the threshold and out into the open air. My eyes shut to slits as I took a moment to adjust to the brightness. Would I ever truly get used to it? Zariah didn't look too bothered by the sun.

Before I could fully open my eyes, gold scales surrounded me and black, narrow pupils waited with impatience. I pushed his head down and he huffed, a small ball of flames bursting from his snout. But he held it still and let me climb on his neck and down his back.

"Alright," I mumbled under my breath, my fingers tightening around the hard spikes at his neck. "Let's go."

I didn't think that I'd ever be used to flying. After a lifetime of hiding under the dome, the sky itself was an almost intangible idea, and now I was soaring through it! I only screamed a little as Zariah's massive wings flapped on either side of me, and he dove off the dome and into the sky.

We flew due west, away from our kingdom, which had seemed so large and encompassing to me before. But out here, the vastness of the desert stretched out to the horizon, further than my eyes could see. Our kingdom was nothing compared to the mountains and landscape that stretched for miles once my eyes looked beyond the immediate blackened earth. For the first time, I wondered about visiting all the other kingdoms in the world—past all the sand and red rocks I could see in the far distance. They probably didn't worry about dragons and curses. They probably didn't build giant domes.

I thought we'd fly to the mountains, but we landed just before them in a cluster of low-lying rocks. Zariah's scales were hot under my hands as I wrapped my arms around his neck, nearly falling off during the rough landing. He buffeted me with his right wing, slowing my descent to the ground.

Using my hand to shield against the sun, I frowned at the rocks. "I see nothing."

Zariah lurched forward in his dragon form, tearing at the pile of rocks with his claws and armored snout. Some of them were larger than me!

"I'll just ... let you handle that," I said lamely, crossing my arms over my chest. I wasn't sure what he was doing until he backed away, trying in vain to wipe the soot and dirt from his nose.

"Let me."

His snout was softer than the rest of him as I took it in my hands, wiping his nose clean with my shirt. I trailed my fingers up his face until they met the hard, unyielding scales of his brow. Gold eyes met mine, then flicked back to the rock pile. I followed his gaze, blinking at the massive black hole that went straight down.

"Oh. That's it? I guess I expected something more ... I don't know. Grand?"

Zariah huffed and pushed me forward with his nose, showing I should go down.

"Real cute. Why don't *you* go down first, then shift back into a dragon and roast anything that gets too close?"

He growled in his chest, but a second later, Zariah stood naked in front of me, scowling. Without hesitation, he strode over to the black hole and shoved himself in, feet first, with his arms over his head. He disappeared in an instant, and worry immediately blossomed in my chest.

I stood at the edge of the hole, my fingers gripping the dirt. "Zariah? Are you—" The surrounding dirt near my hands crumpled inwards, and I fell face first into the hole. I let out a loud shriek, my fingers scrabbling uselessly at the smooth dirt walls as I looked for a root or a rock or anything to grab onto.

WHUMPF.

I bounced off something firm, but not too hard. It wasn't the ground. Scales and warmth surrounded me, and then Zariah twisted around so I rolled from his soft belly to the ground. I didn't think dragons could have the same expressions as humans, but I swear one scaled eyebrow rose at me.

"Thanks," I grudgingly let out, brushing myself off. Zariah belched out a long line of flame outwards, simultaneously lighting the old wooden torches the lined the corridor in brackets and showing what lay ahead. The path wasn't really large enough for Zariah's dragon, but he stubbornly tucked his wings in against his sides and pushed forward.

"If you insist," I mumbled to no one, sticking close behind him.

I shouldn't have worried about the tightness of the space— after only a short walk forward, the path opened up into a huge, cavernous space. Zariah leaped into the air at once, flying around an area that was as large as the entire mud quarter! He spit out bursts of fire every few seconds, illuminating the space for me. Massive pits were scattered here and there, diving deep into darkness. Narrow, steep staircases cut into the stone itself around the edges, leading toward more tunnels and more darkness.

And the bones.

They littered the ground in front of me like the dust did in the mud quarter. I told myself they were animal bones, and it worked for a few steps. I made it down the first set of stairs to the main floor when I saw the first human skull.

This wasn't an abandoned mine. It was a mass grave.

"Zariah. ZARIAH!"

I heard him before I saw him. The surrounding air turned into a wind tunnel and then he descended, skidding wildly on the piles of bones before nearly face-planting on the ground. He crashed into an old cart and a pile of tools, pushing it forward along the tracks until it smacked into a large metal frame. The resulting echo reverberated in my chest, pinging off the stone walls so loudly I had to cover my ears.

Zariah picked himself up, giving me a sheepish look. I sighed, picking up the skull and holding it out to him.

"These aren't animal bones…. I think they're all … What did you call them? Oh yeah. *Not* slaves."

His head ducked onto the ground as if asking for forgiveness. I turned away, not yet ready to give it. It was one thing to be ignorant; it was another to willfully choose it. I studied the skull carefully, noting the fine layer of black dust covering it. In fact, everything had the same sheen. It covered the bones, the ground was, and even my boots now had a layer that rubbed off on my fingers when I bent down to swipe at it.

"You've never been here before, right?" I asked Zariah, my voice barely above a whisper.

His massive head shook back and forth even as his ears pricked, flattening against his head and turning to the right.

I was too busy imagining what could have possibly happened here to result in so much death and destruction. *You already know*, my traitorous brain thought.

Soot everywhere. Scorched bones. A dragon had done this.

"Zariah, this makes little sense—"

A scream permeated the air from far in the distance. It was high and twisted, and sounded nothing like any scream I'd ever heard before. It sounded like a rat in its death throes. Zariah went still, his body flattening to the ground as his ears stayed against his skull. His tail tensed, quivering.

A chorus of screeching joined the first scream until it got louder. And closer. Zariah leaped to his feet and pushed me back toward the tunnel with his nose, both of us panicky and not thinking clearly. I slipped on some bones and my ankle rolled under my body, sending me to the ground. I stifled my gasp of pain, but only just. Zariah made a frustrated, pained growl as I grabbed my ankle.

I tried to stand up and hobble, but white-hot agony raced down my leg. "I can't walk," I panted. "I can't—"

The shrieking exploded into our cavern, and Zariah pushed me into the tunnel. I ignored the pain as I landed, ducking under his legs as he put his massive frame between the tunnel's entrance and whatever was approaching. With a massive roar, he spread flame everywhere in the cavern, and I caught a quick glimpse of dark creatures pouring out of the opposite tunnel before the flames forced them back. Their screams modulated and kept going. In a burst of madness, I tried to crawl under Zariah's legs and get a better glance as they came toward us—yellow, stained teeth, crazed eyes, and long black claws and fangs—black silhouettes of fear and death streaking toward us.

Zariah's head swung down to me and he roared again. The message was clear: get out. "You'd better be right behind me!" I screamed back, then crawled frantically on my hands and knees down the tunnel.

Heat rolled around me, making it hard to breathe as Zariah blasted fire into the cavern over and over again. I coughed and choked, reaching the bottom of the black hole, but having no way to get up. Not without Zariah.

I pulled myself to standing by using the dirt walls and waited. Zariah roared again, and then a sickening feeling crept over me. It was nausea and fear all rolled into one: the pain in my ankle flared higher, making the pain almost unbearable. I couldn't breathe from the tightness in my chest, and it felt like thousands of bugs were crawling all over my skin. I wanted Zariah to set me on fire to make it stop. I wanted the pain to end. I wanted to *die*.

I screamed as something jammed itself under me and tossed me up into the air. I landed and all the air was shoved out of my lungs. Large, leathery wings wrapped around me like a cocoon as the world rocked and tilted crazily. Dirt fell on my head and my mouth, and I spit it out.

Sunlight exploded into my world, and the wings released me. Hard claws caught me as I tumbled and air buffeted around me, whipping through my hair and making it impossible to open my eyes. The animalistic screaming faded into nothing.

The claws holding me opened, and I fell a few inches to the ground. I rolled onto my back and looked at the blue sky above me, then yelled as I realized I was at the edge of a cliff. No, make that *mountain*. I crawled a safe distance away and collapsed.

Turning my head, Zariah crashed next to me. He was back to his human form as his knees hit the ground, panting like he couldn't catch his breath.

"Are they ...? Are they coming out?" I coughed out, reminding myself to breathe.

Zariah shook his head, his dark curls bouncing against his ears. "No ... pushed the rocks back in with my back claws. Cave in."

"What ... was ... that?" I asked in disbelief.

"C-creatures. Black creatures. White teeth. Screaming ... so much screaming. And then ..."

He fell silent, and I knew what he was remembering. That awful, horrible feeling that had invaded our senses and brought us to our knees.

"What was that?" I moaned, fighting the urge to vomit all over myself. Was it something the creatures had done?

"I know what it is. I've felt it before," Zariah gasped out, on his hands and knees and visibly looking as nauseated as I felt. At least my ankle appeared only bruised, and not broken. I gave a few experimental steps, and found I could walk with only a little pain.

"What? What is it?" I demanded. I had no idea what that horrible feeling had been, but I knew without a doubt I never wanted to experience it ever again.

"I feel it every time I shift," he confessed, his voice pained.

"What?!" I asked again. Zariah didn't seem completely there. Then those silver eyes swung toward mine.

"Magick," he whispered.

CHAPTER
SEVENTEEN

I don't know why the thought of magick was so shocking. I'd seen men shift into giant dragons, so I could hardly not believe in it.

"Are those ... demons?" I asked incredulously, not having another word for the dark, mindless creatures I'd seen.

Zariah panted, still trying to catch his breath. "I-I don't know."

I caught the hesitation and fear in his voice, and seized it like I was back in the bathing pools and it was the edge of the tub.

"Yes, you do," I challenged.

"I don't!" Zariah roared back, his face red and flushed.

I refused to back down. "You have a guess."

Zariah went silent, glaring at me.

"You have a guess," I spat again, giving him just as much venom in my stare, "about these demons, and the *not slaves* who worked in the mines."

Zariah grit his teeth as if in pain, then grabbed his head

and put it between his knees. My anger stepped aside as worry shot through me.

"Zariah? Are you alright?"

His eyes were closed as he took deep, measured breaths. "We can't argue now. We have to leave. Zion figured out I shifted and that we're out here. He's ... not happy."

Yeah, I bet that was an understatement.

Zariah grunted in pain as he slowly shifted back into his dragon form as if this time it was laborious and painful, each scale and talon costing him something as he forced the change to come.

I clambered up his neck as soon as he was done, knowing he was losing strength. He took off into the air, in a direct path for the dome that was a distant shimmer in the distance. I kept my screams internal as he dipped low suddenly, then straightened out. Was he going to fall? If he didn't get higher, we'd crash right into the walls of the kingdom!

"Come on. You can do this," I shouted over the wind, not knowing if he could hear me or not. The dome was growing closer, but we weren't high enough to land on it.

"Zariah! Up!"

The dragon groaned and rumbled under me, but the heavy wings on either side of me flapped hard, straining. Little by little, we rose.

"We're going to make it! Just a little more!"

I reached forward and stroked my hand down Zariah's neck, trying to offer what I could. We rose a little more, and I yelled as the dome rose in front of us and we skidded across the very top, Zariah's belly sliding against the bottom. He shifted as we stumbled across, both of us rolling together until we landed, me on top of him.

A dragon roared from behind me.

Vaguely, I realized it wasn't Zariah because he was

currently under me and obviously a naked man and not a dragon.

The dome shook as Zion landed in his dragon form, identical to Zariah's, except for a slight narrowness to his snout that Zariah didn't have.

I shouted, but Zariah's movements were sluggish under me. I don't know why I did it, but I stood over him and put myself between him and his enraged dragon brother.

Zion's massive body came hurtling at me, and there was no way he was going to stop in time.

I yelped as he crashed into me, but it wasn't as hard as I thought. And instead of hot scales, flesh and bony elbows crashed into me. All three of us rolled six feet before coming to a stop. Zariah lay trapped under me, and Zion pinned me down on top.

"Get off her!" Zariah reached around me and took a wild swing at Zion, who grabbed me with both arms and yanked me away from Zariah.

"ME?! You're the one who risked shifting while I was already a dragon! You took her beyond the safety of the dome and the walls! And for what? I felt your terror! Whatever you were doing out west, I could kill you for risking her!"

Zion's arm tightened around my waist, refusing to let me go.

Zariah threw his arms in the air, exasperated. "She asked me to go! The whole thing was her idea—"

Zion yelled, and sucker punched his twin. I gasped as blood flew, but didn't have time to check on Zariah as Zion grabbed me by the back of my neck and claimed my lips with his.

Before, when I'd kissed him, it had been cocky. He was someone who was used to getting what he wanted at all times without argument. My first instinct was to kick him between the knees, but then I realized the kiss was different.

It was desperate.

The way he clung to me as the wind whipped around us took my breath away. His fingernails dug into my skin, unable to bring me as close to him as he wanted. The grip on my hip would leave bruises, but I didn't care.

Zion had always tried to take from me, but there was innocent despair in the way he simply held his lips against mine, not pushing me or dragging my body against his as he'd tried to in the past.

So I kissed him back.

Zariah growled from behind us, and Zion's grip loosened as I melted against him, both of us raw with each other for the first time.

Another pair of arms ripped me away, and I gasped at the loss, only to have Zariah devour me. His kiss was demanding, and I fought him for dominance, refusing to let him cow me about anything, let alone this.

His tongue pushed into my mouth, so I pushed mine into his. His hands tangled in my hair and pulled me to him, his grip tight as I refused to yield. I put my hand on his cock and squeezed hard, letting him know he wasn't going to just boss me around.

Zion stepped up behind me, trapping me between the both of them. Instead of anger or panic, I only felt .... intrigue. Zion's hands went to my waist, then left. Zariah went still as death, and that's when I noticed the knife Zion had pressed against the back of Zariah's neck; the same knife that had just been in my waistband.

"Let her go," Zion demanded, his voice still rough from his time as a dragon.

Zariah grinned, keeping his head still. "She likes it, don't you, flower?" His voice was gravelly and full of need.

I didn't want to move, lest one of them did something stupid.

"You're the one who tried to force her, from what I heard anyway," Zariah continued, anger bleeding in his voice. "But I'll forgive it, since your recent spurts of madness seem to be more uncontrollable than usual!"

"Give me the knife, Zion." I twisted around in Zariah's arms and held my hands out. He growled, but reluctantly released his hold on his brother and gave me the knife. I slammed it back into its sheath at my waist, glaring at both of them. "No one is leaving this dome until you tell me what the curse is about."

Zariah tilted his head to the side, still smiling. But he wasn't looking at me; he was looking at his brother. "Zion, just accept it. Let it settle in your blood. We don't have to fight over her. I'm sure she'd accept us both."

"If you both don't want kneed in the groin ..." I threatened, only for Zion to kiss me again. He pushed me up against Zariah, who laughed and braced himself so I didn't go anywhere. His arms locked around mine, pinning me against him with nowhere to go.

I didn't exactly mind.

My mind went blank as Zion's tongue dove into my mouth, claiming and taking over. One hand went to my neck and squeezed while the other caressed the curve of my breast through my leathers. Behind me, I could feel Zariah's hardness pressing against my bottom.

"I want her officially declared as our future queen. I want it to happen as soon as possible," Zariah growled. "You'd like that, wouldn't you, flower?"

Zion's fervor increased, a low groan emanating from his chest. He nipped my lower lip and bit down. I gasped at the delicious pinch of pain.

"Accept it, Zion. You and the dragon are one, and we've both chosen her. We can share. Can't we, Mari?"

My brain felt like mush. I fought through the sludge and the sensation of hands all over me, touching and feeling.

Zariah chuckled darkly, and I felt the vibrations from his chest against my back. He leaned down and bit down on the back of my neck. I moaned, loving the sensation of both of them working me at the same time.

"Not much is known about dragons, but what I found in our library suggests they mate for life. It's a deep blood bond that breaks for nothing except death. And we choose you."

But they weren't dragons all the time, so ...

My mind screeched to a halt, realizing what he said.

"You're choosing—"

"The bravest, most beautiful girl we've ever seen," Zariah interrupted. Zion made a noise of assent in his throat, moving lower down my neck to suck at my collarbone.

"Your mother—" I protested weakly.

"Will not be queen forever. Think of how much you could help those in the mud quarter as queen."

My eyes widened as Zion's grip around my waist tightened. I could make a change. As queen, I could learn to read, and have access to everything in the archives. I'd solve the mystery in due time, and maybe be able to break the curse they were under, and save the kingdom! Yes!

"Look how her eyes burn with ambition, brother," Zariah growled at me. Zion didn't answer, his teeth busy tearing a rip in the collar of my shirt. I made a move to stop him, but Zariah kept a firm hold of my hands.

"We can help each other. Yes?" Zariah pushed.

I nodded, unable to do anything else with him pressing wonderfully against my backside and Zion working me over like a machine.

A strange whistle shrieked overhead, causing both of them to freeze.

"What? What is that?" I asked, panic flaring in my veins.

Zion huffed, pulling away.

"We will have to finish this another time, darling," Zariah told me, grasping my chin in his hand and pushing up so it forced me to look straight up at him. He kissed me hard, then let me go. I stumbled backwards into Zion.

"Mother is calling," Zariah grit out.

CHAPTER
EIGHTEEN

Apparently there was going to be a large ball to conclude the games, and announce me as the 'winner.'

Yet, we didn't go to the grand ballroom. The ball wasn't even going to be today. Apparently, the queen wanted an audience.

Zion went ahead and dismissed the two servants lingering in my suite and the fireguards outside my door, allowing Zariah to carry me over the threshold and into the bathing room as Zion set about checking the temperature of the water.

"I can walk, you know," I protested weakly, not entirely minding being coddled a little. It was nice to just be cared for, for a charge.

Zariah set me down on my feet next to the bathing pool, the humidity in the air thick and promising a warm bath. "Strip," he commanded, him and Zion immediately turning on their heels to face the opposite wall.

I was sure he'd insist on watching me get naked. That was

more his speed, wasn't it? Or was it Zion's? As I forced the light leggings down my hips, my mind whirled.

Based on what I'd experienced, I was ready for them to get fresh with me, or one of them to try something while the other argued and fought. Yet, none of it happened. Not only did they give me privacy until I disappeared into the pool, but they were business-like in handing me different soaps and oils, letting me bathe myself and helping me reach my back or hold up my hair so I could get between my ears.

When I was done, Zion handed me a towel and clicked his fingers at Zariah. Both left the room. Mystified, I toweled myself dry and wrapped it around myself, not seeing any other clothes laid out. I shuffled out from the bathroom into the shared living quarters, seeing the boys looking over a selection of dresses a nervous maid had brought in on the rack.

"You're inspecting them like they're swords or armor, looking for any weakness," I joked, trying to bring levity to the situation.

Zion raised an eyebrow. "They are. This will be your first official appearance to Mother. We should make a statement."

My lips puckered with distaste. "I'd rather have the daggers and armor."

Zariah snorted. "We can arrange that, I'm sure. It's always a good idea to have daggers when Mother is around. Several, if you can manage it."

I remembered the cold steel of her blade against my neck, and shivered.

Doubt crept in around me. I wasn't some pampered princess who grew up in the Seat's heart. I was a mud girl. I wasn't fit to even be in the throne room, let alone sit on it.

I took a deep breath, quelling the panic in my veins. Despite my own misgivings, I was the only one in a position to help my people. If I didn't do it, no one else would. So I steeled my nerves and pointed to a deep chocolate brown dress made of a cloth that shined in the light. It was gilded at the edges with a dusting of gold and bronze shimmers, and had no straps to hold it up around my neck. I knew the dress would show off the strength of my arms. I wanted people to be reminded that I was strong; that I had faced down a dragon and lived. I wondered vaguely where my diamond dress had got off to.

Zion nodded at my choice while Zariah smirked, picking the dress off the rack. He held it up to me and I snatched it from him.

"We'll leave you to it, then," he remarked, and they both sat down in the cushy chairs the girls and I once shared, eagerly picking up delicate porcelain plates and loading them with small sandwiches and fruit.

I missed the other girls horribly. At least if I went through with this, I'd see them around. The thought gave me courage, so I took the dress behind the changing screen set up next to the dress rack. I dropped the towel to the ground and stared at the dress. There were a lot of strings in the back I didn't understand, and I wasn't sure if it went over my head or if I was supposed to step into it. Over my head seemed safer, so I flipped up the hem of the dress and pulled it over myself.

I tugged the dress down over my breasts, but it got caught just underneath them. I tried to wiggle an arm down to create space, but only got myself stuck.

"Everything alright over there?" Zion asked.

I didn't need help with a stupid dress. Admitting defeat would only reinforce that I was just some dumb mud quarter girl who didn't belong in society.

"F-fine," I squeaked out, steeling myself and then pulling down harshly on the dress with my free hand.

Rrrrrrriiiip.

The dress slid down my hips, but only because I'd practically split it down the middle. I stared at it in horror.

"I'll uh ... just get the servant, shall I?" Zion cleared his throat, and I heard him cross the room and open the suite doors. Zariah cursed, his footsteps disappearing frantically. Quick steps followed behind Zion as hot tears leaked from the corners of my eyes.

Maybe I *was* nothing more than a stupid mud girl. Hurried footsteps danced into the room and over to the screen.

"Oh dear. Don't worry. We can fix this. Haza will make it right."

An older woman with a short brown bob peppered with grey touched the edge of the dress with worn fingers. She gave me such a warm smile that a bit of my panic melted. The expert was here. I would be fine.

"Sorry, Haza," I whispered. "It's such a nice dress."

"I don't know what the prince was thinking," she grumbled. "These dresses usually take two or three people to get into. You start by loosening the corset strings. See?"

She had me step out of the dress, and for once I didn't care I was naked. The woman's attention was fixed firmly on the dress. Carefully, she picked out the strings that were on the back of the dress, letting them out.

"Now, in you get. Arms up." She got her hands under the hem and lifted, sliding the dress over my head. "Hold please," she asked, pinching together the two ripped edges of the seam, and I looked over my shoulder and held them in place. Haza dug into the worn pouch hanging from her dress, and withdrew a needle and the thinnest, most translucent thread I'd ever seen.

Haza caught me staring. "I've been here the longest, so I get the good stuff," she remarked with triumph. "Spidersilk is tough as nails but looks light and fragile. No one will see you've ripped it once I'm through."

Haza set to work repairing the tear, and I wondered what other important skills I had yet to learn in life. Needlework seemed incredibly droll, but the ability to repair and strengthen your clothes was not one to be overlooked lightly. I fought the urge to twitch or move as she worked, an uncomfortable feeling of bugs crawling on my skin coming over me.

"There. Hold still."

The odd feeling vanished as Haza put the spidersilk away and attacked the laces in the back of my dress.

"Not too tight!" I protested as it became difficult to breathe as the dress tightened around my waist. Haza clicked her tongue at me, but the laces loosened. I glanced down at the rip, but it wasn't there. That had been where it was, hadn't it?

"Good stuff, isn't it? Now stay put and I'll do your hair."

Haza dragged a chair from the living area back behind the screen and pointed at it. I sat carefully, not wanting to damage the dress even more than I already had.

"Have to be honest, I'm tickled to finally meet the dragon-tamer mud girl," Haza chattered away as she ripped the leather thong out of my hair.

I grunted in pain, but soon her fingers were combing soothingly through my scalp, rendering me boneless. Pleasure hummed in my veins that I hadn't known existed.

"You've shaken things up. I like that," she continued, twisting my hair this way and that, and digging out a handful of brown pins from one of her many deep pockets and jamming them into my hair. I winced, but stayed still.

"I'm going to leave off with the jewelry: makes a better statement. Plus, your shoulders look lovely on their own."

Haza helped me up and clapped her hands together in dismay. "Oh! You need shoes! Silly me!" She darted from behind the screen and went to the dressing rack, then returned with bright gold and red slippers. "A pop of color suits; plus, it reminds me of the dragon!" She whispered conspiratorially, grinning like a loon. I smiled back, finding her attitude infectious.

"There we are. All ready. Call for me anytime you need it, you hear? I'd love more excuses to stick around."

Before I could respond, she pushed me out from behind the screen. Zion's eyes snapped up to me from the book he'd been perusing, which then fell out of his hands and landed on the floor. Haza clucked her tongue and rushed to pick it up, smoothing down the cover and its pages. Zion ignored her, standing immediately at the sight of me. His silver eyes trained on me, his face oddly blank.

"Majesty," Haza mumbled, giving a little bow before excusing herself from the room.

"I want Haza as my f—maid," I said quickly, wanting to get it out there before I forgot or became too intimidated to ask again.

Zion smiled. "Of course you can have her. You can have anything you want. Zariah has explained this, hasn't he?"

I sighed. He grabbed my hands, kissing them. Zariah must have slipped out of the suite when Haza was with me because he was nowhere to be found. A sudden roar came from high above us, confirming it.

"It can't be fun having one of you constantly ducking out like that," I remarked wryly. "Why don't you just reveal your-selves? Even by 'accident' or something?" Sure, the queen would be furious, but it would be too late to do anything about it, wouldn't it?

Zion's eyes shuttered. "Our existence brings enough fear and chaos to the kingdom. We don't wish to cause any more."

I wanted him to explain further, but a short blast of trumpets came from directly outside my door. Trumpets only meant one thing—

Two fireguards swept my doors open as the queen strolled in, dressed in a sparkling silver gown with diamond jewelry that made her look like a star come down to earth. Did she ever wear another color? I couldn't help but compare it to my diamond gown and fought down an inappropriate grin. Was the queen trying to subtly outdo me? Well, not so subtly, really. Two more fireguards followed behind her, making the spacious common area feel suddenly cramped.

"Darling, there you are. I haven't had to blow the whistle in years, but I couldn't find you."

Her smile was sweet, but her eyes were hard. Zion blinked, but otherwise didn't show any other signs of surprise. "Mother."

The queen's eyes flashed, a cruel smile playing on her lips. "I called for you, didn't I?" She tossed her white braid over her shoulders.

"Mari wasn't ready for an audience. She'd been in the same clothes for—"

Zion shut his mouth hurriedly, realizing that revealing my previously soiled state wouldn't exactly endear me to the queen.

Her eyes snapped to me as if she was just deciding to acknowledge my existence. They narrowed, then slowly raked me up and down as if looking for fault. "Bare shoulders. How gauche." The queen took in my uncomfortable stance and smiled, reminding me of a satisfied predator who'd just picked out the juiciest prey in the pack.

"I wish to have a word with her before our first public appearance tomorrow at the ball. You may wait outside."

My heart pounded in my chest as Zion took one step forward, then stopped himself. "Mother, I don't think that's necessary. Anything you have to say to her, you can say to me."

The queen's own silver eyes were so different from her sons': they were cold and lacked any source of warmth. "Now, dearest. I'd hate to make a scene. She doesn't mind, does she?"

Zion glanced at me, and I made my best panicked face. He looked at his mother, who was glaring. He sighed, running a hand through his hair, and went to the door.

My hand ached to reach out and snatch his, keeping him from going.

"It's not like I'm going to feed her to the dragon." The queen laughed as if it was a hilarious joke, but Zion didn't react and the fireguards weren't allowed to. Anger churned in my gut as Zion walked through the open doors. Zariah wouldn't have left me alone with the woman who'd tried to kill me, mother or not. Perhaps that's why Zion was the heir and Zariah the beast; the queen knew which son she could control and which one would fight her.

The door closed with a finality that made me twitch.

"There now. Why don't we sit down?" She gestured toward the couches and the leftovers from where the boys had raided my food. Her tone was the most gracious I'd ever heard it, and there was no real reason to say no, so I slowly walked to the nearest couch and sat down. My bottom sank into the cushions.

"Would you care for some—"

"What do you want?" I cut across her, refusing to play her little social games and niceties.

She sniffed, picking up a porcelain teacup and sipping delicately from it. "You're a horrid little thing, aren't you?"

"Only to those trying to kill me," I quipped back, unafraid. Knowing you had two dragon boys behind you gave you a huge burst of confidence.

"So you don't want my gifts, then?"

Her voice was all honey and sweetness, and I didn't trust it.

"What gifts?" I asked warily.

The queen withdrew a chalk tablet, and a large chart covered in letters lined up neatly in rows. "I never thought I'd see the day where I'd be teaching a full grown woman to read, but here we are."

My eyes bugged out of my head. She was giving me an alphabet—a way to learn how to read! It took all my self-control not to snatch them out of her hands.

"If you need more chalk, let me know. Any old rag will do to wipe it away. Perhaps your old clothes?"

I brushed the barb away as the queen stood abruptly, brushing off her skirts. I thought about demanding to know about the demons, or my suspicions about the mud quarter. Fear held my tongue, though.

"Well?" she asked, crossing her arms.

"I won't say thank you, if that's what you're waiting for," I ventured, snatching the writing materials as if she'd take them away any second.

She laughed, but it didn't reach her eyes. "I wouldn't dream of it. See you at the ball tomorrow."

The fireguards opened the doors as she swept away, leaving me alone. Outside, I heard Zion confronting her. I didn't know why, but I felt compelled to hide my materials. I chalked it up to a lifetime of hoarding whatever little bits I'd ever procured for myself. This was no different. The fireguards likely had reported to her that her son had taken me to the archives and allowed me free access.

I shoved the chart and tablet under the cushions of the long couch, just sitting on top as Zion strode through the door.

"What did she want? She wouldn't give me an answer."

I kept my eyes down. "Oh, you know. The usual. Behave at the ball, blah blah blah."

Zion's eyes narrowed, but he didn't push further. "Will you be alright if I'm occupied this evening? There are quite a few arrangements to be made for tomorrow. Zariah says he'd rather be in the air and burn off some energy."

Good. Fine. I was eager to study my new letters, after all.

I gave Zion a strained smile. "That's fine. I need to rest a bit after all the excitement."

Zion nodded, then gave me a kiss on my head. "Excellent. Stay out of trouble, and one of us will return for you."

I waited an hour after he left to creep down the corridor and steal my way back toward the archives.

NINETEEN

I had almost made it there on my own, only getting lost toward the very end. The fireguards were more than ready to be helpful now, which I thought was ironic. Just a few days ago, they'd been willing to watch me die. Now, they were falling over themselves to be the ones to help me find the archives. In the end, I chose the tall one with familiar, kind eyes who I suspected was the fireguard who used to feed me extras in the mud quarter. It was hard to tell through the helmets. He insisted on carrying my tablet and chart for me.

"I'll just stay outside. Come get me when you wish to leave, and I'll escort you back to where you'd like to go."

"Thanks, that'd be great."

I took my materials from him and waited until he was back outside the doors, then sprinted down to the tables Zion and I had been at. I thanked the gods he hadn't bothered to clean up after himself, and apparently servants weren't allowed in here to tidy up. All the scrolls Zion had read to me were still out.

I took one look at the tiny, scrawled words and letters, and my heart sank. Did I really think I could teach myself to read?

There were so many letters and so many combinations! I didn't even know what the letters sounded like.

My face burned with humiliation. Had the queen given me this only to frustrate me and make me fail? It was the kind of passive aggressive, shitty thing she'd do: lord her knowledge and skill over me, laughing as I tried to teach myself in vain. She either didn't think I could do it, or... or she wanted me to discover something. I didn't like either idea.

Well, I had two options: give up or swallow my pride and figure it out.

Giving up wasn't part of life in the mud quarter.

I shuffled back to the double doors, knocking. The fireguard outside heaved and opened them just a crack.

"Yes?" he asked, surprised to see me again so soon. My lips were dry and my words stuck in my throat, but I forced them out, anyway. "Do you ... do you know these letters?"

I gestured at my little chart pathetically, eyes firmly trained on the floor. I didn't want to see the look of pity or amusement that would cross his face. Instead, he nodded to the other guards and slipped inside. The others closed the door behind him.

"Yes. Are you learning?"

I looked up when I heard his tone. It wasn't accusatory or pitying. His voice held no traces of contempt or mockery; it simply held curiosity.

"You're the fireguard who would give us food in the mud quarter. I remember you. You'd always give me more than the others," I accused.

He chuckled quietly. "You were always skinnier than the others."

I thrust the chart out at him again, a silent question in his eyes. His eyes fell down on it. "I don't want no trouble. But ... perhaps I could oversee you while in the archives. It would be irresponsible of me not to keep a close eye on the prince's promised."

He moved past me into the archives, glancing around. Spying the table filled with scrolls, he hummed and sat down in one of the old, aged leather chairs.

I stood next to the table, warring within myself. I needed his help to understand the letters, but ...

"You let them take me from my home" was what came out instead.

His head jerked at me, and he sighed. To my astonishment, he took the great metal helmet with its tassels and red horse hair off, setting it down on the floor. Underneath the helmet, it shocked me to see ... an old man. I don't know what I was expecting, but fireguards had always been this hard, immovable force in my mind. Seeing just a ... man with gray hair was the last thing I expected.

"You got more time than most of them, you know," he remarked, looking me up and down. "And it did you a lot of good to come here. You look healthy. Muscled. Much different from the little mud rat I was used to."

I wouldn't let him dodge his own part in all of this. I missed my mother. I worried about how she was doing without me.

He cut me off as my mouth opened. "Your mother is fine. The others on the street keep her fed. They pool their leftovers together for her."

My brain stopped. "W-why would they do that?" Our quarter was every woman and child for themselves. The last thing anyone would do was share food.

The fireguard's face was lined with wrinkles and lines, like a worn piece of leather. "They know it's only a matter of time before the new mud queen comes back for her mother, and they don't want to suffer your wrath. They pray you will care for them as they care for your mother."

Tears welled in my eyes. The mud quarter was a dark and wretched place. People would rather beat you and steal from you than give you a kind look. And now suddenly there was camaraderie? Hope?

"You did that," he continued. "I volunteered for extra shifts at the palace, hoping I'd be able to talk to you. To tell you."

None of this made any sense. "Why?" I asked.

"Because ... Well, you know what it's like there. Most of us are lucky to get out. They teach the men to fight, and the pretty girls get to live as Noble wives."

"But not everyone gets out," I corrected him, thinking of my mother.

He sighed, running a hand through his short, graying hair. "No, not everyone does. The Nobles want their girls pure, after all. They don't want the crippled or the feeble-minded. They refuse anyone disfigured or sick."

"Or used," I spat back. I couldn't think about it anymore. The more I did, the more nausea welled in my gut. I was here living the high life, trying to decode letters while they were out there starving and dying.

Was that guilt in his eyes as he glanced away from me?

I eyed the scrolls of our history with determination as he patiently started lighting the candles all around the room. "Tell me what these letters are and what they sound like."

The fireguard raised a bushy eyebrow at me. "That, I think I can do."

Hours later, the fireguard was leaning back in his chair, snoring lightly.

"T-the k-king ... d-dom o-of Ah ... Ahllddd ..." I groaned and gave up on the word, too odd for me to make out. "T-traaad. Trade. Trade in j-joools—jewels—f-from the m-moun ... nnnnn ... ten. Mountain."

My head throbbed as I struggled to make out the words in the dim light. The candles had burned down to the stubs, and would go out soon.

Perhaps that was my cue to quit for the night. Or at least for what was left of it.

I didn't want to; this scroll mentioned mining and jewels, which meant it might contain the information I was looking for about who worked in those mines! Yet, if I tried to do this myself, I'd be the king's age before I could read any of it.

Gently, I elbowed the fireguard, who snorted and straightened instantly in his chair, trying desperately to look like he hadn't just been caught sleeping on the job. I ignored his twitchiness and pointed to the scroll.

"Can you read this?" I asked curiously.

He yawned, his jaw cracking as he glanced down, bored. "Thought you figured out I was from the mud district, too. I picked up my letters here and there, but I can't string 'em together. Not much use for it as a foot soldier."

He pulled down the back of his tunic, exposing an old, raised brand on the back of his shoulder. F1143.

Tears gathered in my eyes as emotion rose unexpectedly in me, closing off my throat and tightening my chest.

"Of course," I managed. I stood quickly, then regretted it as the world teetered around me and my legs shook. The fireguard steadied me, and I took a deep breath in. "Thanks. We've been here awhile. I need to eat."

He picked up his helmet, settling it back over his head. "I'll pass word to have a plate brought up. Your quarters or the prince's?" He gathered my materials in his hands. I took a step away from the table, then on a whim grabbed the scroll I'd been trying to decipher and rolled it up tightly, deciding to take it with me. Zariah had insisted it was worthless 'day-to-day minutiae,' but I couldn't help but feel as if there was more to it.

I was so fucking thankful for the lack of judgement in the fireguard's tone. "The prince's," I answered, wondering who I'd find in bed tonight. Zion or Zariah?

As he led me down the dim hallways, exhaustion slowed my steps.

"What's your name?" I asked.

The fireguard laughed, as if it were the most ridiculous question ever. "At least there are many more flower names than names for fire. In my unit I'm known as Flame Eleven Forty-Two, since I was the eleventh boy taken into the Seat in the forty-second year of the reap. The others in my unit call me Ell."

Wow. That was way worse than my name.

He snorted. "The look on your face. It isn't so bad. Most of us have nicknames or something else more clever or meaning-ful. It doesn't matter what the kingdom calls us."

Now that was a thought I could get behind. "Well, thank you, Ell. You were very helpful."

We paused in front of the archway that led up to the prince's tower. Ell looked down at me like he had something of utmost importance to say, his eyes glistening a bit underneath the shine of his helmet. Then he bowed, handed me my mate-rials, turned on his heel, and left.

I ascended the spiral steps to the prince's tower myself. The door easily pushed open on its own, but the room was empty. I was both relieved and put out by this, but at least I

could hide my scroll now. Not that I didn't trust the boys—
Well, ok, maybe I truly didn't yet. The queen clearly held at
least Zion in her palm, and this mission felt personal, like
something I had to do for myself. So, I tucked the scroll and the
materials under the prince's mattress and crawled into the
large bed. A knock sounded a few minutes later, a servant
bringing in a tray of porridge and some fruit. I smiled as she set
the tray on the table and hurried away. Even in the palace, Ell
was making sure I was getting extra food. The thought made
my chest seize for some reason.

The porridge was thick with honey, and the fruit dripped
down my chin. As soon as I finished eating, my eyes went
heavy, and I put the tray on the floor next to the bed. I bundled
the covers around me and went to sleep.

A heated pounding on the prince's door woke me the next
morning. Momentarily confused, I blearily peered around my
surroundings until I remembered I had, in fact, gone to bed in
the prince's tower, and not my suite. I stumbled to the floor in
yesterday's clothes, my hair a mess and drool stuck to the side
of my face. It was still dark outside. Who could it be?

"ZION! SO HELP ME—"

I unbolted the lock and opened the door.

Zariah blanched at seeing me unkempt, and with sleep still
clinging to me like a blanket.

"Ah. Oh. I …"

"What?" I demanded.

Zariah put a hand behind his head, embarrassed. "Apologies. Zion was supposed to take over with the dragon bits last

night. I haven't seen him around, and then you weren't in your rooms, so I thought—"

"What, that he'd stolen me away or something? Like you had?" I interjected, raising an eyebrow at him.

He blushed. "Like I said, I'm sorry. This ... whatever this is between us makes it difficult to control what my inner dragon has been screaming at me."

"Which is what?" I asked, curious.

He gave me a deadpan look. "To take you to the top of the tallest mountain, squirrel you away in a cave, and fuck you until you're pregnant with my child."

Uh. Woah.

I blinked at him. "That's a bit ... aggressive."

He gave me a weary grin. "Like I said, instincts are being a bitch. Luckily for you, I have much more practice at controlling them than Zion. Now, where is my brother?"

I shrugged and stood aside as Zariah came in, closing the door behind him. "Maybe he's just out fly—"

I didn't get the rest of my suggestion out because Zariah seized my face with one hand and my waist in the other. He pushed me back up against the closed door, our lips meeting in a blistering kiss. When he pulled away, both of us were panting.

"I thought something had happened to you. My dragon was inconsolable. It's taking everything I have to keep him in check."

His skin glimmered gold in the waning candles, scales appearing and then disappearing underneath his skin. His eyes kept oscillating between silver and green and his dragon's black and gold.

"I'm here. I'm fine," I tried to reassure him, touched that anyone had been concerned about me. It was a new feeling, and I found I liked it.

"How can I help?" I asked, my voice its usual self-assured self.

He lifted me up in the air against the door in response. My legs wrapped around his waist automatically. His hands stroked my face while his nose nuzzled in the side of my neck. "Let me hold you. Let me know you're alright. Hopefully, it will satisfy my dragon long enough so that the other ... urges will subside."

I swallowed. "The ... mountain and the babies bit?" I clarified.

His eyes were gold now, and completely feral. "More than that. My seed, filling your belly and growing into our child. Your cries of pleasure that will echo along the entire mountain range, letting everyone in this kingdom know who you belong to."

That sounded ... oddly fine. Need and lust grew into an ache between my legs, and I had a sudden desire to see his manic urges released on me.

I crushed my mouth to his in a kiss, sliding my tongue inside to battle with his. He groaned in appreciation, then hurriedly broke away.

"If you push me," he cautioned, "I won't stop. The dragon needs reassurance. Hell, I need reassurance. I just ... we need you."

"Yes," I breathed out.

Zariah growled and spun us around, dumping me on my back on the bed. He ripped his clothes off, standing before me nude as his eyes devoured me like a snack. My eyes dropped to his cock, at full attention between his legs.

Zariah hissed as my fingers wrapped around his length. It was so firm. And this went inside of me during ... the act?

It made me nervous, but also intrigued.

I'd seen other women put their mouths on it before,

women who did it to the fireguards patrolling our quarter for an extra crust of bread or wedge of cheese. The fireguards seemed to enjoy it. Perhaps Zariah would too.

I opened my mouth and leaned in, letting the tip of my tongue swirl over the top of his cock as my hand held him in place.

"Shit, Mari!"

His hands tangled in my hair, holding me in place. I grinned and settled on my knees. Without warning, I took him fully in my mouth.

He gave a half-shout, half-roar, pulling at my hair so tightly it burned my scalp. I didn't care; I loved the roughness of it all. Pain was real. This was real. Zariah moved slowly in my mouth and I went with it, hollowing my cheeks to give him more room to work with.

"So wet ... so warm ..."

I ran my tongue up and down his length, and that made him move faster in and out of my mouth. What if I sucked on him?

"Ah! Mari!"

Hearing my name come from his strangled voice gave me a sense of power and confidence I'd never felt before. I moved against him with gusto, alternating sucking and licking, taking him deeper into my mouth and throat little by little. Could I make him lose control completely? The thought was its own aphrodisiac, and—

"Fuck me!"

Zariah pulled away, his cock leaving my mouth with a small pop. I wiped my mouth, frowning. Had I been doing it wrong?

"I don't ... I don't know what would happen if I came. The magick ..."

I pulled him down to sit next to me on the bed as he regained his breath, wrapping his arms around me.

"If you came?" I asked, unsure what he was talking about.

Zariah laughed, the sound choked and desperate. "Oh, my gods. You've never ... holy shit."

He pinned me down to the bed, licking and nibbling at my neck. My brain worked furiously to pay attention despite such distractions.

"Coming is when a man spills his seed inside a woman. That is when his part of the act ends."

His teeth bit down at the hollow of my throat, and I moaned.

"T-that's how babies are made?" I gasped out.

He chuckled darkly against my neck, the vibrations from his voice rumbling against my skin. "Just so."

"I don't want a child," I managed. "... yet."

His mouth went lower, nuzzling my chest and ripping open my tunic. "It does not always result in a child. Just sometimes."

Well, that didn't seem very encouraging.

"With the curse I'm under, I do not know if my seed would produce a child, or burn you, or do something else horrible. I know when I'm in my dragon form, it's very toxic and can burn through stone."

My jaw dropped as my mind spun, imagining him as a dragon ... doing it. Doing me? I was a confused bundle of hormones and lust.

"Oh. Maybe ... best not to, then?" I suggested weakly.

"Or I can come here and now, and we can see what happens." Zariah gathered a marble bowl from the nightstand, setting it on the bed next to me. "I never wanted to risk coming and destroying something. Mother has ordered us to have the utmost discretion."

There it was again: that unquestioning obedience to the queen. I hated it.

"How does one ... come, then?" I asked.

He bent down, nuzzling my neck again, then pulled down the neckline of my dress and seized my breast with his lips. I gasped as his teeth lightly bit down, and he sucked.

"Won't take much," he rumbled against me. "Just seeing you naked and coming undone should do it."

He made short work of my clothes, pulling them off and throwing them to the floor. I was on fire and too needy to care about my nakedness.

Zariah sat back on his heels in the bed, staring at my naked form. His hand went to his cock, stroking and pulling on it. "You're magnificent," he rasped, his hand moving faster and faster. I watched, mesmerized, trying to commit what he was doing to memory. I wanted to try it sometime.

It didn't take long. One moment he was staring at me, and then the next he bent over, grabbing the marble bowl and pointing his cock at it. Intrigued, I leaned in to see. A white, milky substance shot from the tip, and didn't look like it was burning through anything.

"Is that what it's supposed to look like?" I asked.

Chest heaving, Zariah put the bowl on the floor and fell back against me. "Yes," he panted.

"That's good then, yes?" Curious, I leaned over and put a finger in the white substance, sniffing it.

Zariah made a strangled sound. "D-don't do that." His hand was back on his cock again.

"Why not?" I asked, sensing he liked what I was doing. Convinced it wouldn't kill me, my tongue swiped out for a taste. It was salty.

"Fuck! Mari!"

He yanked my hands away. I squeaked as Zariah rolled me

over on my stomach, pinning me to the bed underneath him. "You're going to be the death of me," he growled into my ear.

I wiggled my bum into his pelvis in response.

Zariah caught my throat with his arm, and turned us both so we were on our sides. Holding me still with the pressure against my neck, his hand went to the apex of my thighs and sought my center.

"I—"

His arm went tight against my throat, cutting off any protests. It felt so deliciously dark and dangerous to be held immobile while his hand snuck lower and lower ...

"Open for me. There's a good girl."

I whimpered with need as his fingers touched my innermost parts, slick and wet for him.

"Let's find out what makes *you* come, shall we?"

I tensed in alarm. Surely, I wouldn't spew white liquid like he did?

"Relax, my flower."

He slid one finger inside of me while the other found a small nub toward the top of my entrance and circled it slowly.

My hips pushed back on their own accord, needing more pressure.

"That's it."

The arm around my neck loosened as he teased my nipples, pinching and rolling them between his fingers.

A whine emanated from the back of my throat.

"Good. Feel it. Let it consume you."

I relaxed into Zariah, his fingers continuing their patient, effective rhythm inside of me. The sting on my breasts and the pressure around my neck pushed me further toward something intense and dark ... and I wanted it so badly.

"Let it happen. It will feel so good."

I may have not trusted him in anything relating to his

mother or the kingdom, but in this, I trusted him completely. The realization was sobering, but allowed me to surrender completely. I moaned loudly as his pace increased. My body was nothing but glorious sensation after sensation, my hips grinding against his hand, desperate for release.

"Yes. Yes. Good girl."

I cried out as something broke inside of me, a dazzling crescendo of feeling that left me boneless and teary-eyed as it rocked my body. After the initial wave, smaller ones followed until my thrusting against him slowed and eventually stilled. Every muscle in my body was loose, a feeling of such lethargy washing over me it had to be its own type of magick.

I couldn't breathe. Was I dead? If that was dying, it wasn't so bad.

Zariah's lips found my temple. "Beautiful."

I blushed, suddenly extremely aware of our nakedness.

"Oh no, flower, we aren't done."

My lips parted in shock. "Not ... done?"

He pushed me over onto my stomach again, lightly directing me to get on my knees as he settled himself behind me. "My dragon demands I claim you. May I? Please?"

He was trying hard to stay in control, but I sensed the tight tension in his voice. I remembered my mother, stuck forever in the mud quarter after a man had left her alone with a child growing in her belly.

And yet ... I was already here, wasn't I? That fate wouldn't be mine. I'd already escaped.

Fuck it. Consequences be damned. I needed to be queen to help my people and uncover the truth about the mines. My feelings for the boys were growing day by day.

And I *wanted* it.

"Yes," I whispered into the pillow.

"I'm sorry," he mumbled back, then entered me from behind with one hard, deep thrust.

I gasped in pain even as his arm hooked around my neck and held me tight. "Breathe, Mari. Breathe, my flower."

I obeyed instantly, and with each breath out, the pain dulled. In its place, something else was growing. The same lust from before: the same itch, but deeper inside of me. I moved slightly against him, and he loosened his hold on me.

I felt … gloriously full. And if he just moved *so*, he'd scratch that itch—

"Mari, not so fast. I'll embarrass myself."

I had no idea what he was talking about. I needed to move. I needed him to move. I propped myself up on my arms, arching my back into him. He groaned, fingers digging into my hips.

"Mari, I need—"

"Take it," I ordered him, wanting all of it and more.

He started a pounding, punishing rhythm behind me, one hand digging into my hips, the other putting delicious pressure on my neck as he pumped himself in and out of me.

SMACK.

I gasped in pleasure as he smacked my ass, my face flushing red.

"You'll take it all, won't you? Won't you?" he growled.

He smacked me again, harder. I was mortified by how I flushed in pleasure.

"Yes! I will! I want it all!" I cried out, only able to ball the sheets into my fists and hold on.

A massive roar sounded around us as well as a haze of heat. Wings clipped by the nearest window, gold and black eyes peering in at us.

"He is jealous. But I get you first. We can share later," Zariah called out, his voice raw.

My eyes widened at the thought, doubling my lust. Both of them working me at the same time, just like on the roof, but more. Sweet gods above.

"Oh, you dirty girl."

Zion roared again from outside the window. My mind ran away with my fantasy, imagining both of them on either side of me until I screamed with pleasure. The thought was enough that I reached the cliff again, but this time I didn't pause at it. I sailed over it.

"Fuck," Zariah gasped, as my inner muscles convulsed and squeezed around him. It was so intimate, so intense....

He pounded into me from behind like an animal, and I was so sated with my release that I went limp, just enjoying the ride.

Zariah came moments later with a roar, the dragon outside echoing him. He slumped against me and squashed me to the bed with an 'oomph.' I laughed and rolled, feeling incredible.

Zion screeched in the air and pulled away, flying. Zariah gathered me in his arms, nuzzling into my neck. "Sore sport," he mumbled.

I raked my nails lightly up and down his side. He groaned in appreciation.

"Oh! I nearly forgot." He shot up from the bed, grabbing the marble bowl and disappearing through a door I had assumed earlier was a closet. He came back without the bowl but with a wet rag.

Delicately, he cleaned up the wet mess from in between my thighs, meticulous and careful.

"Thanks," I managed, shifting side to side. I felt a little sore, but nothing unmanageable.

Zariah gave me a rogue grin, closing his eyes.

"Dragon happy?" I asked, raising an eyebrow.

"Ecstatic," he purred back, drawing me in for another deep

kiss. He broke away, frowning. "Though he is insisting Zion get his turn. Odd. I didn't expect my dragon to want to ... share."

My mouth went dry.

"Up you get!" Zariah suddenly intoned, his manner bright and chipper. He gave my bum a firm pat.

"What? Why?" I hated the whine in my voice, but it was comfortable here. It was warm and cozy. I didn't have to worry about who was trying to kill me next. I could just be ... me.

"The ball is in seven hours. You need to get ready." He quickly shucked on his clothes, sitting on the side of the bed to tie his boots.

"Seven hours? How much time does it take to get ready for a ball?" I asked in abject horror.

He laughed at me. I used his distraction to grab the scroll from under the mattress and shove it down my bosom.

CHAPTER
TWENTY

He walked me back to my room and left.

After what felt like only minutes later, primas came knocking on my door. I couldn't help the twist of my face as I glared at the two of them standing in my doorway. The last time I'd seen one had been when they'd been actively trying to drown me and any other girl who couldn't swim.

"Come with us, princess," one intoned. She appeared a little older than me, if at all. Her hair was covered by a long headdress, and her body by the prima's long, flowing black robes.

"Princess? Quite an upgrade from dead girl," I muttered to them, but they either didn't hear me or didn't react. We marched in stoic silence down the palace, taking a long, stretching corridor that seemed to connect to another building that was outside the castle itself.

"You'd better not be taking me back to the bathing chambers, because—"

My mouth shut as we came out into the large marble halls

of the same bathing chambers where two of the girls had died. Anger boiled in my gut, and I opened my mouth to refuse, and demand to be taken back to my chambers where there was a perfectly good working bath.

"Mari! Oh, it's really you!"

My head whipped to the side as a voice called my name and nearly bowled me over. The two primas at my side tutted with disapproval as the figure hugged me around my middle, then withdrew to get a good look at me.

"Leilani!" I gasped, recognizing the small blonde instantly. "I—What are you doing here?"

She giggled against me and waved the two primas away. They frowned, but obeyed. I'd have to remember that.

"We're here for the same reason you are—to get ready for the ball! Apparently, it's a big tradition that all the noble ladies get ready together. Isn't that fun?"

I didn't see the queen skulking about, but that was probably for the best. I looked across the bathing halls, packed with about two dozen other girls. Freesia was already in a bathing pool, being supported by primas as she floated on her back while a third massaged oil into her hair. Her eyes were closed and relaxed.

"Mari!"

Azalea called out and waved to me from across the room, and Leilani and I made our way over to her pool. Each was big enough for ten people, so I didn't see why the three of us couldn't share.

I looked around in awe as Azalea and Leilani unhooked their long robes, completely unbothered by getting nude in front of everyone. There were so many girls here ... more than had competed. I spotted Heather and Hyacinthe three pools down from us, clinging to each other and refusing to go any further in the water than their knees. "Where did all these girls come from? They weren't picked up from the quarters like we were...."

"Oh, they're all noble daughters. They're to be given to the primas. That's what my prima said, anyway." Leilani seemed unbothered by this, though Azalea's smile seemed forced.

"Why? Wouldn't they want to marry into the noble families like you are?" *Like we all are,* my brain corrected.

"They can't. Too many of them are related, I guess? Something about bloodlines and birth defects. I don't know." Leilani waved away my concerns and stepped into the pool until the water came up to the tops of her breasts. "Ooh, it feels so nice!"

I shot Azalea a look. She looked as unsure as I did.

"It's really not our business, I guess," she offered quietly. "We will be provided for here. Our families back home will be provided for. It's a good calling."

I highly doubted anyone would be back to the mud quarter to give my mother anything. I tried to imagine any of the mud girls back home surviving in this cold palace with its gleaming surfaces, and couldn't. Not Shava, not the lost little girl clinging to her mother's hand, and certainly not me. No one here had troubles or imperfections. I wondered again about Oleria, burned all over her body from Zariah's heat in the throne room. Would they cast her aside? Send her back to her quarter? Had Zariah tried to save me the pain and embarrassment of the examination, and Oleria had just been collateral damage?

It made my head hurt.

"But why can't the nobles marry their own girls? What are the specifics?" I insisted, shooting a prima a dirty look as she gestured at me to get on with it, and get into the tub. I quickly shucked my clothes and jumped in with a large splash to the horror of the watching primas.

Leilani shrieked with laughter, and Azalea cracked a small

grin. I popped up close to the edge, but I needn't have bothered —this pool wasn't full to the top, so I could easily touch the bottom. No need to kill us now, I guess.

To keep the primas away, we had to scrub every inch of our bodies to perfection—first with a porous stone, and then with a soap that smelled like honey. Next, we had to massage the oil into our hair, then wash everything off. The worst part was when the primas lined us all up in a single row, naked. It reminded me of the reaping time in the mud quarter. And when the queen had watched as Vession 'inspected' everyone.

I shivered, remembering I'd been the only girl not examined.

"Just go along with it, please," Leilani implored me as she saw the rising storm in my eyes.

I tamped down my anger and bit my tongue. Just because I was a loose cannon didn't mean I'd ruin whatever chances of happiness my friends had. Even if I disagreed with it.

After an embarrassing but blessedly touch-less inspection by the oldest prima with wrinkled skin like worn leather, we could retreat to our pools. They had set chairs up as primas waited with pins and brushes.

I stopped, my feet firmly planted on the ground like a tree.

"Come on," Azalea grit at me, poking me hard in the side. "It's just hair."

Yeah, easy to say for the beautiful redhead with straight hair that was easy to brush. A braid could only control my wild mane or putting it up like Haza had earlier.

The younger prima from before stepped in front of me, gesturing to the first chair. I sat down moodily, crossing my arms over my chest. Gently, she untied the leather thong, keeping my hair tied at the base of my braid as she smoothed her fingers through my hair against my scalp.

Ooh. That felt ... nice.

I relaxed at the impromptu massage, not even minding when a second prima came over and took over untangling my hair as the first prima continued with her magick hands. This was one perk I wouldn't say no to.

The first swipe of the large, long-toothed comb caught me off guard, and I winced in pain as it tackled the snarls and knots in my hair.

"Stop moving. It will be quicker that way."

I didn't care if it was quick or not—just less painful! The older prima glared at me, wielding her comb like she'd swat my nose with it. I huffed and settled in my chair, determined to bear this with grace. None of the other girls seemed to have the same problems I did.

"Such coarse hair and so dark." The prima sniffed.

I wanted to turn and show her just how 'coarse' I could be, but seeing as she held the weapon of my demise, I bit my tongue and bore it. After a few minutes, the pain ceased, and her comb went easily through my hair, which had given up its struggle and now hung limply down my back in submission, even though it looked like a giant puffball.

"Finally. Now we start," grumbled the prima.

For what felt like an hour, she twisted and plaited, tucked and pinned. The prima waged war on my hair while I was nothing more than a neutral third party standing by. At long last she ran out of pins, and stood back.

"It will have to do."

Thank the gods. I stood, eager to get as far away from her and that chair as I could. "Oh Mari! It looks great!"

Leilani and Azalea were sipping from chilled goblets, their hair twisted and pinned in an elaborate updo. I supposed mine looked similar, from what I could feel on top of my head.

"We have to return to our rooms to dress. We'll see you at

the ball. I can't wait for you to meet my betrothed—he's so handsome!"

Leilani was nearly beside herself. Azalea gave a happy grin, but there was some sadness behind it. While Leilani turned to ask the prima a question, I leaned in close to Azalea. "Is there any chance you can slip into my room to read something to me? I've been trying to learn, but I have to know what it says now."

Azalea's brow lifted in interest for the first time since we'd been in the bathing chamber together. "I suppose. Can you sneak it to the ball? We're all being watched closely."

I considered this. "Probably. What, you don't have a boy to introduce me to at the ball?"

She winced. "I will introduce you if you insist."

Immediately I felt bad. "Azalea, I didn't mean—"

"I'll see you there."

The primas were moving with concentrated effort, herding and shepherding all the girls away like we were cattle. The girls I didn't know all looked plain, their hair unadorned and worn long around their face. Apparently, my friends and I were the only ones with fancy hairdos. From across the room, I heard Freesia's dainty little laugh. Her too, I supposed.

"Alright then, I'll bring it."

I didn't even argue as my two primas appeared on either side. I led the way back to my room, surprised I even knew it myself. Perhaps I was learning.

They didn't allow me any moments to myself as the primas stuffed me into a ridiculous gold dress and painted my face. I had my eye poked with black kohl twice before the prima snapped at me to stay still, or the next one would go *through* my eye.

Vicious woman.

They added gold jewelry and trinkets to my hair, my wrists, and my ankles. The dress was low cut with a deep v and clung to my hips before flaring out and trailing down the back. The front hem ended high enough to show off the heeled death traps forced on my feet, death traps that they claimed were shoes.

If this was another attempt by the queen to kill me, I had to give her points for creativity.

"Hold still. Almost done."

The old prima reverently held out a small canister to the young one, who carefully dipped a fuzzy brush into it. Golden powder covered its bristles, and without warning, she dusted it on my dark hair, my cheeks, lips, shoulders and arms.

I blinked, feeling like a small sun with how much I shined and glittered. It would be neater if I hadn't started coughing like I was about to hack up a lung. "It's for Elio," the young prima whispered into my ear conspiratorially. "He would have wanted it."

"Why?" I shot back. "Won't he be there?"

The young prima bit her lip and shook her head, her eyes downcast.

The old prima rolled her eyes, then they both bowed. "We will escort you now to the ballroom."

Inwardly, I panicked. "Uh, may I have a moment first? To uh ... send thanks to the gods!" I made up wildly, remembering these technically were religious women. The old prima's eyebrow rose, but she nodded in grudging respect. She held up her thumb and middle finger.

"Two minutes."

They slipped outside my door, and I hobbled toward the cushions where I'd stuffed the archive scrolls. The one I wanted Azalea to read was too big to take with me.

Oh man, she was gonna kill me. But there was nothing for it, so I took the old, sacred scroll and folded it up as tiny as I could, and stuffed it down my bosom again just as the primas knocked. In a gown like this, it was a handy hiding spot. I wondered if I should stick a knife down there as well.

"Ready! Coming!" I called back, hoping the paper didn't stick through my cleavage. I took a few stuttering steps toward the door, then grabbed my knife in its leather sheath and stuffed it down my front as well.

I frowned at my shoes. Surely they weren't serious about me walking in these?

Outside in the hall, the primas waited with hands on their hips. The older one's eyes flew to my stutter steps, a look of utter disdain on her face.

I guess we were going to find out.

TWENTY-ONE

I tried to sneak into the ball without fanfare, but the primas put an end to that, insisting they introduced me properly. The grand doors of the ballroom opened wide just for me, and every head whipped toward me as the 'dragon tamer of the west' rang in my ears. I turned my head, wondering if she was behind me.

Oh. They meant me.

I walked forward stiffly, ignoring the people and taking everything in. The ballroom was beautiful. They had hung the room with flowing, gauzy canopies, giving the normally cold, empty room an air of coziness and intimacy. Candles hung everywhere, perilously close to the curtains, but watched dutifully by fireguards every few feet. They piled mounds of food upon silver plates, with most of the nobles steadfastly ignoring it.

It made my blood boil to see so much of it go to waste. When I was queen, that would be the first thing I would fix.

Speaking of the queen, she stood at the end of the aisle, rising from her throne. Zion stood far more quickly, his eyes on fire. It was definitely Zion, all coiled tension and barely contained wildness.

"Now that our guest of honor has arrived, I welcome you all. Our kingdom will be in safe hands as the new princess ends the menace of the dragons and their curse once and for all!"

A litany of cheers went up around me as my palms grew moist. I hid them in the folds of my dress and tried to keep up an unbothered, stoic expression. The queen was bold in announcing this to the whole kingdom—she would make sure I failed, then blame me when I did.

Clever.

Freesia swept over to me a moment later, giving the shallowest of bows and the smallest inclination of her head to show respect.

"Princess. I hope we can set aside any difficulties from our past as we both move forward in life." Her face was calm, but a hint of worry lurked behind her eyes.

I sighed, tired of it all. "Fine. Just—"

Her shoulders fell with relief. "Oh, thank goodness! I'd like to introduce you to my husband, Berthold. He was just dying to meet you!"

My jaw dropped as Freesia produced a man so quickly at her side it was as if he'd appeared from midair. He was tall and handsome and with blond hair that was more golden yellow opposed to Freesia's white locks. His eyes were blue and watery, his smile strained, but I couldn't find any other faults with him.

"Uh ... husband, you said? When—"

"Last night," Freesia interrupted, locking arms with him and giving him a small smile. "He just couldn't wait to have me, he said."

I'll bet, I thought viciously. Freesia was the queen's favored and likely the most sought after girl. This man no doubt wanted to stake his claim before anyone else could. Smart. Ambitious. I'd have to monitor him.

"Nice to meet you," I managed, giving a slight nod of my head. I turned and shuffled away on my death-trap shoes as quickly as I could without seeming rude. A small crowd was gathering, eyeing me hungrily. My throat closed up and my mouth went dry.

"There you are. You thought you would sneak away before dancing with me?"

My savior grabbed my hand and pulled me toward him. I took in the blue sash across his jacket with its gold embellishments, finally landing on the ornate crown on his head, noticeably smaller than his mother's.

"If you value your feet, you'll reconsider," I warned Zion, pointing at my heeled shoes.

As if anyone from the mud quarter had ever learned how to do anything as frivolous as dance.

"It's easy," Zion assured me, every inch the pompous prince today. The crowd shrunk away, giving us room. I could breathe again.

"Thanks," I muttered reluctantly.

"When I step, do the opposite. So if I step forward like this," he paused and put one leg in between mine, "you do ... that. Wonderful."

I brought my leg back to match his, stepping behind me.

"Just do that ... over and over again. You're naturally coordinated."

I let the compliment roll over my back, trying to relax into the moves. It was like fighting: don't think too much, just go with it and move.

Except everyone was watching me—no, waiting for me to fail. I forgot to step with Zion and stepped on his toe. He grit his teeth in pain, his grip on my hand crushingly tight.

"Sorry," I whispered.

He shook his head, smiling the next moment. It was odd how he was so calm and collected when playing the perfect prince, but out of control with his dragon and emotions in private. Zariah was his exact opposite—wild and spontaneous in person, but in control with his dragon.

They'd both drive me insane.

Zion jerked me to the side unexpectedly, and I tripped over him, nearly falling on my face. I couldn't dance. I wouldn't embarrass him or myself like this. I'd rather face the hordes of people.

"I-I need a drink," I begged him, letting go and running (well, hobbling) through the crowd. People pressed in around Zion with no shame in taking advantage of my absence to snag his attention.

I made it to a table with drinks and kept to the wall behind it, hoping the dim lighting and the shadows would give me a moment or two to breathe. I pressed myself into the darkness.

"Mari! Mari? Oh shoot, I thought I saw her come this way."

Leilani paused at the table in front of me, worry in her eyes. Her white dress was stiff and puffy, but suited her light, bubbly personality perfectly. Brightly colored embroidered flowers dotted the hem and her sleeves, snaking down her chest and around her collar. Wooden shoes on her feet gave her added height.

I almost stepped out of the shadows to greet her, but a man followed behind her, a satisfied smirk on his face. I hesitated, not feeling up to meeting another 'new guy' just yet.

"Well? Where is she?"

His red hair was a beacon in the ballroom, bright orange instead of the usual dark red hue I'd seen on other nobles and Azalea. His face pinched, and lines crinkled around his eyes. He looked much older than her and me.

Leilani flinched, but smiled brightly. "I'll keep looking; don't worry. She's my best friend! She'll want to see me."

"Find her. That's your job tonight." His hand landed heavily on her shoulders, and she nodded. He turned and disappeared back into the crowd. The moment he was gone, the happy smile vanished, leaving only tired defeat behind. Leilani closed her eyes and took a deep breath, then spun around to face the crowd, her dazzling smile back in place.

I didn't know what to make of it at all.

"It's the same for all of us."

I flinched violently as Azalea materialized next to me, having snuck up on me while I was watching Leilani. "Gods above, Azalea, I—"

My mouth shut at the dead expression in her eyes. Her face and makeup were perfect, but something was very wrong.

"Do ... do you have a betrothed as well?" I asked lamely, then remembered she'd already said that, hadn't she?

She stared numbly at me, then nodded once.

"Right. Well, uh ..." The hidden piece of paper in my bosom poked at me sharply, and I grabbed at it. "Here!" I thrust it at her, hoping a change in conversation was exactly what we needed. "This is the paper I was telling you about. What does it say?"

A bit of her old self sparked when I showed her the torn paper. She gasped in horror. "Mari, where did you get this? Is this from the archives? Did you rip it out?"

I gestured with my hands that she should keep her voice down, glancing around to make sure no one had spotted us. "It's important, Azalea. It's about the mud quarter, and something terrible that happened long ago. It might lead to defeating the dragon!" I knew that would get her. "Please, what does it say?"

Azalea bent over the parchment, squinting. "Ledgers for who brought in what... mining records, I guess."

My shoulders drooped. That's what Zariah had said.

"But that ... Wait. That makes little sense," she continued. "Look here." I followed to where she pointed, about halfway down the sheet. "They listed the amounts next to each numbered individual, and then it lists a date for 'shipment' and that they've all come from ... Hoveria. So it can't be referring to the jewels. The jewels come from here." Her forehead wrinkled in confusion.

I wasn't confused though. In fact, it all made a horrifying amount of sense.

"What? What is it?" Azalea shook my hand, realizing I'd figured it out.

"It's not a ledger of how much each person dug up," I managed, feeling faint. "It's how much each person cost; they sold them from their home to be slaves here in the jewel mines. I, and everyone else in the mud quarter, are descended from slaves. That's why we have dark hair. That's why we live so differently than you. And Zariah lied to me about it."

Azalea blinked at me. "Slaves? But that—"

"Makes complete sense," I argued, anger and realization fueling my outburst. "It explains why people from the mud quarter look so different. The shape of our faces, our noses, our dark hair.... It explains why we starve and live in squalor, praying for the good fortune to come here. Gods, I'm an *idiot.*"

Azalea looked stricken. "I don't—don't jump to conclusions."

Of course I would jump to conclusions! I knew Zariah was hiding the truth from me; he'd brushed my questions about the parchment under the rug. We had been slaves, and he lied about it!

"I ... I need to go."

"Mari, wait! There's something I have to tell you!"

It would have to wait. I snatched the parchment back, holding it limply in my hand and not bothering to hide it. My feet took me automatically toward the queen, who was looking over the entire ballroom from her throne on the raised dais at the end of the hall.

She saw me coming. She saw the parchment in my hand and the look on my face.

And she fucking smiled.

That bitch knew.

She'd handed me the tools to read because she wanted me to know the truth. But why?

"Sit down," she commanded, pointing to a small stool directly on her left. I went down instantly, not knowing what else to do.

"It's true then," I accused her.

"You don't know the half, sweetheart," she purred at me, eyes still on the crowd below us.

"Tell me," I demanded.

She laughed airily, her hand to her chest like I'd just told the most amusing joke. "Don't be ridiculous."

"Tell me, or I'll go back to the mud quarter. I'll tell everyone. We'll rise, and—"

"And do what, exactly?" She drawled, ice dripping from her voice as she turned to fully face me. "I have two dragons that obey me. And dragons around here seem to have a habit of turning your people into ash."

My jaw dropped as my heart sank into my feet. She knew *everything*.

I opened my mouth to argue that Zion or Zariah would never, but I hesitated, remembering how they always obeyed her, no matter what. Suddenly, horrifically, I wasn't so sure who'd they pick if forced to choose between their mother or me.

"What dragon?" I insisted, remembering the charred remains in the cave. "It wasn't Zion or Zariah—"

The queen huffed, looking away. "Haven't you heard the proverb never to poke a sleeping dragon? I suggest you go down there and have a nice time. This—" she gestured between us with her fingers, "is not a nice time." Her eyes sharpened, as if a sudden idea just occurred to her. Nausea rose in my stomach.

"Actually, stay awhile. I have someone I'd like you to meet."

The queen clapped her hands twice, and a young man stepped up to the dais. He was dressed as a noble in long, silver flowing robes that matched the queen's, now that I saw them standing next to each other. He was handsome with brown eyes and shoulder length hair that was black. He was probably only a little older than I was. I stared at the short hair that was exactly the same shade as mine. Something about him felt familiar.

"Yes, my queen?" he asked, his voice smooth and cultured.

The queen held out a hand to him and he kissed it, his lips lingering on her fingers. She giggled like a schoolgirl and my dread only increased. Where was the king? He was conspicuously absent. "Tell our new princess who you are, dear."

He cleared his throat. "Ah, Flame Six Seventy-Six. The others call me Ess."

For all the S-sounds in his name, I bet. Oh boy.

My brain struggled to remember what the other fireguard had told me about the significance. "So ... the sixth boy taken during the seventy-sixth reaping?"

His eyebrows shot up in surprise, grinning at me. "Yes!"

"Maybe you knew my brother," I said faintly. "He might be

older, though." I couldn't stop staring at the shape of his eyes. The shape reminded me of my mother's.

The queen had a sick smile on her face that didn't bode well for either of us.

He blinked. "Do you know his flame number?"

I shook my head.

"What does he look like?"

Again, I shook my head. I'd been too young when he left.

"Ah. Well, fifteen of us got reaped my year, but five went back, eventually."

"He would have been from the third row; like me," I added.

Ess beamed. "I'm from the third row. I had a little sister like you, barely toddling. I wonder—"

He stopped short, staring at me as his lips parted in shock. I flinched backwards.

No.

It would be too much of a coincidence. And if I let myself believe it was really him, it would only hurt all the more if he wasn't.

"My sister is the infamous dragon rider of Barcenea?!"

"Barcenea? What's that?" I demanded.

He smiled as if I'd uttered a clever joke, his expression faltering when he realized I was serious. "It's ... it's the name of our kingdom."

Oh.

"Ess is a *personal* friend of mine. Our current king is looking a bit worse for wear. Ess would make a fine sight standing next to me with a crown, don't you think? I thought it only kind to make you aware of each other since you both have such recently ... *elevated* roles."

My stomach flipped and I savagely pushed the urge to vomit deep down. "How recent?" I managed to ask, my mouth dry.

"The queen has been very kind to notice my work and relieve me of my fireguard duties for ... other pursuits," Ess said emphatically, his eyes on fire as they devoured the queen's form.

I was going to be sick. The queen was grooming a new king, and it was my long-lost brother.

My heart pounded in my chest and my hands shook. I had dreamed of the brother I'd never known for ages. To have him suddenly drop into my lap only to learn he was queen's little lap dog was worse than knowing he was dead.

I stumbled down the dais only because I didn't know what else to do. Someone called my name, but I didn't hear it. I tried to run, but tripped on one of my ridiculous heels. It broke off, and I lurched forward, only to be caught by Leilani's betrothed. His hands felt cold and rubbery around me.

"Oh! Princess! How wonderful—"

"Excuse me. I must be going."

His grip around my arm tightened painfully, so much so that I knew it would bruise. I didn't hesitate.

I drew my dagger and nicked him on his hand, just enough to encourage him to drop me.

He yelled and dropped me in shock as a thin line of black appeared on his hand. He rushed to cover it, running off as I flung off my shoes and ran out of the ballroom, putting my entire weight into the heavy oak doors. They opened, and I fell through, ignoring the fireguards and ducking around the corner.

I wiped my sweaty face, trying desperately to regain some sort of composure. The sound of quiet sobbing lifted me out of my own problems, and let me know I wasn't alone. I seized any excuse to push my problems away.

Where was it coming from? I walked along the corridor and ended up in front of a small closet. I pulled it open, only to see

Hyacinth on the floor, dress and all, curled up into a ball and sobbing.

I shut the door behind me, and darkness shrouded us.

"Hyacinth? What's wrong? Why are you here?"

She hiccuped. "Mari ... it's awful. It's all so awful. It's all a lie...."

Her breaths came in large, gulping gasps, her arms flailing out to reach for me. I grasped her hands, willing her to calm down.

"Tell me. It's alright."

I couldn't see her, but I felt her shake her head vehemently back and forth. "No. NO! It will never be alright. They're *all* cursed ... gray skin and rotting bodies. Don't make me go out there. Don't make me!"

She was talking nonsense. "Where is your sister?" I asked. Perhaps I could get Heather, and she would talk some sense into Hyacinth. At the mention of her sister, though, Hyacinth only sobbed harder.

"Has something happened to her?" I tried, figuring it was one of the few things that would put Hyacinth into such a state.

"She tried to run away from him.... I heard her screaming and crying. I went to help.... He tied her up so she couldn't run away. He gagged her so she'd stop screaming."

I put my hands on either side of Hyacinth's face to ground her, and she clutched tightly to me.

"Who, her betrothed?"

It had to be. It was a dumb question, but it helped her focus.

"Yes ... yes. I went to help and saw. And then ... and then I ran away. Here. Hiding here. You'll help get me out, right? I don't want to marry one of them. They're all like that. He said I couldn't escape it!"

I resisted the urge to slap some sense into her, reaching deep for patience instead. "Hyacinth, listen. Tell me what you saw."

She took several deep breaths, still clinging to me as her lifeline. "Gray skin. It was rotting off in places where their clothes rubbed it. The eyes are normal. That's how they get away with it...."

"You're saying all the nobles have ... gray skin?"

She trembled violently. "Can't have babies. Cursed. That's why they need us. That's why all their girls are primas. Help me get away. We need to get away!"

She stood, frantic, as she threw my arms down and stumbled toward the door. I pulled her back, alarmed at her panic.

"Hey, hey! Wait! Just hold on! I—"

Her fist came up and landed hard on my temple, knocking me back. She opened the door and ran, slamming it shut behind her. I had to wait for the room to stop spinning to follow. Once I could, I darted out into the hall, looking to see which way she went, or at least to ask a fireguard.

She wasn't anywhere, and neither were the fireguards.

Unease churned in my gut. Azalea had tried to tell me something, hadn't she? I regretted brushing her off. There was nothing for it; I'd have to go back into the ball to find her.

I ignored my shoeless state and heaved at the heavy doors myself, since the guards were gone. It opened just enough for me to slip through, but the left door fell back on my shoulder before I could get the entire way in. A grunt escaped me as white-hot pain shot through my shoulder, but I made it back inside.

I scanned the crowds, looking for red, curly hair. Combing through the shadowed corners and alcoves failed to reveal her.

"Mari! Are you alright? Your face is—"

"Have you seen Azalea?" I asked Leilani intently. "She had something important to tell me."

Leilani blinked, taken aback. "Oh. Well, I don't know if I'd take anything she said that seriously, Mari."

Her tone was more like Freesia than I'd ever heard. I did a double-take. "Why is that?" I demanded.

Leilani rolled her eyes. "A fireguard came in and removed her. She was drunk and causing a scene, fighting him and yelling. It embarrassed the queen. It might cost her a betrothal." Her voice was hushed, her eyes wide and serious. To her, there clearly was no worse fate.

"Wait. She's gone? Where did they take her?"

Leilani shrugged as if it wasn't her problem. Irritation surged through me. "Leilani! She was helping me figure out a bunch of secrets from an old piece of parchment I found in the archives! The queen admitted to killing a bunch of people from the mud quarter with a dragon! I need to know where she went!"

Leilani's nose crinkled. "The archives? Aren't there more important things in life than some old words and bits of parchment?" She gestured widely with her arms. "Everything I've ever dreamed about is here, Mari! Why are you so sad and worried? Look at this life!" She frowned. "Have you seen my betrothed?"

I backed away, knowing I'd lost her. And she hadn't even had that hard of a life to begin with as a daughter of a baker. I turned on my heel and left her standing there, confused.

Freesia's white hair flashed before me, and I reached out to grab her hand without thinking. She turned in alarm, but the haughty look on her face settled into something more neutral when she saw it was me.

"Princess. What is it?"

My hand gripped her wrist as I weighed my options.

Freesia didn't like me, but we were more alike than I wanted to admit. She had a cynicism about the world I knew well, and she had a tendency to lean toward a conspiracy that I was counting on.

"May I speak with you? In private?"

Her pale eyebrows rose as Berthold popped out behind her like a prairie dog sticking its head out of the ground.

"Darling, the princess wishes to speak with me in private. I will return."

Berthold's face flushed in pleasure at that, and he gave me a brief nod. I studied his face and hands, not seeing any gray skin or ... rotting anything. What had Hyacinth been going on about?

I hustled Freesia across the dance floor, taking the most direct path to a shadowed corner. People moved out of my way, but I ran into the one person I didn't want to see now all the same.

"Mari? Are you alright? Something's wrong." Zion stopped us, one hand on my shoulder, and Freesia slowed. His face showed me nothing but honest concern, and to be fair, he hadn't been the one who lied to me about what was on the parchment. That had been Zariah. But I couldn't confide in him. Not until I knew for sure he had nothing to do with the killings or that he wouldn't obey his mother if she told him to scorch the mud quarter.

I couldn't trust him.

It made my chest ache, but I turned away from him without answering. Hurt broke over his features before he visibly hardened them, turning away quickly so no one else would see.

I saw.

Freesia stumbled behind me, no doubt confused and horrified I would snub the prince. I tugged harder.

"Slow down! What is this about? You're acting like a lunatic!"

Ah, yes. There was the Freesia I knew and loved.

"Listen. I just ... I need you to listen. I know we haven't exactly been friends, but we could all be in danger. Have you ... noticed anything odd about your husband?"

I winced, because it sounded just as ridiculous as I thought. I couldn't think of where to start, though.

Freesia drew back, offended. "Berthold is the perfect gentleman. He holds my hand, opens doors, and—"

"And is anything off about his skin? Hyacinth was going on and on about the nobles having gray skin, or rotting sores."

Freesia laughed. "I always suspected she was touched in the head. That confirms it."

I pushed harder. "So Berthold's skin is normal? Even under his clothes?"

She scoffed. "How would I know what's under his clothes? That's most improper. His hand is cold when I hold it, but I hardly see that as grounds to accuse him of being some sort of ... demon."

I tilted my head at her. For all her posturing and puffing, surely she wasn't more innocent than ... Leilani or the twins!

"Freesia," I grit out, "have you and your husband spent the night together?" Images of Zariah and I filled my head, but I refused to blush. Not now.

Freesia blinked. "Stay up all night? Why would we do that?"

Oh, gods above.

"Freesia. Did you and your husband ... make your marriage official? Did he sleep in the same bed as you? Did you have sex?"

I had to say the last one, because she was still staring at me in confusion. When the word 'sex' rolled off my tongue, she went white. It was clear to me when I first met the other girls that they weren't as... *worldly* as me, but I'd made it my business to know exactly how babies were made so I didn't end up stuck in the mud quarter like my mother. I knew it involved that ... white liquid from the man after he put his cock inside of you. Out of all the other girls, I didn't expect Freesia to be ignorant of such things.

"Don't speak so—"

"FREESIA!"

"No!" she stammered, most likely just to shut me up. "He bids me goodnight and leaves!" She smoothed down her hair and dress as if my words had physically attacked her. "Now if you don't mind, my husband awaits."

I grabbed her arm, pulling her back. "I do mind, because something foul is at play here. It either traumatized most of my friends, or they're willingly turning their noses up at any sign of suspicious activity, and you're the only intelligent one left I trust."

That got her. She gawked at me, her lips parting in shock. Then she shook her head. "No. No. Absolutely not. You're just trying to ruin a good thing. The prince chose you. Why can't you be happy like all of us?" Freesia's hand swept the length of the hall, showing the nobles and the party in full swing.

"Hyacinth isn't happy!" I roared back. "Heather isn't happy! Azalea was apparently just hauled out of here for questionable reasons, because you and I both know she doesn't drink to excess."

Freesia's nostrils flared, her arms crossing over her chest. "Heather and Hyacinth were always lacking. If you ask me, they're a little dim. And how do I know Azalea wouldn't drink? This is the first time we've had free rein to drink whatever we wanted! Why is it so hard to believe she overdid it? You're fearmongering and ruining everything!" She cut herself off, realizing her voice had gotten high and shrill. "If I wasn't already married," she continued slowly, her tone rigid, "then I'd take the prince for myself since you can't properly appreciate what you have." She gave me a brief once over and apparently found me lacking. "Dragon rider or not."

She walked away, and I found myself alone in a room full of people.

TWENTY-TWO

I walked right out of the party, and no one seemed to care. The fireguards hadn't returned to man the doors, so I tried to navigate back to my rooms on my own.

"You've lasted longer than I thought."

The voice startled me as I whipped around, unsteady on my ridiculous shoes. My ankle rolled under me and I would have likely twisted *again* it had it not been for the strong pair of arms that caught me. Stupid shoes.

The king's dark eyes studied me curiously as I got my feet back under me, and he let go.

"What do you mean?" I asked harshly. It wasn't like he didn't know what was going on, after all.

One dark eyebrow lifted. "You rode on his back right? At least one of them?"

I nodded, not seeing where this was going. He was talking about the queen having me killed, wasn't he?

His head tilted to the side, puzzled. "Surely you've noticed. Dragons are possessive and vengeful."

"OK ..." I said slowly, still not understanding.

The king's brow furrowed and with a sigh, he grabbed the neck of his tunic and pulled it down. My lips parted in shock as horrific scars met my eyes; three monstrous claw marks that started near the top of his chest and disappeared down his torso. He let go of the tunic, hiding them once more.

"I was lucky to survive, and that was *accidental*. You should leave now while you can. I know you probably want to help everyone … but I already explained this. You can't. They are too powerful."

His warnings rang true in my ears, but despite their reluctance to give me information, I felt the need to defend my boys. "They haven't hurt me," I insisted. "Either of them."

The king's lips tightened. "Yet. They will."

"What is happening to the nobles? Why do they need to marry us so badly?" My hand went over my shoulder to touch the raised brand on my skin, hoping it would remind him we were both from the same dust and earth and compel him to help me.

"It all comes back to the curse, doesn't it? She was a young, new queen, looking to mend the errors of the past and move forward. It was an honor and my duty to accept. I was lucky. The others who've met the dragon … haven't been."

I stepped closer, noting the bags under his eyes and how unkempt his clothes were. The streaks of gray in his hair were more pronounced than the last time I'd seen him, with a few new white ones. When was the last time he'd changed clothes?

"Why aren't you at the feast?" I asked even though my brother's face flashed before my eyes, smiling widely at the queen.

"Why aren't you?" he fired back, crossing his arms over his chest.

Silence stretched between us.

"You say … they haven't hurt you?" he asked delicately.

I gestured dramatically to my whole and uneaten body.

The king smirked. "Perhaps ... there is more hope than I thought. If you can get away from here, there will be answers. That I can promise you."

How vague and unhelpful.

"Get away from here ... to *where*?"

The king smiled again, his eyes unfocused as he took another swig from his flask. A new flask to replace the other one he'd dropped, apparently. "Goodbye."

I watched him glide down the hallway, not a care in the world. Gods, that man was odd.

I only missed two turns the rest of the way to my rooms, so I was getting better at navigating the palace.

Once inside my room, shuffling noises made it apparent I wasn't alone.

"Who's there?" I called out, grabbing a thick, heavy candlestick from its holder next to me.

"Oh! My lady! Apologies! I was told—"

Haza spun around, clutching onto the pillow she'd been fluffing. She gawked at me as I stood in front of her, a candle raised like a weapon. I lowered it, blushing and putting it back in the holder.

"Sorry. Didn't expect anyone to be here."

Her eyebrows rose carefully, but her gaze remained on the floor. "Prince Zion told me you requested me to be your personal servant?"

Oh. Yeah. I had asked that.

"Sorry," I said again, collapsing into the chaise lounge. "Can you get me out of this?"

Haza came around to my side, frowning. "The party's over already? I—"

"No, I left," I muttered, distracted. "Haza, what quarter do you come from?"

Her hair was lighter than mine, but not by much. She smiled. "Why, right here in the Seat. My parents were nobles, but before I was born, they disagreed with the king and queen about something, so we are working folk now. I don't mind. The nobles seem ..."

"Yeah," I finished, still feeling like I was missing something important that was right in front of my nose.

"Come now, let's get you—"

KNOCK KNOCK.

Both of us glanced at each other.

"Who is it?" Haza called out, already rounding the chair and heading toward the door. It wasn't the queen since she always had a large fanfare. It likely wasn't Zion or Zariah, who usually knocked, then barged straight in.

No one answered.

Frowning, Haza cracked the door open.

I leaned over the side of the chair, straining to hear their quiet voices from out in the hallway. I tore the jewels and flowers out of my hair painfully until Haza clucked in warning and batted my hands away. She took over herself, deftly disentangling the jewelry and undoing the multitude of pins in my hair.

"You're a suspicious thing," Haza tutted, pulling the last pin out. I groaned in relief as my hair tumbled down my shoulders, wild and free.

"I'd like to say I'm realistic. Assume the worst, and you're never disappointed: only pleasantly surprised."

Haza huffed.

Another knock sounded on the door.

"Oh, for the love of the gods ..."

Haza went to the door, and Ell stepped in with a small, frail figure at his side.

Mother.

She shrieked when she saw me and I cried out, rushing forward to take her into my arms. She was so, so frail, nothing but skin and bones. My arms wrapped too easily around her, and I was forced to be gentle. A small wind would topple her over! Her dress was threadbare and stained, her feet dirty. I threw an accusing look at Ell, who was standing next to her. "You said she was being fed!"

His lips tightened into a thin lie. "She was when I was there. I came here then, if you recall. I went down to check on her the moment I was able to, yesterday. What I found was ... unacceptable. So I brought her here." He paused. "The queen said it was ok."

My head spun.

"My baby. My *baby*," my mother cried, her hands over her face. Gently, I guided her down to sit on the sofa, lest she topple over from shock.

"Your room is beautiful," my mother said quietly, her breath puffing lightly on my shoulder. She gasped out loud as she caught sight of the food just sitting out on the table.

"Come. Sit and eat." I led her to the couch, and Haza was right beside me, offering my mother a plate. She looked lost like she didn't know where to start.

"Everyone, stop hovering, and sit down!" I yelled at them all. Despite the size of the rooms, it felt crowded with everyone in here like it never did with the rest of the girls.

"And for the sake of the gods, *eat*," I admonished them, slinking down beside my mother on the couch.

My head spun. This was ridiculous. And Ell kept sneaking glances at my mother and my mother was glaring at him. I paused. My mother never glared at anyone. In fact, this was more emotion I'd seen from her in the past decade combined. My suspicions grew.

One last firm knock sounded on the door, and my eyes

closed in dismay. I groaned and kneaded my temples, praying for strength.

"Mari! I—"

The prince stopped dead in his tracks, seeing I wasn't alone. His face split into a wide grin. "Oh! Hello! Who are you all?" I could tell it was Zariah by the bounce in his step and the happy, carefree look in his eyes.

It was too much. I stared from my mother back to Ell. My mother kept her arms crossed and her body purposefully turned away from him. Odd behavior toward the one who'd saved you from the mud quarter, wasn't it? Ell's hair matched mine. We shared eye color and the same facial shape.

I pointed an accusing finger at Ell. "You're my father. *You're* the one who knocked my mother up and made her lose her chance to go to the Seat."

Ell blushed and glared at the floor, his face going bright red. Zariah's lips parted in shock.

I waved my arms around vaguely toward Zariah. "Uh … this is … my family, I guess." Saying it tugged on something in my heartstrings, making me simultaneously proud and terrified. I refused to mention my brother and the queen. It felt too personal, and too raw. Maybe once I recovered a bit from shock, I could gently break the news to my mother. She deserved to know, and she deserved a chance to see him again.

Zariah's eyebrows rose clear to his hairline.

I sighed. "My mother. My father, Ell. And Haza."

Everyone did the proper nods and bows, and the room descended into awkward silence.

"I see mother made good on her word. Isn't that wonderful?"

Zariah's voice grit against my nerves. What did he mean by his mother's word? Had he just confirmed that all this was the queen's doing, which meant it couldn't be anything good? I was going to explode from the tension and anxiety.

"Ell, how about you take my mother on a tour of the castle? Haza, tag along. Mother would love to see the gardens. We don't have flowers in the mud district." I laughed at the near absurdity of the phrase. We had plenty of flowers, just not the kind that grew from the ground.

There was no room in my tone for any disagreement. Ell and Haza shot glances between themselves, but led my mother from the room quickly, Ell with one arm around her thin shoulders. I glared at his back.

The moment the door closed, I whirled around on Zariah. "Why are you here? Zion was just at the party. Shouldn't one of you be in dragon mode? And what do you mean, your mother set all of this up?"

Zariah raised one eyebrow, grabbing a pastry from my table and popping it into his mouth. "Zion was ... not himself. He was struggling at the party. He communicated to me he needed to go flying, so he left the ball and here I am. Were you the cause of his unrest, little Mari?"

My hands balled into fists. I couldn't break his mouth until he was done explaining things to me.

"And I told Mother you were going to be our queen, and it was high time to treat you like one. I'm pleased she took it to heart and is trying to please you." He spread his arms wide, like it had all been a wonderful gift.

Trying to ... please me? I laughed out loud, but it was an ugly, dark sound. "You're ridiculous. I thought you were smart. Isn't it obvious what she's doing?"

From Zariah's blank stare, perhaps not.

"She's gathering everyone I care about under her nose as a threat! If I don't toe the line, she can kill them all just like that! That's way more effective than threatening to kill me!" My voice twisted at the end, panic setting in as I realized she could do exactly that. It wouldn't take much to kill my mother in her weakened state—a pillow to her face at night would do it. Ell was a fireguard, and they died all the time in the line of duty. And my brother? It would be torture knowing he was secretly (or perhaps not so secretly) warming the queen's bed.

"You're cr—"

I stuck my finger in Zariah's chest, stopping him. "If you say crazy, I will break your nose again. Your mother tried to kill me. She's taken my long-lost brother as a *lover*. None of that is a coincidence!"

Zariah rolled his eyes as if that were such a trivial thing. "Stop fussing. Maybe sometimes good things just happen." He came around to the back of the couch, leaning down and putting his hands around my shoulders. His fingers kneaded into the tense muscles around my neck. Ooh, it felt so nice.

I jerked away. No. I was mad at him.

"Can't relax," I spat at him. "Too busy fussing."

He frowned. "Mari, aren't you being a little paranoid? Mother knows you'll be the queen one day, and—"

"When exactly do I become queen?" I cut him off, suspicious of the answer. "After she's dead? When is that? How old is your mother?"

Zariah laughed uneasily. "I'm unsure. One doesn't exactly ask the queen how old she is."

"But if you had to guess?" I pressed.

He shrugged his elegant shoulders.

Good gods. Men.

"I want all of them housed here with me, then. Ell, Haza, and my mother. I don't trust the queen. I want everyone where I can keep an eye on them."

Zariah pouted. "Then we can't have any fun, and your rooms are so much more spacious than ours."

I glared. "Whose fault is that?"

He sighed. "Not my fault Zion can't control his urges, and needs to be outside the dome in case he transforms." Seeing the resolute expression on my face, he relented. "Very well. Put everyone where you like. It matters not to me."

Alright. Great.

"What's going on with the nobles? I'm hearing rumors about ... gray and rotting skin."

Zariah snorted and my eyes narrowed. If he laughed at me one more time, I'd punch him.

"Yes, it's hilarious," I spat angrily. "That's why every single one of my friends married off to a noble is now crying, traumatized, or dragged away." I thought of Freesia and Leilani. "Except for two."

To his credit, Zariah's brow furrowed in confusion. "I don't know what that's about. Perhaps adjusting to noble life is difficult." He gave me a warm smile. "Not everyone is a warrior like you."

I wished I had the time to luxuriate in the compliment, but I knew his tricks. He was trying to disarm me, whether it was intentional or not.

"Hyacinth was raving about her sister's husband.... She said he had gray and rotting skin. They dragged Azalea from the ballroom after trying to tell me something. Why do nobles only marry quarter girls, and their own daughters become Primas? Is it about breeding like my friends say? You must admit it's suspicious."

Zariah walked out onto the large balcony and I followed, my eye skating around the giant scorch mark left from when either he or Zion had killed Ivy. Were they even aware of what they'd done?

He leaned over the railing, taking in the glittering Seat beneath us, and the lights of the quarters even further away. It was so quiet up here. It was like none of the pain and suffering down below existed, let alone mattered.

"The nobles face a crisis," Zariah began. "They have inter-bred for several generations now, and have rendered themselves infertile to each other. That is why they must take wives from the quarters, and that is why we have the games. It's why Mother has a king from the mud quarter."

He turned and took my hands in his. "I understand your reticence. Mother isn't the kindest person, but she does her best."

I pulled back, but he held on tight. "She tried to kill me. I watched her order those fireguards murdered, the ones who saw both you and Zion at the same time. She's taunted me about killing—"

"She is protecting Zion and I, her only children. What she does is out of love. Can't you see that?"

No, I couldn't. He was wrong.

Zariah's grip on my hands tightened. "For the sake of the gods, Mari, she married and bred with a mud quarter flame! What more proof do you need? She bears you no ill will because of your heritage!"

I ripped my hands out of his. Surely he wasn't this willfully blind.

"She bred with one of my people because she had no choice; you said it yourself. Does your father rule the kingdom, Zariah?" I asked cruelly. "Or does he stand at your mother's backside, a withering accessory that she can point to as proof she isn't the monster she truly is? Does the king make any decisions or have any power? I rarely even hear him speak! And even now she fucks my brother on the side, openly taunting me about him becoming the *new* king."

Zariah's mouth bobbed open and closed, his face flushing. "That's not—"

"Inbreeding doesn't cause rotting and gray skin," I stressed. "Something else is going on, and you're just believing everything you're spoon-fed. I—"

"You just think everything is a grand conspiracy against your people—"

"—killed hundreds of us when we were slaves in the mines, bought from another country—"

"—completely unfounded when she's only doing her best—"

"—not to mention all the dead girls from all the quarters, or do they not matter? And—"

"—you people always see the worst in everything. That's why you were slaves!"

My mouth slammed closed at Zariah's admission, my heart stopping in my chest. His face blanched, realizing what he'd just said.

"No, that wasn't what I meant. Mari, I'm sorry."

He reached toward me, but I flinched back.

"I see," I said slowly. "I ... see."

I was the real idiot here, wasn't I? How could I think anyone from the noble Seat would care about me, or view me as an equal? I was such an idiot.... They only wanted me to breed new princes and kings. I was a nameless body; an accessory just like the king to be controlled and put on display to hide the festering rot underneath. That I knew about both of them and the dragons was only a nice bonus.

And now my mother is here. And my long-lost brother. And Ell ... and whoever the hell else the queen had gathered. They were the carrots that the queen's giant stick dangled over me, easily snapped and broken if I stepped a single toe out of line.

"Please leave," I said quietly, trying not to shake with rage. "And don't come back unless I call for you. I need ..." I pulled myself together. "I need some time."

Zariah's hands twitched like he physically ached to touch me, but he drew back, respecting my wishes.

"Fine," he grit out, clearly unhappy about it. "I will return when you are ... more yourself."

Before I could answer, he strode out the door, leaving it wide open.

And me, all alone.

" 'More myself,' *asshole*."

I slumped down on the couch, staring at the far wall. It was clear no one in this damn palace would give me the answers I craved because they wouldn't, or couldn't. The archive's records were incomplete, and even if they somehow held the nasty truth within their dusty pages, I wouldn't be able to read it.

And I didn't have months to wait while I taught myself.

The king's words rang in my ears, churning my stomach as fear that nothing he did or I did would ever make a difference. Hyacinth's cries rang in my ears, bringing a blush of shame to my cheeks that I'd been so worried about the bigger picture that I'd forgotten to take care of those right in front of me.

I had nothing to lose, did I?

I stood, shucking off my dress and fancy clothes, letting the dagger hidden in my chest fall to the ground. When I couldn't reach the buttons or undo the latch on the back, I simply ripped it off. My only regret was ruining Haza's handiwork.

I wasn't running away. I was simply going to check on something. I'd come right back as soon as my questions were answered.

I stormed to my wardrobe in my room, the other two beds still conspicuously neat and absent. The fighting leathers from my 'talent' had been meticulously cleaned and hung up. I pulled them on, grabbing the new leather boots and lacing them. I slammed my dagger into the sheath at my side.

Racing to the balcony, I peered over the edge. It was a sheer drop to the bottom, but if I could get down halfway, there was a thin rock ledge I could probably skirt the rest of the way down on if I was careful.

I tore up my dress into strips, uncaring of the damage. It held no good memories for me. Then I took all the blankets from Azalea and Leilani's bed, and did the same. The result was quite long. Tying the scraps together into a makeshift rope, I secured the end to my railing and threw the rest over.

Silently, it fell into the night. At least the moon was full, providing something with which to see. With a smile, I watched as the rope fell far past the rock ledge. This should be simple, assuming I didn't slip and fall to my death.

Breathing out, I put one leg over the balcony, grasped the fabric in my hands, and pushed off.

CHAPTER

TWENTY-THREE

T he silky sheets were hard to grasp, and I slid far too fast as I desperately grabbed at them to stop my fall. I twisted the fabric around my wrist and finally stopped, my arm shaking to support my weight.

Perhaps this hadn't been such a great idea.

Just don't look down.

Nothing for it now, I had to continue. I reached down by my knees and wrapped my free wrist around that fabric, then slowly unbundled my first wrist. I dropped a few inches, and no further. Even that small distance sent bolts of pain through my wrist, so I knew I was risking serious injury. My heart pounded out of my chest and sweat snaked down my back, but I'd found a workable solution as long as I did tiny, tiny little intervals.

Bit by bit, little fall by little fall, I descended. I refused to look down and simply kept moving with my mind on my goal. Eventually, my feet touched a lip in the rock, finding purchase.

The ledge!

It was wider than it looked from way above, allowing both

of my feet to comfortably stand on it. Using the sheet to anchor myself, I leaned far back and saw the ledge wrapped around the side of the cliff, disappearing around a corner. Intrigued, I carefully shuffled along the edge, hanging onto the sheet for extra balance as long as I had slack.

Around the corner, the ledge widened to a proper path, and my sheet and dress rope was taut as it reached its full length. Reluctant to let it go completely, I found a sharp, jagged rock and jammed it into the dirt at my feet; it was just deep enough to hold the end of the rope in place.

Perfect.

I continued on carefully, keeping my knees bent and my arms out at my side. The path kept getting wider, disappearing behind a large rock. Frowning, I went right up to it. It was massive and unable to be moved. I moved around to the back, surprised to find a large, black space that led into a large cave mouth. I stared at the inky darkness, unsure.

Did anyone else know this was so close to the palace? Surely they did. From above, it likely looked to be blocked by the rock, but surely the fireguards wouldn't overlook such a breach in security.

Would they?

Time to find out.

I had no torch or light to find my way, but the path under my feet was smooth as it sloped gently downward. The air became much cooler, and I resisted the urge to shiver. It was utterly silent except for my footfalls, which echoed loudly around me despite the muffling leather on the bottom of my boots.

I wasn't sure how long I walked, but I started counting just so I wouldn't go insane. Maybe it gave me an odd sense of control over the situation where it was clear I had none. Either way ...

1 ... 2 ... 3 ...

Zariah was a jerk. Zion wasn't much better. Both of them were blind to the real issues facing the kingdom.

4 ... 5 ... 6 ...

And they'd involved my mother in all of this! At least ... at least she'd get to eat as much as she could during the day. I didn't like how thin she was.

9 ... 10 ... 11 ...

The queen was definitely hiding something, and it likely had something to do with the nobles. It wasn't a coincidence that my friends had found out, and were quickly being silenced.

15 ... 16 ... 17 ...

The echo from my steps grew, and I sensed the tunnel around me widening. How far underground was I? *Where* was I?

FWOOSH.

Something flew at me through the air. My instincts screamed as I threw my body to the ground. Whatever it was sailed over my body, right at the level of where my head had been. The breeze whipped up a few stray hairs as it went by.

There was a grumble and a muffled curse, and I blindly punched out where I heard it.

My fist connected with a fleshy underside, and I didn't let up as I kicked, pummeled, and took the figure down to the ground. Whoever they were, they were wearing a long, rough cloak. I wasn't about to take any chances. I withdrew my knife and held it up to their neck.

"Ow! OW! HELP SHE'S GONNA KILL ME!"

Hands seized me and lifted, separating me from the man. I wrenched away, desperately wishing I could see. My knife clattered away onto the ground noisily.

Someone struck a torch, light and fire flaring into life. It took me a few moments of blinking to adjust after so much darkness, but a face stared back at me after flinging her hood off.

A mass of twisted, melted flesh greeted me, only one crack of an eye visible while the rest was a mess of stretched skin and scar tissue. There were two slits instead of a nose, and the mouth was lopsided and gaping, showing teeth and gums as the lips looked burned away. The others said she'd be burned, but never in my nightmares could I have imagined *this*.

"Oleria?" I whispered.

"Help her up."

More cloaked figures hustled, helping the figure I'd attacked to stand. She removed her hood.

"Oh, my gods. Oleria! What are you—"

Shock rendered me silent as the last person threw back their hood, revealing dark hair and skin like mine. Tears blurred my vision, and I hurriedly wiped them away. Surely, it was a trick of the light.

"Shava?" I whispered.

My childhood friend smirked and jerked her head back at Oleria.

"Welcome to the underground, dragon tamer," Oleria said proudly, her face twisting in a macabre imitation of a grin. "Want to meet the demons?"

ACKNOWLEDGMENTS

Thank you to my close friends who put up with reading all the early drafts and sticking with me to see the full story come to fruition. Thank you to my ARC team for pointing out mistakes and errors. Thank you to my husband for putting up with my long hours of intense focus and making sure our children aren't running around feral in the process. Thank you for believing in me and supporting my dreams to write. Thanks to my editor Carrie, who did a fantastic job and couldn't have been more helpful.

Thank you to all the readers who support me. YOU are who I write for. Join my newsletter or reader group below to stay up to date with the latest in releases and contests!

-Raven Storm-

Newsletter: https://dashboard.mailerlite.com/forms/83943/ 73668655639955300/share

Reader's Group: www.facebook.com/groups/ 207690987663684

About the Author

Raven Storm is an emerging author of dark fantasy & why-choose romance. She loves to write, has three amazing children, and resides in the northeast with her husband and cat, Arthur. When she isn't writing, Raven is teaching and performing music, or coaching softball.

Follow Raven on all of her social media platforms below

Tiktok: @writerravenstorm

IG: @writerravenstorm

FB: http://www.facebook.com/writerravenstorm

Patreon: www.patreon.com/writerravenstorm

Youtube: www.youtube.com/@writerravenstorm

Also by Raven Storm

The Lost Siren

The Lost Alliance

The Lost Kingdom

The Lost Nation

The Lost Princess

The Lost Child

The Lost King **Coming Fall 2023**

Rise of the Alpha Series

Chained: Rise of the Alpha Book 1

Claimed: Rise of the Alpha Book 2

Changed: Rise of the Alpha Book 3

Box Set with Bonus Scenes

Aggie's Boys

The 40-Year-Old Virgin Witch

The Witch Who Couldn't Give Amuck

Hex Appeal

The Demon Chronicles (YA)

Descent

Feud

Royal Hunt

Kingdom of Flames & Flowers

THE STORY CONTINUES...

The princes have lied. The queen controls everything, including the dragons. At first I just wanted to save my people in the mud quarter, but I can't do it alone. I'm not running away; I'm regrouping so I can return to finally free everyone from the dragon's curse.

In order to defeat evil, I'm going to have to embrace the darkness, and journey into the abandoned mines on the outskirts of the kingdom, meeting the demons themselves. And the princes? If they have truly chosen me, then we will see in time just how much weight a dragon's promise holds.

I won't end up like the king, discarded and forgotten. No one will forget the name of Marigold Mudthrice; Queen of Bones & Ashes.

GET IT NOW.